Dear Reader,

I still remember the steamy summer day my husband and I visited Heavener State Park in southeastern Oklahoma and I saw the runes for the first time. The idea that Vikings might have carved those weathered symbols grabbed my imagination and never let go.

When I decided to write a thriller featuring the men and women of the Oklahoma Air National Guard, it seemed natural to weave in the runes. Like the Vikings of old, these modern-day warriors sail into dangerous and often uncharted waters to protect our freedoms.

So here it is, a blend of old and new, of ancient symbols and modern technology, with suspense, intrigue and passion thrown in for good measure. I hope you enjoy reading *Eye of the Beholder* as much as I did writing it.

All my best,

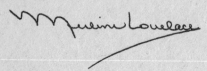

MERLINE LOVELACE

eye
of the
beholder

ISBN 0-7783-2230-0

EYE OF THE BEHOLDER

www.MIRABooks.com

Printed in U.S.A.

This book is dedicated to the men and
women of the National Guard
serving in these tough times.
You do our country proud!

With special thanks to:

Brigadier General Rita Aragon, commander
of the Oklahoma Air National Guard, for
being such a great inspiration and role
model for all women in uniform.

Colonel Mike McCormack, who commands
one of the finest wings in the United States
Air Force. The personnel of the 137th
haven't looked back since 9/11.

Captain Russell Kohl, 185 AS/SGB,
who briefed me on closed head injuries
and what it was really like at K-2.

Captains Liz Kettler, 137 AW/XO, and
Crystal Stitner, 137 AW/PA, for sharing their
insights on the challenges of combining
motherhood and military service.

And John Graves, handsome young attorney
extraordinaire, who fielded my questions
on paternity and grandparental rights.

FOREWORD

I am honored to recommend *Eye of the Beholder* to all American servicemen and women, and to all romantics everywhere. Once again, Colonel Lovelace has captured the honor, dignity and devotion to duty of military members.

Eye of the Beholder is a great suspense, mystery and romance novel that explores in part the mission of the Air National Guard.

Sit back and prepare to be entertained and enlightened with a great story. Thank you, Merline. God bless America and the wonderful men and women who serve her.

Brigadier General Rita Aragon Commander, Oklahoma Air National Guard

1

"Ready."

Seven rifles thudded against uniformed shoulders. Steel barrels glinted in the bright October sun.

"Aim."

USAF Captain Miranda Morgan laid a hand on her son's shoulder, bracing the boy. Bracing herself.

"Fire!"

The shots ripped through the somber stillness of the afternoon. Randi felt her son's small body jerk in shock. She drew him closer against her thigh, preparing him for the volleys yet to come.

"Ready."

The riflemen whipped up their weapons.

"Aim."

The barrels pointed at the cloudless sky.

"Fire!"

Cordite from the second volley added to the first, stinging nostrils and burning eyes. A small arm circled Randi's pants leg and squeezed tight.

Shoulders square, chest aching, Randi stood at rigid attention amid a phalanx of blue. The officers and enlisted personnel of the 137th Airlift Wing of the Oklahoma Air National Guard had gathered at Fort Gibson National Cemetery to say farewell to one of their own.

Or what was left of him, Randi thought with a sharp, slicing pain. It was only by chance that an army patrol had stumbled on his dog tags in a remote village high in the mountains of Afghanistan and forced the villagers to dig up a few charred bones. Now, four months after he'd been listed as missing in action and presumed dead, Captain Tyler Keane had come home to the rolling hills of southeastern Oklahoma.

Randi gripped her son's shoulder as the squad leader rapped out the command for the third and final volley.

"Ready. Aim. *Fire!*"

With the shots still echoing through the hills, the commander of the Oklahoma Air National Guard rose from her seat and stepped forward. General Sanders's white-gloved hands held a flat case. The first female commander of an air guard unit, Sanders epitomized energy, efficiency and smarts. She'd also served as a role model and mentor since the day Randi transferred from the active duty air force to the 137th Airlift Wing and moved back to Oklahoma.

Petite and ramrod-straight, Sanders approached the gaunt, hollowed-eyed man seated between the governor and the two-star Adjutant General of the State of Oklahoma. Opening the flat blue case, she displayed a wreathed gold cross dangling from a blue ribbon edged in bloodred.

"On behalf of a grateful nation, I present the Air Force Cross awarded to your son, Captain Tyler Keane, for extraordinary gallantry against an enemy of the United States."

Stony-eyed, Sam Keane accepted the award, second only to the Congressional Medal of Honor in order of precedence. He didn't utter a word, didn't blink away a tear as General Sanders saluted and then stepped back.

A single drummer tapped his sticks against the rim of his instrument and beat out a solemn cadence. In lock step, the honor guard marched forward. Randi's chest cramped as the six airmen positioned themselves on either side of the flag-draped casket. Taking the edges of the flag, they snapped it taut and began the time-honored ritual of folding it into a triangle that revealed only white stars showing on a field of blue. The lieutenant in charge of the honor guard accepted the flag and carried it to the man Randi had always thought of as a surrogate father.

Sam Keane's eyes burned in their sunken sockets as he took the proffered flag. With the stars against his chest he sat stiff and silent while the lieutenant saluted, executed a precise about-face and left the father staring at his son's coffin.

A faint drone rumbled in the distance. Nothing moved, no one stirred as the rumble gathered sound and fury. Moments later the oaks shading the cemetery shook to the thunder of four C-130s flying low and slow.

Randi squinted into the sky. There they were, the multi-engine cargo aircraft that had come into the air force inventory before she was born. Indispensible to the state and federal governments, the four-engine transports had more than proved their worth both stateside and overseas since the early days of the Vietnam war.

The silhouettes grew larger, the details clearer. Suddenly, Randi's stomach tensed. She could just make out the tail number on the lead aircraft. It was her bird. The same C-130 Hercules she'd flown into that murderous crossfire in Afghanistan all those months ago.

Swallowing hard, she fought the images that screamed inside her head. When the 130s banked left and disappeared beyond the trees, the air rushed from her lungs and a cold sweat trickled down her temples.

The drone of the transports' engines died. In the

distance a bugler sounded "Taps." The silvery notes echoed through the rows of crosses, a last, lonely call that cut into the heart of every military man and woman present.

With the notes pouring out like liquid tears, Randi turned her head and met Sam Keane's eyes. His fierce stare stabbed across his son's casket like an unsheathed sword.

She absorbed the shock of it, forcing herself to stand tall, refusing to look away. Then his gaze dropped to the boy at her side.

His stony facade cracked for a moment, only a moment. Randi glimpsed the desolation and knew what he was thinking. Tyler Keane would have no son to carry on his family name. Sam would have no grandson to mold and shape and bequeath his billions to.

"Mommy!"

The whisper was accompanied by an urgent wiggle. Realizing she'd tightened her hold on her son's shoulder, Randi murmured an apology.

"Sorry, Spence."

The minister said a final prayer. The dignitaries rose, and led by the governor and his wife, they offered their condolences.

Family members came next. Aunts, uncles, cousins. Row after row, they left their chairs to file past the man who sat unmoving beside his son's coffin.

Close friends followed, murmuring words of comfort and sympathy. Randi's very pregnant sister, Sarah, her husband, Cal, and their two children were among them. So was Randi's younger sister, Melissa.

Her eyes red and puffy, Lissa paused in front of Sam. She didn't speak. She knew how meaningless words would be to a man who'd centered all his love, all his pride, on his golden-haired son. Head bowed, she turned and laid a single red rose on the casket. When she ducked under the canopy, tears slid down her cheeks.

Those glistening tracks unlocked so many painful memories. Randi could almost hear Lissa's clear, piping voice announcing that she was going to marry Ty Keane. Could almost see his grin when he ruffled her hair and told her they'd talk marriage when she started wearing a bra. Lissa being Lissa, she'd browbeat her older sisters into taking her shopping for one that same afternoon.

Aching, Randi watched Sarah wrap an arm around Lissa's shaking shoulders and lead her to a dust-covered Cadillac Escalante. Sarah's two kids trailed after them while her husband detoured to take charge of his young nephew.

"C'mon, Hoss. Let's get you to the car while your mom pays her respects."

With a nod of thanks to her brother-in-law, Randi

relinquished her son into his care and joined the line of military personnel and their families moving toward the casket.

Many of these men and women had flown with Ty. All of them knew him. The 137th Airlift Wing was a tight unit, combat tested in Korea, Vietnam, Afghanistan and Iraq, with skills honed by disaster relief, counter-drug and antiterrorist missions here in the States.

Finally, it was Randi's turn. She stepped forward, halted a few paces from the bronze casket and brought her arm up in a final farewell to the man who'd been her friend, her first love, her comrade in arms.

Goodbye, Ty. Sleep well.

Her arm came down. Caught in a morass of grief, guilt and regret, she looked at his father.

"I'm sorry, Sam."

Keane rose, the flag still clutched to the breast of his hand-tailored suit. His eyes were dark and searing. When his lips curled back, his whisper rattled like dry leaves skittering over the open grave.

"Not as sorry as you will be."

Randi clamped her jaw shut. She knew he was grieving. He'd lost his only child. He couldn't accept that accidents happened, especially in the chaos of war.

"Now get the hell out of my sight," he hissed. "I want to say goodbye to my son."

* * *

There was no gathering after the funeral, thank God. Not one Randi and her family had been invited to, anyway.

As Cal's SUV whisked the Morgan sisters away from Fort Gibson and headed south on State Road 64, the three kids strapped into the rear seat chattered nonstop. Cal and Sarah talked quietly in the front. Lissa clung to her sister's hand and stared blindly at hills ablaze with the first colors of fall.

Randi kept her face still and her gaze on the distant smudge of mountains, but Sam's words coiled inside her head like a nest of vicious diamondbacks, spitting venom, striking over and over again.

Not as sorry as you will be.

She couldn't possibly carry any more grief or regret. Both the Safety Investigation Board and the Accident Investigation Board had cleared Randi of any culpability in the incident that had cost Captain Ty Keane his life. After exhaustive reviews, both boards had reported no faulty procedures or pilot error. Only flawed intelligence that had seriously underestimated the ground fire the aircrews could expect on that fatal mission and a last, desperate message garbled in the heat of battle. Randi knew, though, that she would live with Sam's poisonous whispers and the image of Ty's plane exploding into flames forever.

Lifting a hand, she massaged her temple in a futile attempt to ease the pain and erase the awful images alive inside her head.

They were still with her when the Escalante hummed across the bridge spanning the Canadian River. The water meandering through the red mud flats had slowed to a mere trickle. So had the creek that spilled down from the bluff and gave Morgan's Falls its name.

"River's almost dry," Cal observed. "If we don't get a wet winter, you'll have to irrigate before spring planting."

Randi nodded, too spent by the funeral to remind him that she leased out the farm and pastureland these days. She'd given up running the thousand-plus acres herself after 9/11, when she and other "weekend warriors" from the air guard and reserves found themselves called to active duty for months on end. Now Randi managed the business aspects of the Morgan timber and ranching operations. That, along with raising her son and meeting her obligations to the 137th, filled her days.

It also satisfied very different needs. She'd been born and bred to the land, but flying was in her blood. The same grandfather who'd taught her which fields to leave for pasture and which to plant had taught her to pilot a fixed-wing aircraft. She couldn't have been more than five or six the first time Granddad let her take the controls of his single-engine Piper Cub.

Bitten by the flying bug, she'd joined the air force right out of college. While on active duty she'd flown big, honkin' tankers and loved every minute of it. The long deployments to hot spots around the world had taken their toll, though—particularly on her marriage to the handsome surgeon she'd met at a D.C. party and tumbled into love with.

David had professed to admire her independence and career choice, but soon got tired of Randi's absences. In a determined attempt to save her crumbling marriage, she'd left active duty and transferred to a D.C. Air National Guard unit.

The transfer had worked. Her marriage hadn't. The final straw had come when Randi discovered she was pregnant. David, never keen on the idea of children, absolutely refused to adjust his schedule to accommodate hers and pressured Randi to terminate the pregnancy. Instead, she'd filed for divorce, worked another transfer—this one to the 137th—and come home to make a new life for herself and her child.

The birth of her son had put her world to rights. Randi couldn't regret anything that had given her Spencer Daniel Morgan. She thanked God every day for the joy he had brought into her life.

Her family's fierce love had also helped. Her sisters had helped Randi navigate the rocky shoals of divorce, sharing the joys of new motherhood, relinquishing with undisguised relief management of the various family businesses into her capable hands. They'd also helped care for Spencer during Randi's absences. Lissa and Sarah and Cal had been there when she needed them.

So had Ty, she remembered with another piercing ache.

Delighted by her return to Oklahoma, he'd soothed her dented ego with repeated invitations to pick up where they'd left off eight years ago. He'd also eased her transition into the 137th.

Randi had found a home in the 137th. She loved being part of a unit comprising citizen soldiers who took such unabashed pride in service to their state and to their country. The men and women of the 137th had proved themselves over and over. They were still proving themselves.

Members of her unit were in Uzbekistan, Afghanistan and Iraq even now. Randi might've been with them if not for the concussion she'd sustained in the same firefight that had killed Ty.

The throbbing in her temple sharpened. She fought the pain and stared unseeing at the red mud flats of the Canadian. Just past the bridge, Cal turned off the highway, passed under the cut-tin sign identifying the Morgan homestead and bumped over the cattle guard. A cloud of red dust enveloped the SUV as it chewed up the sloping gravel road to the house set high atop the bluff.

The white-painted, two-story structure had been

in Randi's family since they'd first settled in this area, almost a century before Oklahoma had become a state. Added to and modernized many times over the years, the house commanded a sweeping view of the river, the broad valley beyond and the distant, grassy airstrip where her granddad had taught her to fly.

Cal circled the giant oak a long-ago Morgan had planted in the front yard to shade the porch and pulled up beside Lissa's midnight-blue Range Rover. He and Sarah had driven down from Tulsa the night before and had to get back. Eight and a half months pregnant or not, Sarah was due to argue a case in court tomorrow.

Cal left the car running while Randi and Lissa climbed out, but concern filled his warm brown eyes. "Sure you don't want us to stay awhile?"

"Not a good idea. Your wife is just ornery enough to go into labor two weeks early."

"I heard that," Sarah grumbled from the front seat. "Ornery is right. This kid better pop soon *or else.*"

"Or else what?"

"She's been talking about having me gelded," Cal drawled as he unlatched the back seat to let his nephew leave. The four-year-old shot out, hitting the gravel with both feet.

"Bye, Aunt Sarah, bye, Uncle Cal. I'm all packed, Aunt Lissa. I'll go get my stuff."

Legs pumping, Spencer raced for the porch while Randi gave her brother-in-law a final hug. When Cal put the Cadillac in gear, she hooked her arm through Lissa's. Together, the sisters walked to the house where they'd shared so much laughter and joy.

They'd grown up in this house. Randi and Sarah and Lissa. Raised by their grandparents after a car accident killed the mother and father Randi could barely remember. Although shares in the land and various business interests had been apportioned evenly among the sisters after their grandparents died, the house had been left to Randi as the oldest.

Strange, she thought, as she mounted the steps. As much as she loved this place, she'd never imagined she and her son would take up residence here. But the house had sheltered Randi after the breakup of her marriage and it welcomed her now.

Shade washed over her and Lissa when they entered the screened-in porch, blocking the bright October sun. The verandah ran the length of the house and had always been the family's preferred gathering place. The sturdy bentwood furniture, mounted buck with a full rack of antlers and antique washtub planted with cheerful pansies were permanent fixtures. The laser swords, scattered action figures and a plastic castle complete with turrets and drawbridge were more recent additions.

Randi tossed her purse and flight cap onto a

rocker and peeled off her uniform jacket. Used to wearing a flight suit on duty and jeans off, she wanted out of her skirt and panty hose in the worst way, but Lissa's red, puffy eyes concerned her more than her own comfort.

"You okay, Lis?"

"More or less. How about you?"

"I'll make it."

Lissa hugged her arms, looking pale and subdued. She and Randi shared the same glossy black hair, warm complexion and slender build. They'd also shared a lifelong fascination with Tyler Keane.

"I miss him, Randi. I know you were the one he loved, but I miss him."

"He loved us both."

"Not in the same way. I was always just the pesky kid following you two around. You were the one he wanted."

Randi swallowed a sigh at the memory of those hormone-driven high school years. God, they'd been so young then. So hot for each other.

"I never understood why you didn't marry him," Lissa murmured.

Randi had her reasons, but none her sister would understand. Lissa had always worshipped Ty Keane.

"What can I say? My judgment sucks when it comes to men."

"He still wanted you, Randi. After your divorce,

he would've hustled you right off to Vegas if you'd let him."

"I wasn't going to jump out of one mess into another."

Her sister's delicate black brows drew together. "There was more to it than that, wasn't there?"

There was. So much more. But Randi's tangled relationship with Ty Keane had been buried with him this afternoon. It would stay buried.

Thankfully, a series of thumps announced her son's rapid descent from his upstairs bedroom and diverted her sister's attention.

"You sure you want me to take Spencer back to Dallas?" Lissa asked quietly. "I don't like the idea of you being alone out here."

Randi wasn't too keen on it, either. She'd lost so many months with her son during the long stretches the 137th had been called to active duty. Her sisters had cared for Spencer during those absences and he'd thoroughly enjoyed staying with his aunts and lively cousins. Now that she was home, though, Randi hated giving up even a few precious hours with him. But Lissa had uttered her rash promise weeks ago and the four-year-old never forgot a single word of any conversation about fishing expeditions, visits to Chuck E. Cheese's or the Texas State Fair.

"He's been looking forward to the fair so much, Lis. And it'll help me out. I've got drill this weekend."

Spencer barreled onto the porch at that point, dragging his Power Rangers backpack behind him. He'd changed into his favorite jeans and Tyrannosaurus Rex T-shirt. His Redhawks baseball cap sat sideways on his burnished gold curls.

"All set?" Randi asked, a smile forming for the first time that day.

"All set." He made a beeline for the screen door. "Bye, Mommy."

"Hey! Hold on there, bud. How about a kiss?"

He spun around, charged back and scrambled up onto a chair. Randi bent over so he could reach her. She ached to wrap an arm around her son and hold his warm body against her heart, but he was revved up and eager to go. She settled for tugging on the brim of his ball cap.

"Have fun."

"I will." He jumped down and grabbed Lissa's hand. "C'mon, Aunt Lis."

"Hang on a sec." Resisting his tug, she appealed to Randi. "Why don't you come with us? Enjoy the big-city lights for a few days?"

"I can't. I missed too much drill time in the past four months."

"Because you were recovering from a severe concussion! And I know you're still having headaches."

"Not so much anymore."

Lissa pursed her lips. "Just promise me you'll take it easy, okay?"

"I can't do anything else. I'm flying a desk until the flight surgeon clears me to climb back in the cockpit."

Two more months. That was all Randi had to wait. Assuming the headaches remained manageable and she didn't develop delayed complications from the injury that had grounded her for a mandatory six-month observation period.

She itched to get back to flying. She was a trained aviator. One of the best. She had the medals, the citations and the scars to prove it. It was what she did. Who she was.

Once she returned to flying status, though, she'd face a tough career decision. Almost as tough as the decision to leave active duty and transfer to the guard.

In the past few years, the 137th had pulled long stretches of active service in support of the war on terrorism. If the world situation didn't improve dramatically, they'd pull more—and Randi would have to choose between service to her country and her son.

Until then she was stuck with administrative work. And even that took its toll. She didn't like to admit it, but the two-hour drive to Oklahoma City, the long days and the pressure of her temporary duties had Randi's head pounding when she crawled into bed at night.

Lissa understood how much those weekend

drills took out of her. "I know you. You're so damned stubborn, you'll push yourself too hard and—"

"You're not supposed to say damn," Spencer chirped. "Or hell or shit."

Caught in the act, Lissa grinned. "That pretty well leaves me high and dry, doesn't it, champ?"

He tugged on her hand again, eager to go to the land of corn dogs, Ferris wheels and Big Tex. "Let's *go*, Aunt Lis!"

"Okay, okay."

"Call me when you get to Dallas," Randi said.

"We will."

The silence hit her the moment she passed through the front door into the wide hallway. It wasn't the welcoming quiet of a house that had been home to generations of Morgans. Nor the comfortable calm of a refuge. Utter stillness surrounded her, hushed, brooding, haunted.

Without her family's presence to hold it at bay, the ugly scene at the cemetery came rushing back. Sam was grieving, Randi told herself again. He was hurting. He'd clung to hope for more than four months, unwilling to accept that his son had died in a fiery disaster high in the mountains of Afghanistan.

He had no choice now. The dog tags had been the first proof. Then DNA testing had confirmed that the bone fragments found buried in that shallow grave belonged to Captain Tyler Keane.

Weary beyond words, Randi changed out of her uniform into jeans and a royal-blue sweatshirt bearing the 137th wing logo of an Indian chief in full war bonnet. The headache she'd refused to acknowledge until now hammered at her temples, so she unclipped her hair and raked a hand through the dark, heavy mass. The relief was instant, if not complete. She could live with the throbbing, she told herself. The docs had prescribed painkillers, but Randi resorted to them only when absolutely necessary.

Shoving her feet into comfortable loafers, she started for the kitchen to brew a pitcher of iced tea. The crunch of tires on the gravel drive caused a change of direction. Thinking her son had forgotten one of his favorite toys, she detoured back to the porch.

It wasn't Lissa's Range Rover that circled the towering oak, however, but a dusty red pickup. When the Ford F-150 slowed to a stop, a stranger got out.

He stood for a moment, looking around. A maroon University of Oklahoma ball cap shaded the upper portion of his face. A blue denim shirt stretched across broad shoulders and was tucked into well-washed jeans.

"Can I help you?"

He squinted through the late-afternoon sunlight. "Captain Morgan?"

"Yes."

"I'm Pete Engstrom."

The way he said his name suggested she should know it.

"I'd like to talk to you. May I come in?"

Randi had lived on her own for too many years to invite a stranger into her house, even one with this man's easy smile.

"What's this about, Mr. Engstrom?"

"Actually, it's Dr. Engstrom. I'm heading the University of Oklahoma team."

"Team?"

"The research team Dr. Bruhn spoke with you about."

When Randi remained silent, his smile slipped.

"You didn't get a call from the head of the OU Physics Department, requesting permission for a research team to access your land?"

"No, I didn't."

He tilted back his ball cap to reveal a thatch of dark-brown hair shot with red. "Well, hell! They told me you were contacted last week."

"About what?"

"OU has received a grant to study the runestones in this area. The grant specifically refers to the Heavener stone, the ones in the Kerr Museum and the one on your property."

Randi couldn't quite make the connection between the University of Oklahoma Physics Department and the carvings chiseled into the weathered gray stone high on a bluff overlooking the Arkansas River. A good number of local scholars believed Vikings had carved the distinctive runic inscriptions. This popular—if unsubstantiated—theory held that early Norse explorers had sailed down the coast of America, rounded Florida, crossed the Gulf and rowed up the Mississippi and Arkansas rivers deep into the wild, untamed land that eventually became Oklahoma.

"I don't get it. Why is someone from the physics department the lead on this research team? I would've thought ancient runes fell under the purview of the archeology or history department."

"You'd think so, but…well, it's complicated. May I come in?" he asked again. "I'll explain this project's unique approach."

Intrigued, she lifted the latch. Engstrom brought the tang of some lemony aftershave onto the porch with him. He also brought a good six-three of solid muscle. Feeling suddenly crowded, Randi stepped back a pace.

"You said something about a grant?"

"It's part of a ten-million-dollar gift from a distinguished University of Oklahoma alum. Mr. Sam Keane. I believe you're acquainted with him?"

Her insides went tight. Sam's face leaped into her mind, his deep-set eyes burning with hatred.

"Yes, Dr. Engstrom. I am."

2

Pete blinked, taken aback by the sudden frost Sam Keane's name had brought to the captain's blue eyes.

The newspaper coverage he'd read about Miranda Morgan after her return from Afghanistan indicated she and Keane's son had been good friends as well as members of the same air national unit. The iciness in her face and her voice suggested otherwise.

Then again, that could be grief behind her withdrawal. Pete knew Captain Keane had been buried earlier today. He didn't doubt Miranda Morgan had attended the funeral. The timing of his visit couldn't be worse, but he'd had little choice. Captain Keane's father had included specific instructions with his unexpected gift. Instructions Pete was now obligated to fulfill.

"I'm sorry to take you by surprise like this. I assumed Dr. Bruhn had apprised you of the grant. If he had, he would've told you Mr. Keane made the gift in memory of his son."

Her skin seemed to stretch tight across her cheekbones. She looked different from the pictures in the news stories, Pete thought. The cloud of black hair framing her face made it seem thinner. More fragile. The skin under her eyes was shadowed, almost bruised.

Just went to show how deceptive appearances could be. This woman had to be anything *but* fragile, considering what she'd gone through in Afghanistan. If even half the newspaper stories were true, Morgan and her crew were lucky to have survived at all. Sam Keane's son hadn't been as fortunate.

"In the letter laying out the conditions of the grant, Mr. Keane said his son had often expressed interest in the runes. Particularly the one on your property."

Miranda Morgan's eyes shifted to the mountains just visible in the distance. "That's true," she said after a short silence. "Ty and I used to climb up to the bluff all the time when we were kids. He was fascinated by the runes."

"Archeologists have been attempting to date and validate their source for more than fifty years," Pete said quietly. "Solving their riddle would be a fitting tribute to the memory of your friend."

She brought her gaze back. He saw a keen intelligence in those startlingly blue eyes, along with a slowly gathering suspicion.

"I'm well aware of the mystery surrounding the runes, Dr. Engstrom. I wasn't aware Ty's father cared that much about solving it, though."

"Evidently he does. He's made his generous gift to the university contingent on this study and specifically cited the runes on your property."

"You mean OU doesn't receive the ten million unless I give you access to my land?"

"That's correct."

A crease formed between her brows. "I've known Sam my whole life. He doesn't do anything without a reason, and his reasons are never what they seem. I'll have to think about this and get back to you."

"I hate to pressure you, Ms. Morgan, but I've got an entire team on standby." He slid the cell phone clipped to his waist out of its holder. "Why don't we give Mr. Keane a call and talk about it now?"

"No! This isn't a good time for Sam. Or for me." Her jaw set, she reached behind him for the screen door. "I'll think about this and—"

She broke off suddenly, wincing as the color leached out of her face. When she seemed to sway, Pete lunged forward and made a grab for her arm.

"Are you okay?"

Steadying, she jerked free of his hold. Her rigid

expression suggested she was anything but grateful for his assistance.

"I'm fine."

Well, shit! He was blowing this. Fast running out of options, Pete resorted to the brisk tone he employed in a lecture hall crammed with rowdy freshmen.

"How about we sit down, Captain Morgan? I've driven all the way out here. The least you can do is give me five minutes."

Her quick frown said she wasn't used to being ordered around by civilians.

"You're very persistent, Dr. Engstrom."

He'd been called worse. Much worse. Reaching for one of the bentwood chairs, he scooted it around.

"Yes, I am. Sit."

Her eyes narrowed.

"Please," he tacked on. "If you're not tired, I am. It's been a helluva— Sorry, a heck of a day."

Some of her belligerence seeped away. "You were right the first time."

To his relief, she settled into another chair and swung a jean-clad leg. The leg was as shapely as the rest of her, Pete noted as he pulled another chair around, and the swing decidedly impatient.

"All right, Dr. Engstrom. You've got five minutes."

"At the risk of wasting one of them, I'd like to suggest we dispense with titles and start over." He held out his hand. "I'm Pete."

She hesitated, then returned his handshake with a firm grip. "Miranda. Randi for short."

The short, boyish name fit her, Pete decided. Those striking features and trim curves came with a no-nonsense attitude and the assurance of a combat-tested veteran.

"Now about this project?" she asked pointedly.

"As I said, the OU physics department has the lead, and we're approaching it more as a scientific experiment than an archeological survey. We'll be field-testing a new imaging process, one we hope will have significant value in the study of three-dimensional objects incised in stone or other hard surfaces. The tests won't disturb or damage your property in any way. Nor will we be in your hair for very long. We're operating under rather severe time constraints."

To put it mildly. The grant specified that the study had to be completed within sixty days.

Despite the short notice and restrictive operating parameters, Pete had managed to assemble a team of unquestioned experts and consultants that included a noted cryptologist from the University of Chicago and the curator at the Oslo Museum of Medieval and Viking Heritage. Good thing Sam Keane was footing the bill for their airfare. Pete was flying both men in first class.

"We'll employ nonintrusive methods to date the runes. Our spectrographic equipment is state of the art and uses axial transmissive holographic imaging to—"

"How are you going to get to them?"

"Excuse me?"

"The runestones at Heavener State Park and the ones in the Kerr Museum are easily accessible. The stone on my property sits on a high, steep bluff. So how do you propose to transport your state-of-the-art equipment up there?"

"We plan to bring the equipment here by truck, then transfer to all-terrain vehicles."

"Won't work. You say you don't intend to damage my property. Yet ATVs chew up pastureland and adversely affect noise levels."

So much for their brief truce.

"I didn't incorporate ATV decibel levels into the project's environmental impact assessment," Pete admitted, "but I'm confident the noise these vehicles emit is within acceptable standards."

"You think so? My sister and brother-in-law are attorneys. She specializes in environmental law. What do you want to bet her interpretation of what constitutes noise pollution would hold a whole lot more weight than yours?"

Pete didn't have time for a lengthy court battle. Not if he was going to complete this project by the specified deadline.

"Fine. We'll backpack the equipment up to the site."

She folded her arms, looking both amused and skeptical. "You want to trek up into the mountains on foot. Hauling a load of equipment. It would almost be worth watching you try."

"I intend to do more than try. Those runes have mystified archeologists and historians for decades. Using holographic scanning techniques to determine their origin could open a whole new chapter in Oklahoma history."

Leaning forward, Pete pulled out all the stops.

"Your family is part of that history, Ms. Morgan. Randi. One of your ancestors was a member of the Wilkinson Expedition that charted this area after the United States acquired it in the Louisiana Purchase. As I understand it, he married a half-French, half-Osage woman and was the first Morgan to settle on this land."

"You've done your homework."

He didn't mistake the terse comment for a compliment.

"Yes, I have. A key member of my team is an archeologist. History is her passion as well as her profession. She's informed me that another Morgan served at Fort Gibson and assisted in the resettlement of the eastern tribes following the Indian Removal Act of 1831. Whatever your view of that forced resettlement, it constitutes one of the major milestones in the cultural evolution of this state."

Her gaze drilled into him, but Pete was damned if he could tell what the woman was thinking.

"You owe your heritage to those who came before you, Randi. And you owe it to your children to let us study what could be an important piece of their heritage."

That registered. He caught the flicker of acknowledgement in her face, saw her gaze shift to the distant mountains again.

"Give me a number where I can get hold of you," she said after a moment. "I'll get back to you."

Not good enough. Pete wanted her approval before he left today.

"I mentioned that we're operating under rather severe time constraints. I need to conduct the initial site surveys next week. I'd planned to go up to the runestone on your property on Monday, since it's the most difficult to get to."

"Leave me a phone number."

The response was flat and unequivocal. Pete considered his options and knew they'd narrowed to just one. Reaching into his back pocket, he produced his wallet and dug out a business card.

"This has my office and cell phone numbers on it."

She studied the embossed lettering that encapsulated his life. Dr. Peter Engstrom, Professor, Department of Physics, University of Oklahoma.

"Answer me this, Dr. Engstrom."

"Pete."

"Answer me this, Pete. What do *you* get if you solve the riddle? Academic glory? International renown? Or something more substantial?"

"Our department hopes to validate axial transmissive holographic imaging as a means to—"

"No, you personally. What do you get out of this?"

"My associate and I developed this process. We've also applied for a provisional patent to protect it. If these field tests are successful, we intend to market it commercially."

"I thought so."

Her lip didn't exactly curl, but it came close. Pete refused to let the almost-sneer put him on the defensive. Sure, he hoped to validate the process he'd worked on for more than a year. And yes, it could result in significant profits when commercial and government agencies recognized its potential.

The FAA had already contacted Pete about the possibility of using his imaging techniques to analyze metal fatigue and stress fractures, with the goal of preventing catastrophic failure of aircraft parts.

The potential to save hundreds, maybe thousands, of lives drove him far more than the possibility of personal gain. As Pete's former fiancée had so often—and so bitingly—commented, he could easily have earned a six-figure income in private research. Brilliant, beautiful, ambitious Alison had never understood why Pete would "settle" for being a college professor and poke around in a university lab. She certainly wouldn't have understood the thrill of the hunt. Or why he was so eager to take his process into the field and, maybe, solve a riddle that had puzzled scientists for decades.

Provided Miranda Morgan agreed to the project. He was damned if he could tell which way she was leaning when she repeated her brisk, "I'll be in touch."

Rising, Pete gave her a crisp nod. "Make it soon, please. I'd like to finish the site prep before the rest of the team arrives next week."

Randi didn't bother to get to her feet as her uninvited guest exited the porch. She wasn't sure if the pain spiking into her head would let her, and she sure as heck didn't want to fall flat on her face in front of the man.

Frowning, she followed his progress across the yard. He walked with a long-legged stride that said he knew where he was going and was in a hurry to get there. Randi added lean hips and a tight butt to her previous inventory.

Gravel crunched under his truck's wheels as he steered around the oak. When he raised a hand in a brief wave, Randi's mouth twisted. She suspected Engstrom would much rather have flipped her the bird.

Only when the truck had started down the hill did she hook his chair with her left foot to drag it closer. Grunting, she lifted her legs and plopped her feet on the cushion. So far she'd resisted the painkillers the flight surgeon had prescribed. She just might have to give in tonight. The stress of the day and the heartache of Ty's funeral had overwhelmed her.

Ty's funeral.

Christ!

Resting her head against the chair back, Randi stared sightlessly through the screen at hills aflame with fall color. She and Ty had roamed those hills as kids. As horny teenagers, they'd driven up to a favorite overlook and steamed the car windows. Their special place, though, was the rocky precipice in the northeast corner of Morgan property.

It was their private retreat, practically inaccessible except by deer and cougar and the occasional heifer determined to get lost among the tangle of scrub oak and pine. At one time, the rocky crag had provided an eagle's view of the Arkansas River snaking along the horizon. The massive Robert S. Kerr reservoir, created as part of the Corps of Engineering's Arkansas River Navigation System, now dominated the vista.

The panoramic view was magnificent, but the symbols carved into a rock tucked under a ledge had always enthralled Ty even more than the scenery.

He'd read every book written about the Oklahoma runes and would fiercely debate their similarity to those found further up the Mississippi. He'd been entranced with the idea of Vikings in Oklahoma and considered himself a modern-day warrior cast in the same mold.

Was that what Sam's gift was all about? A desire to cherish his son's memory by indulging his fantasies? Randi might have believed that if not for their bitter exchange this afternoon.

She knew what was feeding Sam's festering hate. Two lines from the Accident Investigation Board's final report.

Captain Keane calls for air strike to destroy his downed aircraft and deny its cargo of munitions to insurgents.

Captain Morgan radios immediate counterorder.

Randi's breath came faster. Her heart pumped. She could feel the sweat pool at the base of her spine.

The palette of reds and oranges painting the distant hills faded. A barren landscape filled her vision. Brown, all brown. No speck of color, no shimmer of water.

A howling wind and the wash of four turboprops whipped sand into a frenzy. Tracers seemed to come from all directions. Radio transmissions crackled. Randi heard Ty's shout through her headset. Desperate. Urgent.

Clear! Clear! Clear! Roll in hot!
"No!"

The scream ripped from her throat, startling a
clutch of sparrows from the oak towering over the
porch. The birds cannoned through leaves and
branches, beating their wings, yanking Randi back
from a fiery hell.

She dragged in great, painful gulps of air. The
firestorm died. The howling winds faded. All that
remained was the searing image of Ty pitching forward into the dun-colored dirt.

3

Pete pulled into the university town of Norman, Oklahoma, a little past 6:00 p.m. The drive back from Morgan's Falls had left him tired, thirsty and frustrated.

The fifties-era brick bungalow he rented on Elm Street offered relief from at least two of those conditions. It came with a sagging porch and minuscule one-car garage, but he liked its convenience to campus and the fact that the owner had bumped out the wall in the master bedroom to make room for a man-sized shower.

He'd get around to buying a place of his own one of these days. Maybe. If he stayed at OU. He'd be up for tenure next year, but hadn't decided whether he wanted to become a permanent fixture. He enjoyed teaching and his relative freedom to muck around with optics, but the politics of academia constituted a definite downside to his chosen profession.

When he climbed out of the truck, he saw the nose poking at the miniblinds a half second before a series of ecstatic woofs blasted through the front window. Grimacing, Pete unlocked the door and braced himself.

Claws scrabbled on hardwood flooring. One hundred and thirty pounds of sheer joy streaked out of the living room. Two oversize paws landed on Pete's chest and knocked him back a couple of paces.

Part Great Dane, part mastiff and all energy, the animal shoved a velvety black muzzle in Pete's face and unrolled a tongue at least a foot long.

"Get down, you idiot." He tried to stiff-arm the dog. "Get— Aw, jeez!"

Grimacing, he dodged a near-slurp. The animal took that as an invitation to play. Dropping onto his haunches, the half dog, half horse gathered the muscles under his tan hide. A powerful lunge brought a brindled forehead smacking into Pete's chin.

"Get *down!*"

The message finally penetrated. Dog sank to his haunches. Tongue lolling, he grinned at the man whose truck bed he'd climbed into a few weeks back and refused to climb out of. Like a fool, Pete had brought him home until his owner stepped forward to claim him.

No one had responded to either the ads Pete had run in the newspaper or the flyers he'd tacked up around town. After dealing with these ecstatic greetings and industrial-size deposits in the backyard, he figured he knew why.

"You're going to the pound," he swore. "First thing in the morning."

Since he'd uttered the same threat at least a dozen times in the past two weeks, the animal didn't seem particularly fazed by it. Shooting him an evil glare, Pete headed into the kitchen.

Dog sprang up and galloped ahead in joyous anticipation. Pete let him out the back door into the postage-stamp yard. After a quick dash out to drench the one scraggly azalea, he raced back in. His tail whapped from side to side with lethal force as he waited in front of the fridge for the beer that had become part of their evening ritual.

"Okay, but only one tonight," Pete muttered. "I've got work to do."

Dog slurped his Coors from a plastic soup bowl. Pete downed a long swallow of his standing in the kitchen, then carried the bottle to his bedroom. He needed a shower before hitting his laptop.

A flick of the remote brought the TV to life. With half an ear tuned to Cherokee Ballard, anchor for the six-thirty local news, Pete stripped off. He was down to his jockey shorts when Cherokee captured his full attention.

"Captain Tyler Keane was buried today at Fort Gibson National Cemetery with full military honors. A local hero, Captain Keane was listed as missing in action and presumed dead in Afghanistan four months ago. His remains were recently recovered and returned to Oklahoma for burial."

Pete heard the echo of a bugle sounding off-screen. He'd done a hitch in the marines right out of high school and had racked up a number of unforgettable experiences during those two and a half years. The mournful notes of "Taps" could still give him a kick to the gut. Without thinking, he squared his shoulders and remained rigid until the announcer picked up the story again.

"Captain Keane was based at Karshi-Khanabad, a former Soviet air base in Uzbekistan called K-2 by the men and women based there. Captain Keane was flying an Air National Guard C-130 Hercules like this one—"

The newsroom cut away to show stock footage of a four-engine transport plowing across a stormy sky.

"—on a mission to resupply a firebase inside Afghanistan when his plane was hit by a surface-to-air missile. According to official reports, Captain Keane executed an emergency landing at another abandoned Russian airstrip. He and his crew held off hostiles attempting to overrun their position until a second C-130 piloted by fellow air guard officer, Captain Miranda Morgan, swooped in to pick them up."

The scene switched back to the Fort Gibson cemetery. Telephoto lenses zoomed in on the woman Pete had met only a few hours ago. She was in full dress uniform, shoulders stiff, expression closed.

"Her aircraft also sustained severe damage from small-arms and mortar fire, but was able to return to K-2. In a heartbreaking twist of circumstance, Captain Morgan and Captain Keane were not only comrades in arms, they were also close friends from high school."

The camera then shifted to the female general who approached a gaunt, stiff-backed figure.

"Brigadier General Rebecca Sanders, Commander of the Oklahoma Air National Guard, presented the Air Force Cross posthumously to Captain Keane's father this afternoon. The award cited the captain's extraordinary heroism in providing covering fire for his crew while they ran for Captain Morgan's plane. Captain Keane then called in an air strike to destroy his aircraft and deny its load of munitions to the insurgents. Tragically, when he himself made for the rescue plane, he triggered one of the millions of land mines sowed by the Russians in their twenty-year conflict with the Afghanis."

Helluva way to go, Pete thought grimly as the announcer's voice assumed a somber, respectful tone.

"Captain Keane's father, oil magnate and noted philanthropist Sam Keane, has made a ten-million-dollar gift to the University of Oklahoma in his son's memory."

No word of the special provisions attached to that gift, Pete noted. Or the fact that the entire ten million was contingent on a project requiring Miranda Morgan's consent.

Interesting.

"In another story, the Oklahoma Highway Patrol closed a portion of I-44 today after a semi hauling a load of steel beams overturned."

Half listening, Pete headed for the shower. Dog followed, his tail pumping. Only a securely locked bathroom door kept the animal from leaping into the stall.

It was still dark when Pete left his house the next morning. And cold! A front had moved in overnight. The temperature was supposed to reach the mid-sixties by noon, perfect for the eighty-three-thousand fans who'd crowd into the football stadium later that afternoon, but hovered in the low forties as Pete drove to the campus.

Wishing he'd stopped for coffee, he let himself into the red brick building housing the Department of Physics and Astronomy. Nielsen Hall had been constructed in the forties, but hefty grants by alumni like Sam Keane had ensured the interior lived up to the standards expected of a world-class teaching and research facility.

A scarred oak table stretched the length of the main lobby. This table had long formed the nerve center of the physics department. Faculty, staff, grad students and undergrads gathered on weekday afternoons for "tea," which took the form of black coffee, oatmeal raisin cookies and the occasional pizza. The chalkboard dominating the wall behind the table sported its usual array of formulae and graffiti.

The table was also a favorite gathering place for late-night cramming and bull sessions. More than one student had spent the entire night slumped on its surface.

Sure enough, a fuzzy-bearded student snored softly beside his flickering laptop. This early in the semester, Pete figured it was more likely beer than late-night studies that had gotten to him. Leaving the kid to his sonorous dreams, he made for the second-floor optics lab. He wanted one more shot at calibrating the holographic imaging spectrograph before he took it into the field.

If he took it into the field.

"Call me," he muttered to the distant Miranda Morgan as he entered the lab. "Today."

"Are you talking to me?"

Brought up short, Pete blinked at his lab assistant. "What are you doing here so early?"

The second-year grad student curved her pink, glossed lips. "I figured you'd want to run another test on that sample the archeology department sent over. I brought coffee. And French crullers."

"Bless you, my child."

Her smile lifted in a sardonic tilt, and Pete was forced to admit Anne Gillette looked nothing like a child as she nudged the green-and-white Krispy Kreme carton in his direction. Her silky blond hair played peekaboo with one cheek in classic Veronica Lake style. Her mouth was red and full and all too seductive. With some effort, Pete managed not to stare at the generous breasts stretching the front of her spandex T-shirt.

The woman certainly didn't fit the mold of your typical physics grad student. They tended more toward baggy sweatshirts, scruffy jeans and scraggly beards, like the kid slumped over the table in the hall.

The other profs had ragged Pete unmercifully when gorgeous, stacked Anne Gillette requested Professor Engstrom as her faculty advisor. Pete hadn't wasted his breath reminding the horny bastards that Anne attended OU on a full scholarship. Or that her IQ exceeded her bust size by exponential degrees. They'd figured that out for themselves when she'd aced every one of their classes.

Nor had he told his colleagues—or anyone else—that Anne had come on to him early in their association. God knew he'd been tempted. Okay, he still was. Any man whose pecker didn't sit up and take notice when she sauntered by needed a double dose of Viagra.

But Pete had been burned once by a woman almost as brilliant and ambitious and competitive as Anne Gillette. He wasn't about to get burned again.

"Do we have the go-ahead on the runestone project?" she asked as Pete bit into a honey-glazed cruller.

"Not exactly."

"Come again?"

"Morgan didn't give me a yes, but she didn't turn me down flat, either." He wolfed down the rest of the pastry and dusted his hands on the seat of his jeans. "Hopefully, I'll hear from her today."

"You'd better. You've got a whole team hanging fire, waiting for the signal to move."

"Tell me something I don't know. Let's get to work."

Thirty minutes later, Pete had one lens of the spectrograph aligned on a fragment of inscribed stone borrowed from the Sam Noble Natural History Museum on campus. He'd almost finished calibrating the second lens when his cell phone began to vibrate.

Cursing under his breath, he shot a glance at the caller ID display. The name and number on the screen caught his attention instantly.

"I need to take this."

Anne yelped a protest. "No! We almost have the FT definition fixed."

"This is the call I've been waiting for. Cut the beam splitter."

Groaning, she switched off the power source. Pete got the phone to his ear on the second ring.

"Engstrom."

"This is Randi Morgan. You have my permission to access our land for your study."

That was it. No *Hello, I enjoyed talking to you yesterday, hope you'll keep me posted on your progress.* But what the hell. She'd just handed him exactly what he wanted.

"Great. I'll be at your place early Monday morning."

"How early?"

"Around eight."

"Make it nine. I drop my son off at preschool at eight-thirty." She hesitated several beats before extending a grudging offer. "I'll show you the way up to the bluff. The path is difficult to find if you don't know where to look for it."

"Should I wear my hiking boots?"

The question produced a short, charged silence.

"No," she conceded with something less than graciousness. "And you don't need to haul in an ATV. We keep several heavy-duty utility vehicles in the barn. We can take those or go by horseback if you prefer."

Pete couldn't remember the last time he'd swung a leg over a horse. "I'm a whole lot better with mechanical conveyances than I am with the four-legged variety."

"All right, ATVs it is."

"I'll see you Monday. And thanks. My department head will do cartwheels when I tell him about your call. I'm sure Mr. Keane will be pleased, as well."

"I'm not doing this for your department head." Her response was so sharp it could have etched glass. "Or for Sam Keane. This is for Ty."

She hung up and left Pete wavering between exhilaration, irritation and anticipation. Miranda Morgan might be prickly, but she'd given him the green light and that was all that mattered.

"The runestone project is a go," he informed his lab assistant.

"So I gathered."

"I've got to make some calls. How about packing things up while I find Dr. Hawkins? He'll have to cover my lectures for the next few weeks."

Pete hated having to dump his classes in the middle of the semester, but the OU president himself had directed him to give this project his full and undivided attention. Ten million bucks was ten million bucks.

His mind racing with everything that needed to be done before next week, he started for the door.

"Hawkins can cover my senior optics labs. You'll have to take the freshman intro sessions, Anne."

"No way!" With a dismayed squawk, his assistant rounded the table. "I've been working with you on this high-NA polarization technique for more than a year. This is our first chance to test it in the field. I want to be part of the research team."

"It's already too big."

"So bounce Dr. Lockwood's graduate assistant. What's his name? Grady?"

"Brady."

"You need me more than you need another bonehead from the archeology department."

Determination narrowed her emerald eyes. Pete had always suspected the luminescent color came more from tinted lenses than pigmentation. Whatever the source, Anne knew how to use it to stunning effect.

"You know I want to focus on coherent imaging of birefringent samples for my doctoral thesis. I need hard data to support my thesis proposal."

"Dr. Bruhn will never go for both of us taking off in the middle of the semester."

The head of the physics department hadn't been particularly thrilled about Pete's involvement in this interdisciplinary project to begin with. Academic politics and funding wars played heavily at OU, as at any university. Or they had until Sam Keane dropped his bomb.

"I want in," Anne repeated stubbornly. "I'll speak to Dr. Bruhn."

"He won't buy it. Dan Tobias is down with mono, so we're short a teaching assistant as it is."

She looked him straight in the eye. "I'll speak to Dr. Bruhn."

That answered one question in Pete's mind. He'd wondered about Anne's propensity to hang around Nielsen Hall more than usual lately. He had a good idea of the reason after he'd spotted her leaving Bruhn's office past midnight a few weeks ago. Obviously, she'd shifted her attention from Pete to a target higher up the food chain.

Well, that was her business. And Bruhn's. The department chairman wouldn't be the first professor to jeopardize his marriage, his reputation and his career by getting involved with a graduate student. And the blunt truth was that Pete could use Anne on this project.

"If Bruhn concurs, you're in."

"Good. I'll take a miss on my classes this week and reschedule the labs—"

"I don't need you until the full team assembles."

"Didn't I just hear you tell the Morgan woman you're beginning the site surveys Monday?"

"I am, but I can handle those on my own. You'll help more by staying here and working the logistics. Let's go down to my office. I've got the detailed requirements list on my computer."

His mind in full gear, Pete almost sprinted down the stairs to the first floor. The zoned-out student was still slumped over the table. Pete and Anne detoured around him and left him to his twitchy dreams.

Pete's office was halfway down the south hall, next to the one occupied by his associate, the guru of quarks and gluons, Tom Hawkins. The office boasted a single window that overlooked the historic South Oval, a fact that attested to Pete's seniority. The more junior profs got a view of the alley behind Nielsen Hall.

Anne followed him in, clucking as she always did at the books, journals, papers and coffee cups occupying every horizontal surface. She'd tried a number of times to organize both Pete and his private space, but had finally written them off. Thank God. He functioned better when surrounded by chaos.

Booting up his computer, he printed out the schedule he'd created using a tentative start date of Monday, October 20th. Good thing Morgan had come through. If she hadn't, he might've had to resort to the big guns for additional persuasion. The OU president. The chairman of the awards and grants committee. Sam Keane himself.

Although…

Everything Pete had read when he was throwing together the proposal for this study indicated the old man was a close friend of the Morgan family. Ditto his son. And last night's news coverage had emphasized Captain Keane's personal and professional relationship with Miranda Morgan.

Yet Pete had sensed a definite chill when he'd informed her about the gift Keane had made in his son's name. She'd come within a breath of turning him down, despite her admission that the runes had intrigued both her and Keane's son. The reluctance had come through again this morning, when she'd given her grudging approval.

Pete's gut told him there was more to the curious conditions Keane had attached to his grant than he knew at this point. And more to the woman who figured large in those conditions.

Captain Miranda Morgan was beginning to interest him almost as much as the puzzle of the rune-stones.

4

Randi sat hunched in the driver's seat of her Jeep
Cherokee. The engine idled, puffing exhaust into
the chilly October dawn. She'd pulled into the
Metro Tech parking lot to make the call to Engstrom
and now trembled inside her green Nomex flight
suit.

Vehicles streamed by on the road just beyond the
parking lot. A steady flow headed for the 137th Airlift Wing's west gate and the mandatory, once-a-
month drill for those personnel not serving on
active duty elsewhere or getting in training hours
by flying sorties during the month. She stared
blindly at the stream of headlights, trying to convince herself she'd made the right decision in allowing Engstrom access to her property.

God knew she'd gone back and forth about it. All

through a long, sleepless night. Well into the dark hours before dawn, when she'd begun the long drive from Morgan's Falls to Oklahoma City. Only after she'd turned south off I-40 onto MacArthur and spotted the hangars at Will Rogers World Airport had she made her decision.

Randi had grown up hearing tales of the Spanish conquistadors, French trappers and Native American warriors who'd roamed the plains and mountains in this part of the country. The stories were woven into her heritage, threaded through her family history. The possibility of adding Vikings to that eclectic assortment had long tugged at her imagination.

Now there was a chance it could actually happen. More important, scientists might solve the riddle of the runes. She understood the importance of Engstrom's research and its potential impact on Oklahoma history. She probably wouldn't have hesitated to agree to his request yesterday if not for the fact that Sam Keane was funding the study.

Her gut told her the funding was somehow tied to Sam's promise to make her pay for leaving his son to die halfway around the world. He couldn't accept what Randi *had* to believe. Ty had been dead before he hit the ground.

Her hands locked around the steering wheel. She'd seen Ty take a bullet. Watched helplessly from the cockpit of her aircraft as he'd spun around, staggered off the runway and triggered the land mine that blew him apart.

In that agonizing instant her responsibility as aircraft commander had shifted to her crew and the members of Ty's crew they'd rescued. So she'd left her friend's body behind and flown her crippled bird back to Karshi-Khanabad. Everyone aboard had survived the bone-jarring, wheels-up landing at K-2. She had that much to be thankful for.

But Sam would never forgive her for abandoning his son, and Randi wasn't sure she could ever forgive herself.

"I'm sorry, Ty." Shuddering, she dropped her forehead onto her hands. "God, I'm so sorry."

She had no idea how long she sat there, alone with her guilt and her grief. Minutes, probably, although it felt like hours.

A dogged sense of duty dragged her from the morass. Lifting her head, she forced herself to put away the past and focus on the present. She wasn't flying today. She couldn't climb into a cockpit for another couple of months at least. She owed the 137th two full duty days, though, and intended to contribute her usual one-hundred-plus percent.

Easing the Cherokee into gear, she entered the still-heavy stream of traffic and drove through the west gate of the 137th Airlift Wing. The base was relatively small—one hangar and a few dozen build-

ings, painted the air force's standard mud-brown—
but the facilities were first rate.

A new fire station with state-of-the-art crash and
rescue equipment loomed on her right. The com-
munications center on the left bristled with satellite
dishes and antennas. The 137th shared the three bi-
secting runways with the Oklahoma City Airport
and the FAA Training Center, an arrangement that
worked well when it came to securing funds for up-
grades but required close cooperation during peak
flying periods.

Randi experienced a feeling of coming home as
she wound her way toward the Operations Building. She'd loved her years as an active duty air force
tanker pilot, but the 137th Airlift Wing gave her a
much stronger sense of belonging to a community
as well as to a military service.

As laid out in the Constitution, all national guard
units operated under a dual charter. The 137th Airlift Wing was no exception. For peacetime operations it came under the control of the governor of
Oklahoma and provided support for the protection
of life and property, counter-drug operations and relief in natural disasters. In this role, the wing had
dropped hay to starving cattle during blizzards,
helped destroy nearly seven million dollars' worth
of marijuana plants in one major bust, airlifted
emergency food and supplies to victims of floods
and prairie fires and tornados, and sent crash and

rescue teams to dig through the rubble to recover victims of the Oklahoma City bombing.

When activated to operate in its federal role, the 137th provided airlift surge capability to the United States Air Force. Operating under the direction of USAF Air Mobility Command, the wing's aircraft, crews and support personnel could deploy within seventy-two hours to any hot spot in the world. They'd done just that many, many times since 9/11.

The half-empty flight line testified to the 137th's continued support of operations Enduring Freedom and Iraqi Freedom. Randi skimmed a glance over the parked aircraft, noting tail numbers and vacant areas. The aircraft and crews she'd flown with at K-2 had rotated home, but another flight of aircraft with accompanying aircrews and support personnel had departed for a classified location two weeks later. The wing was down to half strength—which made it all the more imperative she return to flying status.

She'd talk to the docs, she decided as she parked in front of the 137th Operations Group headquarters. See if she couldn't convince them to waive the remainder of the mandatory observation period. This temporary staff duty sucked. She wanted to get back in the cockpit. She *needed* to get back in the cockpit. She suspected that was the only way she'd exorcise the demons from her last mission.

She could handle the normal flying requirements

with no problem. Most were day flights or involved a single overnight stay. She had sitters lined up for Spencer for the day flights and could leave him with one of her sisters on the overnighters. She'd have to think long and hard about pulling another overseas rotation, though. She wasn't sure she could bring herself to leave Spencer for an undetermined period again. Or risk making him an orphan.

The future weighed heavily on her mind as she arrived at the Ops facility. The building hummed with activity as personnel reported in for weekend drill. Aircrews in flight suits and support personnel in baggy green, brown and black fatigues headed for various offices or briefing rooms prior to assembling for roll call. Making her way down the tiled hall to the Stan/Eval office, Randi exchanged greetings with men and women who'd become as close as family.

Airman First Class Callahan looked up from his computer and flashed her a grin. "Hey, Captain. How's the head?"

"Still there. What time is roll call?"

"Same as always, oh-seven-thirty."

Randi tossed her flight cap onto her temporary desk and grabbed a mug emblazoned with the 137th's logo. Callahan's grin faded as she filled the mug with coffee from the pot he'd keep percolating throughout the weekend.

"That was a grim scene yesterday, at Captain Keane's funeral."

"Yeah, it was."

"His father took it real hard."

"He buried his only child."

She could understand Sam's agony. The mere thought of *her* son being hurt or injured was enough to put Randi in a cold sweat. Thunking down her coffee mug, she dug in her purse for her cell phone. It was still early, but she needed to hear Spencer's voice.

Lissa answered, reported that they were almost ready to leave for the fair and turned the phone over to Spencer.

"Hi, bud. Whatcha doing?"

"Eating Cheerios." A noisy slurp and several crunches punctuated his speech. "Aunt Lis says we can't go until I finish."

"Be good, okay? And go easy on the cotton candy and corn dogs."

"I will," he got out around more hasty spoonfuls. "Aunt Lis says she's not gonna let me throw up on her, like I did last time."

Randi wouldn't bet the farm on that not happening. After a few more maternal cautions she knew would be ignored, she left Spencer to his Cheerios, hung up and switched into duty mode.

"What have we got this weekend?"

With a click of his mouse, Callahan brought up the aircrew examination schedule. "Two check rides and a supplemental eval."

Air force regs required regular evaluation of each member of the crew to ensure his or her proficiency. That generally wasn't a problem in the 137th. Most of the crew dogs had been around a long time, as had the support personnel. They knew their business.

"Colonel Jackson's taking the check rides," Callahan reported. "The first one's scheduled for eleven hundred. While he's doing that, he wants you to pull up the flight evaluation folders and check the Form 8s."

"Again?"

"Again. He's getting goosey about the inspection next month."

Nothing like a pending visit from higher headquarters to get folks goosey. Randi had already done one scrub of the computerized flight evaluation folders for the pilots, navigators, flight engineers and loadmasters assigned to the wing. It looked as though she'd have to scroll through them line by line, entry by entry, once more. Swallowing a sigh, she downed a slug of coffee and joined the herd moving into the assembly area for morning roll call.

Being chained to a desk did have one upside. Randi wasn't required to go into crew rest and could indulge in a beer or two during the traditional after-duty gathering on the patio behind the Ops Building. Since 137th personnel drove in from several states, some from considerable distances, this shared hour provided an opportunity for everyone to relax, catch up on family news and stay connected.

After agreeing to meet some aircrew members from her squadron at their favorite rib place for dinner, Randi checked into her motel. The Comfort Inn was one of several local hotels under contract to the 137th to provide quarters for those who lived too far away to commute back and forth during drill weekends.

Once in her room, Randi dumped her gear bag on the bed, exchanged her flight suit for jeans and a long-sleeved T-shirt layered under a denim jacket, and reached for her cell phone. She'd bet Lissa and Spencer were home by now. Eight hours at the Texas State Fair should have exhausted even her son's seemingly endless energy.

It had, Lissa reported with undisguised relief. "He's zonked out on the bed. I'm about ready to join him."

"Did he chuck up any foreign projectiles?"

"Not today. *I* came pretty close, though, after your little monster insisted on riding that damned loop-the-loop *twice*."

"You're a saint, girl."

"Yes, I am. What time do you think you'll get home tomorrow evening?"

"I should be there by eight."

"Okay. Spencer wants one more shot at the midway before we drive back to Oklahoma. I should have him bathed and in his jammies by the time you reach the house."

"Thanks. And Lissa…"

"Yes?"

"I…"

Randi bit her lip, searching for words to express her gratitude for the way her sisters had rallied after the divorce, through her pregnancy, and during the long months she'd been deployed.

She settled for another simple "Thanks."

"You're welcome."

Shorty Small's was a favorite spot with crews from the 137th. The place specialized in tender ribs and platter-sized country-fried steaks.

Randi joined the group of five who'd already gathered at a round table. They were a mixed lot— an investment banker, a junior high math teacher, two commercial airline pilots, and a vivacious, flame-haired former Miss Oklahoma who now owned and operated a string of tanning salons.

Like Randi, Janice Overton hailed from a ranching family and had learned to fly while still in high school. She and her new husband—a Delta pilot— were both members of the 137th. With five kids between them, they had to scramble to arrange for child care during drills. The fact that Dale Overton was now deployed to a classified location for an indefinite period complicated Janice's situation even more.

"They're with my mom," she said when Randi asked about her kids. "How about Spencer?"

"He's with my sister."

Janice made a face. "Ever wonder why we do this?"

"All the time."

They both knew the answer. Flying was in their bones. Along with the knowledge that they were part of something vitally important.

Both women worked hard to juggle their commitments to the 137th and the demands of their families and jobs. Janice also waged a constant battle with her first husband, who continually gave her a hard time about leaving their kids in order to fly.

Nor was their situation different from that of their male counterparts with working wives. They, too, had to rearrange their lives to accommodate the once-a-month drills, two-week training every summer, and the ever-increasing deployments in support of real-world operations.

It wasn't those ongoing operations that dominated the conversation at the table that night, however. Like AlC Callahan, everyone was feeling the impact of Ty Keane's funeral. They'd had four months to prepare for it, four months to hash over the grim details of his death. Still, the reality of it had hit hard.

Randi didn't realize just *how* hard until her co-pilot on that last, fatal mission stopped her in the parking lot outside Shorty Small's. Night had brought a cold nip. Hugging her arms, she turned in response to Buck Jones's request for her to wait up.

"I got a call from Sam Keane a couple of weeks ago," the math teacher told her. "He wanted to know if I agreed with the findings of the Accident Investigation Board."

A chill that had nothing to do with the night air ran along Randi's spine. The accident board had taken Buck's testimony, along with hers and that of every other aircrew member involved in the incident. So had the Safety Investigation Board. Their findings had been reviewed at every level of command. There was no reason to mistrust those findings.

"What did you tell Sam?"

"What the hell kind of question is that? That I agreed, of course."

Buck shoved his hands in his pockets. Randi could see there was more, see him struggling to put his doubts into words.

"We made the right decision, didn't we? We had to get our bird in the air and get the hell out of Dodge or we would've lost everyone onboard."

"It was my decision," she reminded him evenly. "I was in the pilot's seat. And yes, it was the right one."

She searched his face in the garish glow from the restaurant's neon sign. He'd walked away from the crash that had left her concussed, but not all wounds were visible. She wasn't the only one susceptible to post-traumatic stress disorder.

"You okay, Buck?"

"Yeah. Except…"

"What?"

"I'm having trouble sleeping."

"Have you told Doc Russell?"

The 137th's flight surgeons were integral members of the wing. They lived and flew with the crews. More to the point, Doc Russell had deployed with elements of the 137th on their last rotation to southwest Asia.

Russell had been waiting with the crash team when Randi had brought her crippled 130 back to K-2. His was the first face she'd seen when she regained consciousness and the last before she was medivaced to Bagram for a CAT scan.

"You need to talk to Russell," she told Buck. "You can't fly without adequate crew rest."

"Yeah, you're right. I'll make an appointment to see him tomorrow."

"Good. Let me know how it goes."

"Will do." He hesitated, shoulders hunched

against the cold. "Sam Keane asked about more than the accident board findings. He wanted to know about you and Ty."

Her chest tightened. "What about me and Ty?"

"He said someone told him the two of you got into it the night before that last mission."

They had. Until this moment, though, Randi hadn't realized their heated session behind the mess tent had been overheard.

"Did he ask…?" She heard the tremor in her voice, ground to a halt, and started again. "Did he ask why Ty and I supposedly got into it?"

Buck wouldn't look at her. "I told him I wasn't there when it happened, so I couldn't say what you and Captain Keane argued about. If you *did* argue."

He knew. They probably all knew. It was hard to keep secrets in a unit as close as theirs.

"Thanks for telling me about the call."

"Yeah, well, see you tomorrow, Randi."

"See you, Buck."

She held herself together during the drive back to the motel. After locking the door, she turned on the TV and made another call to Lissa to check on Spencer.

Then she sat on the bed, shaking, while what felt like concrete nails hammered into her temples.

5

Pete hadn't intended to take along a companion when he got into his truck to conduct the site presurveys Monday morning. Dog, however, hunkered down in the passenger seat and wouldn't un-hunker.

Pete tried coaxing, bribery and brute strength. The idiot thought they were playing some kind of new game and rewarded his playmate with joyous, slavering swipes. Cursing, Pete yielded to a superior force and dumped his gear in the truck bed.

"You're going to the pound," he vowed as he got behind the wheel. "Tomorrow!"

He cranked the ignition and lowered the passenger window so Dog could stick his head out. The animal woofed greetings to everything that moved and much that didn't. Pete mouthed a silent apology to the neighbors still tucked in their beds and headed north on I-35.

He hooked a right on 240 and joined the bumper-to-bumper stream of early-shift workers going to work at the state's two largest employers—the General Motors assembly plant and giant Tinker Air Force Base. Traffic eased up once he was past the air base and 240 merged into I-40.

The sun came up shrouded in haze. Most of the fog had burned off by the time Pete stopped at the McDonald's in Henryetta, although wispy gray fingers still drifted among hills showing bright splashes of fall color. He ordered a large coffee and six sausage biscuits, two for himself and four for Dog.

At Henryetta he turned south on the Indian Nation Turnpike. State Road 9 took him across the Canadian and opened a window onto the mountains rising to the south. The Sansbois, the Jack Fork, the Winding Stair, the Kiamichi—all part of the Ozark-Ouachita Highlands that spread across Missouri, Arkansas and southeastern Oklahoma. The same highlands cut by the mighty Arkansas River.

The scientist in Pete had yet to buy into the theory that Vikings had rowed up the Arkansas a thousand years ago, but then he didn't have to buy into it. That was the purpose of the study, to date and source the mysterious carvings, using the latest spectrographic imaging techniques. It was also why he had the lead on the project, instead of his counterparts in the archeology or anthropology departments. They required proof of historical significance to fund a study. Pete had required only the green light from the OU president—and the generous gift from Sam Keane.

He had to admit the idea of Vikings in Oklahoma tickled his imagination, though. The often-told story of Leif Eriksson's voyage from Greenland to a beautiful place he named Vineland had morphed from legend into fact with the 1960 discovery of Viking artifacts at L'Anse aux Meadows, in Newfoundland. Subsequent studies suggested the village had been used primarily as a base camp for explorations further west and south. The recently opened Viking Exhibit at the Smithsonian supported that theory.

Now Pete would lead a team to determine if, in fact, Norsemen had traveled *this* far from Newfoundland.

"What do you think, Dog? Can you see Vikings roaming these hills?"

Dog answered with an ear-splitting bark that Pete took for an affirmative.

"You can, huh? Well, we'll see."

He was determined to remain objective, but excitement simmered below his layers of scientific detachment when he turned onto the sloping road that led to Miranda Morgan's home.

She must have heard the growl of the truck coming up the drive. When she stepped off the porch into a bright patch of sunlight, Pete's scientific detachment got blown all to hell. He knew then his sense of anticipation had less to do with rocks and Vikings than with Miranda Morgan.

Tall, slender, her black hair gleaming in the morning light, she wore jeans, a red plaid shirt, and a somewhat less than welcoming expression. She looked so damned good, though, that Pete forgot to exercise caution when he got out of the truck.

"Good morn—oooof!"

A hundred-plus pounds of brindle exploded through the open door, almost knocking Pete off his feet. When he recovered, the hound was streaking toward Miranda.

"Dog! Stop! Heel!"

Pete took off running, gathering his muscles for a flying tackle. He was a half second from going airborne when Miranda pointed a finger at the charging animal and rapped out a stern command.

"Sit!"

Dog skittered to a halt and sank onto his haunches.

Pete practically fell over him. Jaw dropping, he dragged his disbelieving gaze from the quivering bundle of restrained energy to the woman who'd stopped it cold.

"How the hell did you do that?"

Her severe expression gave way to sardonic

amusement. "It's called projecting authority. Something all military officers, parents, university professors and pet owners should know how to do."

"I can handle a lecture hall full of students. But this guy." He shook his head. "Obviously, Dog and I haven't learned to communicate."

She scratched behind the animal's ears, reducing him to a state of slavering bliss. "Maybe it would help if you called him by his name instead of 'dog.'"

"I don't know his name. I found him in my truck bed a week or so ago, minus any collar or tags. I put an ad in the paper and flyers up on campus, but no one's come forward to claim him. He's going to the pound unless—" Hope leaped in Pete's chest. "You've got lots of room here. Could you use a friendly if slightly oversize companion?"

"Sorry. I have enough trouble lining up babysitters for my son when I pull drill. No way I could palm this horse off on my relatives, too." She wiped her hand on the seat of her jeans and extended a grudging offer. "Do you want some coffee before we head up to the bluff? I just made a fresh pot."

"That would be great." Pete aimed a forefinger and projected stern authority. "Stay."

Dog didn't even blink. Springing up, he pranced after Miranda. She rolled her eyes and reissued her original command.

"Sit."

The animal dropped back onto his haunches.

Shooting him a nasty glare, Pete followed his hostess into the house.

Evidence of her son was everywhere. Toys spilled out of a brassbound trunk on the porch. The long, elegant table in the dining room off the main hall was graced by an antique silver epergne and a plastic dump truck. A kid-size baseball glove and bat occupied the sofa in the den.

In the kitchen, magnetized plastic letters and colorful drawings decorated every metal surface. It was a large, airy room, warmed by a round table with a scarred oak surface and copper pots dangling from the rack above the stove.

Randi poured a mug of steaming black coffee for him and replenished her own. "Cream and sugar are on the counter. I'll fill a thermos to take with us. I also made some sandwiches. I'd better make a few more," she added with a questioning look, "if you intend to take your horse up on the bluff with you."

"My horse? I thought we were going by—oh, you mean Dog. I hadn't planned on taking him along."

He hadn't planned on having his company at all, but didn't want to admit just how little control he exerted over the creature.

"It's probably better to leave him here," Randi said. "We haven't had a deep enough freeze to kill off the ticks and chiggers. He can stay in the barn. We'll lock him up when we get out the ATVs."

While she packed the thermos and sandwiches into an insulated bag, Pete drank his coffee and let his gaze roam the cheerful kitchen. A curious paperweight perched on a stack of bills at the end of the counter drew his interest.

He fingered the two-inch marble square topped by a twisted shard of metal. "What's this?"

Randi glanced over her shoulder. Something flickered across her face, quickly come, quickly gone. "That is—or was—part of a C-130 fuselage."

She left it at that and turned back to her task. Pete got the message and didn't pry, but the small brass plaque affixed to the marble base told at least part of the tale.

To Captain Morgan, from the crew
Thanks for bringing us home, holes and all.

"If you've finished your coffee, we can go."

Pete downed the last swallow. "I'm done."

He took the insulated bag and followed her back down the hall. She stopped at the ornately carved antique coat rack beside the door and pulled on a lightweight jacket. She also collected the padded rifle case that was propped against the stand.

"Think we'll need that?"

"You never know when you might run into a mean-tempered bear or mountain cat." She slid a box of shells into her pocket. "Best to be prepared."

The four-wheeled vehicles she drove out of the barn had been modified for heavy-duty ranch work. Oversize brush guards protruded from the front end, winches from the rear. The cargo racks were large enough to haul moose carcasses.

Dog dashed around the ATVs, sensing an adventure. Pete lured him back into the barn.

"Sorry, pal, you're not invited." He tried the stern, finger-pointing thing again. "Stay."

It didn't work. Shaking her head, Randi took charge.

The mournful howls began as soon as she shut the barn door. They continued unabated while Engstrom hooked his gear bag onto the back of his ATV with bungee cords. As the baying grew louder, he threw a worried look over his shoulder. His obvious concern for an animal he professed to dislike and had vowed to get rid of gave Randi an unexpected insight into the man's character.

"He'll be okay," she assured him. "I keep the fertilizer and other potentially harmful chemicals locked up in a separate shed. Here, you'd better wear one of these."

She passed him a bright orange hunter's vest.

"Deer season started this weekend and runs for the next twelve days. I lease several deer stands to hunters. None up where we're going, but it doesn't hurt to take a few extra precautions."

Nodding, Engstrom put on the orange vest. Like Randi, he wore boots and jeans. The sleeves of his rust-colored flannel shirt were rolled up to display strong wrists and a no-nonsense watch with a plain black band.

She waited, feeling the ATV vibrate under her, while he tested the controls of his vehicle. She'd vacillated from the moment she woke up this morning about accompanying him on this expedition, about sharing her private place with him, about allowing him on her property at all. Twice she'd reached for the phone to call him and withdraw her permission. Once she'd even punched in his cell phone number.

Now, though, the sense that she'd done the right thing in agreeing to the study was growing stronger with each minute. Maybe it was the clean autumn air. Or the earthy scent of the leaves that had fallen to form a spongy cushion. Or the play of Engstrom's shoulders when he twisted around to check the bungee cords anchoring the gear he'd loaded onto the back of his vehicle.

She barely knew him, wasn't sure she trusted him, but the woman in her had to admit he possessed a rugged charm. And watching his lop-eared hound get the better of him this morning had showed an interesting side to his personality. It had also made Randi want to laugh out loud, something she hadn't felt like doing in months.

As a result, her smile was friendlier than she'd intended when he straightened, facing front again. "All set?"

He gunned the vehicle's engine. "All set."

The dog's howls pursued them out of the yard, through the fallow wheat field beyond the barn and into the woods at the far side of the field. Randi caught Engstrom looking back once or twice before the rough terrain claimed his attention.

The first twenty minutes or so were relatively easy going. They took an old logging road that followed the bluff above the river. Randi used visual landmarks and the guide stakes pounded into the ground by a previous Morgan to measure their progress. About a mile from the end of the road, she slowed her vehicle and shifted around in the seat.

"This is where we turn off," she told Engstrom over the rumbling engines. "There used to be a dirt track up to the bluff, but it's pretty well overgrown. You might want to roll down your shirtsleeves and tuck your pants into your boots to keep out the chiggers."

He put his vehicle in neutral and complied. When she saw he was ready, Randi nosed her ATV off the road and led the way up a barely discernible track. Pin oak and dogwood crowded the trail, but the dense underbrush hadn't yet overtaken it completely. Keeping a wary eye out for hanging clumps of poison oak and ivy, she zigzagged upward.

Gradually, scrub pine and spruce replaced the oak. Shale made the going tricky for about the last hundred yards. Randi throttled back, taking it slow and careful over the loose stones. Finally, the track circled a protruding ledge and leveled off atop a high bluff.

She parked a safe distance from the edge and turned off the engine. When Engstrom did the same, a majestic silence enveloped them. Randi sat there for a moment, breathing in the tang of resin and the broad, sweeping vista spread out before them.

Forests of dark, verdant pine and spruce spilled down the steep slopes. Hawks floated above the ridges on an endless blue sky. The Kerr Reservoir lay wide and silver far below, fed by the Arkansas River as it wound through the rolling green countryside.

How many times had she come here? Randi wondered. With her grandfather? With Ty? Both men had loved this spot. Both had puzzled over the mystery of the runes. And both were now gone.

The pain of that cut into her so deeply she didn't realize Engstrom had come to stand beside her until his deep voice broke the silence.

"Quite a sight."

"Yes, it is."

"Can you imagine what they must've thought when they first saw it?"

Randi slanted him a look. "Which 'they' are you referring to?"

"The Cave Dwellers. The Mound Builders. The Osage and Quawpaw and Spanish and French and American soldiers who came after them."

His gaze roamed the stunning panorama, then returned to her.

"And maybe the Norsemen," he added.

She took the hint. "The runes are back there, under the ledge."

She led him to a thick shelf of rock that jutted out at approximately shoulder height. Below the shelf, a thick plastic shield had been bolted into the rock surface. The shield was hinged and could be swung away.

"My grandfather put this up," Randi explained as she worked a key into a rusty padlock. "We had several teams come here to study the runes and word started to spread. He didn't want souvenir hunters or treasure seekers chipping away at the stone."

Pete gave her grandfather high marks for precaution and ingenuity. Then the shield swung to the side and he ducked under the ledge to get his first glimpse of the actual carvings.

He'd studied digital photos and drawings of the symbols in various books and monographs, but nothing compared to viewing them in their natural setting. There were three of them marching across the face of the rock.

Pete's pulse went straight into overdrive. The angular symbols were characteristic of the ancient runic alphabet—straight, slashing lines that could be easily incised on wood or stone. As he stared at the three letters, the research he'd devoured tumbled through his head.

The Vikings were a prehistoric people. Although much was written about them by other sources, they themselves hadn't recorded the events in their lives on paper or in books. They did, however, carve short inscriptions to commemorate great deeds, celebrate kings and queens, and mark boundaries. For this, their ancestors had developed a 24-character futhark or runic alphabet that had remained in use for over a thousand years, until gradually replaced by the 16-character "twig" alphabet around A.D. 1100.

The letters Pete was looking at were definitely old futhark. Those two pointed *P*s set nose to nose represented the letter *M*, a symbol that didn't appear in the later twig alphabet. The question now was whether they'd been carved by a ninth- or tenth-century Norseman or someone from a later era with knowledge of the old symbols.

Either possibility fired Pete's imagination. Resisting the almost overpowering impulse to finger the incisions, he studied the surface they'd been carved on.

"The geology reports I read indicate this is quartzite sandstone," he murmured, "part of a Mississippian Age Savannah Formation. The various strata went through some low-grade metamorphism and the sand grains recrystalized, producing a rock that tests at a seven on the Mohs hardness scale."

"Okay," Randi drawled. "I'll bite. Is that good or bad?"

Distracted from his vision of a muscled warrior hammering into that wall of rock, Pete shot her a grin.

"Good. It means this is *very* hard rock. Whoever carved these symbols had to have used forged iron tools to hack into it. That in turn means the cuts will have relatively precise angles, edges and depths. They'll image beautifully using spectrographic techniques."

"That's what you're going to do? Make three-dimensional images of the grooves?"

"That's the plan."

"I don't get it. How will that tell you when they were made or who made them?"

"It won't, unless we find a precise match with other runes carved by known individuals at known times. It's a refinement of a relative dating technique called stylistic chronology."

She looked as skeptical as the head of the anthropology department had when Pete first proposed this application for the holographic imaging process he'd developed.

"What about radiocarbon dating?" she asked. "Wouldn't that give you a more precise fix?"

"Radiocarbon dating doesn't work in this instance. If the symbols had been painted on, we could date the materials in the pigments the same way we date the linen binding Egyptian mummies. Or if we'd found a broken axe blade lying under the stone, or the awl used to punch the groove, we could date the tool. Without some external object, we have to focus on the incisions themselves."

Cocking her head, she considered the problem from a different angle. "How about the effect of weathering on the rock? Can't you measure the difference between the darker surface and the lighter grooves to get an idea of how long they've been exposed?"

"There are two separate processes that attempt to do exactly what you suggest. One method looks at the oxalates—black surface deposits that contain dust and salt and are thought to reflect changes in the environment. The problem is we don't fully understand how oxalates are formed or how much natural sources such as lichen impact them, so that technique isn't reliable. Another approach is to analyze the silica skins formed on the surface of the grooves by water seepage. It contains all kinds of organic matter that could be radiocarbon dated."

"So why doesn't that work?"

"The silica is extremely thin and there's considerable migration between the layers. It's pretty well impossible to obtain a pure sample."

"So, as you said, all you've got left are the grooves themselves."

"That's all," he confirmed cheerfully.

"I still don't get it. How will examining cuts in a rock tell you who made them and when?"

"We'll do more than merely examine the cuts. We'll image them from every angle and calculate precise mathematical dimensions. Then we'll compare those dimensions to other inscriptions known to have been carved at various periods in history. If we get a match, or anything close to a match, we can theorize that the cuts might have been made at approximately the same time using similar methods."

"Hence the term relative dating."

"Exactly."

"Hmm, sounds like you have your work cut out for you—if you'll pardon the pun."

"Yeah," Pete said, "I do. And I'd better get to it."

Randi found a perch while he dug into the gear bag strapped to the back of his ATV. Minutes ticked by as he shot visuals with a slicked-up version of a digital camera. After making extensive notes, he constructed a three-dimensional site grid on a handheld computer.

Pete took the coffee she poured from the thermos and absently drank a few sips before setting it aside. Randi nursed hers, cradling the cup in both hands, her gaze on the vista below.

After an hour and a half, she started sneaking quick glances at her watch. She'd asked a friend to pick Spencer up when his preschool let out at noon. She'd have to head back soon, to be at the house when he got there. To her relief, Pete began to pack up a few minutes later.

"I could use one of those sandwiches now," he said when he had everything stowed.

"So could I," Randi admitted. "My stomach started rumbling a while ago."

They ate standing up, hips propped against a boulder, eyes on the spectacular view. The river glistened in the distance. Hawks wheeled over patchwork quilts of color. So serene. So still. So dangerous, Randi knew, to the unsuspecting or unwary.

As if on cue, one of the hawks plummeted earthward. It flapped up again seconds later, a squirming creature in its claws. Frantic, piping cries carried on the still air.

Pete followed their flight with narrowed eyes. "The circle of life. Brutal but necessary."

"Which is why I carry that rifle," Randi said with a shrug. "I'd just as soon not become lunch for some critter bigger and hungrier than me. That already happened once up here, according to an old family tale."

Shifting, he bumped a knee against hers. The contact was inadvertent but sent a small, surprising jolt through her.

"Who got eaten?" he wanted to know.

"A French trapper, supposedly. One of my ancestors, Rifle Sergeant Daniel Morgan, apparently met up with him not far from here."

"I read about Daniel Morgan. I think I mentioned that earlier."

She nodded. "This trapper told my great-great-and-then-some-granddad about strange carvings in stone, or so the story goes. When they climbed up to view the marks, a puma leapt down from a pine tree and ripped out the trapper's throat."

"It did, huh?"

He didn't sound particularly worried, but Randi noticed the quick look he sent up the trunk of the pine shading their rock.

"There's another part to the tale," she said. "Daniel later married the trapper's widow. She was a woman of great beauty, with the jet-black hair of the People and startling blue eyes she always believed were a curse."

Pete's gaze met hers. Unlike her sisters, who both had brown eyes, Randi had inherited the clear, electric blue eyes of her long-dead ancestor.

"A curse? They don't seem dangerous from

where I sit. Then again…" A smile tugged at his lips. "You never know. Should I be worried?"

"Maybe," Randi answered, feeling the impact of that crooked grin. "According to legend, men with flame-colored beards and eyes like the sky once wintered in this area. One of them shared a blanket with a woman of the People. After he departed, his woman bore a girl-child with blue eyes—and a series of disasters followed. Ever after, a maiden with blue eyes signified grave danger to the tribe."

"Good Lord!" All traces of laughter left his face. "Has this legend ever been documented?"

"Not that I know of."

"Still, it wouldn't hurt to do a search of tribal records and oral histories. What tribe did Daniel Morgan's wife belong to?"

"Osage, I believe, although there's Quawpaw and Cherokee in the Morgan family bloodlines, too."

He whipped out his Palm Pilot and clicked in some notes. To Randi, the tale had been little more than family lore, woven around the carvings in the rock. It thrilled her to think it might actually have some basis in fact.

She was glad now that she'd agreed to give Engstrom access to her property. Not only did it ease her guilt and honor Ty's memory, but Engstrom and company might turn up some nugget of family history she could share with her son.

Feeling a good deal friendlier toward the scientist than when he'd first approached her, Randi packed up and led the way back down the craggy bluff.

Any and all friendly feelings evaporated, however, when they wheeled into the yard. With a sinking feeling, Randi saw that her son, his friend Joey and Joey's mom had not only arrived, they'd released the hound from the barn.

"Mommy!"

Her son's face was ecstatic as he raced toward her with the animal barking at his side.

"Where did you find him? Can we keep him? Please, please, *pleeeez!*"

Randi shot an exasperated look at Engstrom, who lifted his shoulders with an I-didn't-let-him-out innocence. Swinging off the ATV, she prepared to do battle with her son.

6

"I'll take care of him, Mom. I promise!"

Spencer barely reached the hound's shoulder, but somehow managed to loop an arm around its neck. Dodging playful slurps of a long pink tongue, he begged, pleaded, cajoled and made promises she knew he'd never remember, much less keep.

"I'll pick up all my toys 'n my sneakers 'n jammies 'n *everything*. Honest. 'N I'll scoop seed into the bird feeder, just like you showed me. 'N I'll eat my peas. 'N… 'N…"

Inspiration struck. His face lit up.

"'N I won't hit Joey with the Wiffle bat anymore."

"When did you hit Joey with the Wiffle bat?"

"This morning," Joey's mom put in ruefully as she and her son joined the group. "After my little stinker whopped him with a golf club. Plastic, thank goodness."

Although Judy Hayes lived in Keota some nine miles away, she was Randi's closest neighbor with a son Spencer's age. Her lively brood also included four older children, which made Randi reluctant to impose on her to keep Spencer during drill weekends or overnight flights. Judy had stepped in more than once, however, when Randi got called for a short-notice flight or an unplanned meeting.

"Was it okay to let the dog out of the barn?" she asked with a curious glance at Pete. "He was howling so pitifully when we drove up."

"It's okay by me," he replied. "I just hope he didn't cause bodily harm when you released him. He tends to get a little excited."

"No kidding," Randi muttered, observing the bundle of quivering delight pressed against her son's body.

Spencer had been following the adult conversation with some difficulty, given his attempts to hang onto his new pal. But he grasped enough to produce a scowl and a petulant lower lip.

"Is this your dog, mister?"

"No, I found him. Or rather, he found me. It's just a temporary arrangement," Pete added, avoiding eye contact with Randi. "If I don't find him a home, I'll have to take him to the pound."

"God will get you for that," she whispered as

Spencer's pout disappeared and his eyes grew wide in a plea designed to make angels sigh and mothers weep.

"Can't we give him a home? *Can't* we?"

The entreaty touched Randi's heart and weakened her resistance. Every kid should have a dog. She'd fully intended to get one when Spencer was a little older and capable of taking care of a pet.

"*Pleeeze*, Mom."

"Okay, okay. But only if—"

"Yaaay!"

He bolted without waiting to hear conditions that included feeding, watering and an occasional dousing with the garden hose. The dog galloped after him, woofing at the top of his lungs. Joey scrambled to follow and added his shouts to the din.

"Pretty slick maneuvering," Judy said, grinning at the perpetrator of the crime.

"I thought so. My name's Engstrom, by the way. Pete Engstrom."

"Dr. Engstrom is a professor at OU," Randi explained. "He's directing a research team to study the runes."

"Hey, I heard about that. My sister-in-law works at the Kerr Museum, where the three smaller stones are kept. She said a whole team of experts was coming in to measure them or something."

"That's right. The team should assemble at the museum in a few days."

"I'll have to tell her I met you. Gotta go, Randi. Oh, and Joey has an appointment with the optometrist tomorrow, so I won't be making the preschool run."

"No problem. I'll get Spencer there and back. Hope Joey doesn't need glasses."

"Me, too. Nice meeting you, Dr. Engstrom."

Corralling her son, she dragged him away from his playmate. The dog cocked his head, as though he was trying to decide whether to climb into the car with them or stay and frolic. Spencer settled the matter by throwing himself at the animal. They rolled over and over on the grass, a blur of brindled hide and laughing boy.

"Spencer!" Alarmed, Randi lunged forward. "Not so rough! He's not used to you. He might bite."

Pete got ahead of her in two strides. Before either of them could reach the pair, however, the tussle ended with Spencer flat on his back, giggling helplessly while the dog drenched him with sloppy kisses.

Keeping a wary eye on the twosome, Randi fired a question at Pete. "Has he ever snapped or growled at you?"

"Never. Not once. I swear. But I'll take him back home with me if the possibility worries you."

"Of course it worries me!"

Annoyed though she was, Randi had to admit

the brindled hound seemed anything but dangerous. His dewlaps flapped in a silly grin, and his entire back end wagged from side to side. Still, she didn't doubt those massive jaws could crunch through bone.

"Randi, I'm really sorry. I didn't think about this from a parent's perspective. You're right to be cautious about taking in a strange animal. I'll cart Dog home with me."

"Oh, sure. Make me look like the bad guy in this!"

Engstrom shoved back his ball cap and tried another approach. "Okay, how about we conduct a field test. I'll be at Heavener State Park inspecting the stone there all day tomorrow. If the hound shows any sort of behavior that makes you doubt he'd make a suitable pet, just give me a ring. I'll hustle over and collect him."

"And tell Spencer what?"

"That I made a mistake. That I need to try harder to find his owners. That I'm worried some other little boy might be crying for his lost pet."

She aimed another glance at the dog. He was the one on his back now, with all four legs straight up. One rear leg pawed the air as Spencer tickled his belly.

"All right," she conceded, "we'll conduct a field test."

"If you're sure…"

Looking both relieved and a little worried, Pete transferred his gear from the ATV to his truck and returned to the four-wheeler.

"I'll put it away," Randi said.

He nodded and thrust out a hand. "Thanks for the coffee and the sandwiches and for blazing the trail. If I don't see you tomorrow, I'll see you when I bring up the team next week."

"I may not be here when you're ready to go to the site again. My duty schedule's been kind of erratic lately. Can you find the way on your own?"

"I think so."

"We should've thought to tie some kind of ribbon or marker at the turnoff to the site. If I have time this week, I'll do that."

Pete hadn't really expected her to act as pathfinder and tour guide during the entire course of the project. Nor had he expected to feel this sharp disappointment at the idea that he might not see her again. Luckily, the perfect opening popped into his head.

"I've got a fifty-pound bag of dog food at the house. I'll bring it with me tomorrow and drop it off later in the afternoon, if you'd like."

"Fifty pounds?" She folded her arms across her chest. "That doesn't sound to me as though you planned to take the dog to the shelter."

"I was. I swear."

"Uh-huh."

Pete decided it was time to beat a dignified retreat. Whistling to the dog, he knuckled the animal's broad, flat forehead and issued a set of useless instructions.

"Mind your manners, fella. No drooling on the furniture. No poking your nose where it doesn't belong. And no guzzling all the beer."

Spencer's eyes rounded. "Does he drink beer?"

"He does," Pete admitted, then noticed Randi's lifted brow, "but he prefers water. He also likes to, uh, take a shower with you."

What he liked was to nose the curtain aside, muscle his way in and crowd out any other occupant. The new owners would discover that soon enough.

"What's his name?"

Pete had bestowed several epithets on him, but none he could repeat to this towheaded kid. "I don't know. You'll have to pick one."

"Cool!"

Issuing a stern order for the animal to stay, he opened the pickup door. Dog, of course, leaped for the cab.

"Sit!" Randi snapped.

The animal dropped down.

Wondering how the *hell* she did that, Pete climbed into the truck.

A whine started in the back of Dog's throat. As Pete shifted into gear and drove off, it escalated to a howl loud enough to wake the dead.

Jesus! If he kept that up, Randi would be on the phone within the hour demanding he turn around and reclaim the pest.

She didn't call that evening, nor were she and Dog waiting for Pete when he arrived at Heavener State Park the next morning.

The park was home to the largest of the Oklahoma runestones, a massive slab of rock tucked back in the mountains. The Heavener stone had been the subject of heated academic debate and controversy since its discovery at the turn of the century. Thanks to the dedicated efforts of a local scholar, Gloria Farley, the state had funded this park to protect the stone and offer explanations as to its history.

Pete glanced around the parking lot and breathed a sigh of relief when he didn't spot a black muzzle poking through the window of any car in the lot. Hopefully Dog had found a home.

Hard on the heels of that wish came a curious disappointment. Much as he hated to admit it, he'd miss the overgrown mutt.

The brief moment of regret was followed fast by anticipation. The fifty-pound sack in the truck bed gave Pete a perfect excuse to drive over to the Morgan place after he'd finished here at the park. He'd call first, he decided as he shouldered his gear. Make sure she was there. Check on how Dog was adapting. See if she and the boy wanted to go for a pizza.

That last thought snuck up on him as he walked over to the wood-and-stone visitors' center, but the more he rolled it around in his head, the more he liked it. Pete couldn't remember the last time a woman had piqued his interest as much as this one. Randi Morgan came across as someone who didn't take crap from anyone, yet more than once he'd caught a fleeting glimpse of shadows in her eyes. Like everyone else, she had her worries, her problems, her secrets. She also had a killer smile and a tight, trim butt.

Pete didn't classify himself as an ass man by any means. He enjoyed the complete package, particularly when it included intellect and humor. But he had to admit the view during the ATV ride up to the Morgan runestone had stayed with him afterward.

It was still vivid as he entered the visitors' center. Shoving the delectable Ms. Morgan to the back of his mind, he approached the silver-haired attendant at the counter. Her name tag identified her as Brenda Caldwell, Volunteer.

"Hi. I'm Pete Engstrom. I have an appointment with the park superintendent."

"You're the one heading the team to analyze the runes?"

"That's me."

"Harry told me to keep an eye out for you. Hang on, I'll buzz him and let him know you're here.

We're all really excited about the study," she added as she punched in a number. "Most of us volunteers would like to help in any way we can."

"Thanks. We can certainly use the help when the team sets up on site."

Park Superintendent Harry Dennison emerged from his office at that point and took Pete's hand in a bone-shattering grip that matched his massive frame and booming bass profundo.

"Engstrom! Can't tell you how thrilled we are about your project. We've had plenty of historians and scientists examining our rock, but none who put together a team like the one you're bringing in."

"We're pretty excited about the study, too." Pete slipped his hand behind his back and wiggled his fingers to see if they still functioned. "It's the first time we'll get to test our holographic imaging process in the field."

"You want to go over the data I have here at the office or go up to the site first?"

"Let's go up to the site."

Unlike the rugged climb to the Morgan stone, the two-hundred-yard trail to the Heavener stone was paved and made for an easy walk through stands of tall, rough-barked oaks interspersed with spindly dogwoods. Leaves crunched underfoot, and turns in the trail provided glorious views of the valley and the city of Heavener some thousand feet below.

The path snaked back a final time and cut into a U-shaped ravine bounded on three sides by granite bluffs. Water trickled down the face of one of the cliffs to form a stream that bubbled over mossy stones. Birds flitted through the trees. And there, under an overhanging ledge, was a wall of granite measuring ten by twelve feet. It was stuck in the ground like a giant signboard, framed in wood and encased in plastic.

The symbols were etched on the stone at eye level, stretching halfway across the face. Only one of the eight symbols matched those carved on the Morgan stone—the old futhark *M* that looked like two pointed *P*s set nose to nose.

Pete knew various scholars had interpreted these eight runes in widely diverse ways. One translated them as a date—A.D. 1052—and an invitation to barter by Norse traders. Another argued that a Danish-born compatriot of the French explorer Robert de la Salle had carved the symbols when de la Salle's party explored this area in the early 1800s.

The most compelling theory in Pete's mind had been advanced by Richard Nielsen, who held a doctorate from the University of Denmark. Nielsen had spent weeks comparing the Heavener runes to some found further north, in Minnesota. Nielsen believed these symbols had been incised around A.D. 750 as a boundary marker and transliterated to "Glome's Valley."

The idea that he might be the one to finally verify their date and origin set Pete's blood pumping. Unpacking his gear, he got to work.

It was lunchtime when he and the park superintendent returned to the visitors' center. Business was picking up. Two more cars were parked in the small lot and a third vehicle was rounding the last curve up to the site.

Pete's heart sank when he spotted a massive head poking through the window of the dusty black Cheroskee. Telling Harry he'd join him in the visitors' center, he waited for Randi to pull into a slot.

Dog was a quivering mass of joy when she released him from the back. Bounding out of the Cherokee, he tore straight over to his drinking buddy. Pete managed to dodge a full-frontal assault—barely. With Dog chasing mad circles around him, he walked to Randi and her son, standing beside their vehicle.

The boy shook a finger and issued a stern command. "Sit."

To Pete's utter chagrin, Dog did. "How the heck did you do that?"

"Mommy taught me. She said Absol just needs to understand who's boss."

"Absol?"

"Don'cha know him? He's the one with the blade for an ear."

Pete's blank look drew a grin from Randi. "Absol's a Pokémon character. A big, four-legged creature with a scythe on the side of his head."

"If you say so." He had to ask. "What happened? Did Dog here—"

"His name's Absol," the boy insisted, tugging on a velvety black ear.

"Did Absol flunk the field test?"

The kid's brow furrowed. "He didn't flunk anything. He's real smart. He already knows he has to pee outside. Poop, too." His face brightened. "Mommy says it's my job to keep the front yard clean, so we bought a pooper-scooper. A big one. It works just like a dump truck. Wanna see it?"

"Sure."

While Spencer clambered into the Cherokee to root among the bags in the backseat, Pete's face eased into a smile.

"Whew! I figured you'd come up here to return the merchandise."

"I thought about doing just that last night. Several times. And again this morning when he woke me at five-twenty to let him out. But Spencer's been wanting a dog for ages and..." She knuckled the head leaning against her knee. "This big dope is really good with him."

Pete leaned an arm on the open car door. "So why *did* you come up here?"

"I had to run some errands after I picked Spencer

up at preschool, so I swung by for that sack of dog food you said you'd bring out to the farm. Thought I'd save you the trip."

Well, hell! So much for his plan to drive out to her place later and invite them to dinner. Maybe he should try for lunch. Dumping his gear in the back of his truck, Pete slung the heavy sack over his shoulder.

After transferring it to her Cherokee and admiring the metal jaws of an industrial-size scooper, he dropped a casual suggestion. "The park superintendent and I were just about to drive into town to grab something to eat. Have you and Spencer had lunch? If not, how about joining us for burgers or a pizza?"

"Pizza!" the boy whooped. "Yay!"

His excitement infected Dog. The animal trotted around in circles, barking his fool head off. Randi had to pitch her voice over the din.

"We can't today, Spencer. We have an appointment to get Absol checked out by Dr. Chambers, remember?"

Back to plan one. Using the boy's obvious disappointment to his advantage, Pete offered an alternative.

"How about tonight, then? I should be through here around five. I'll swing by and pick you up."

She cocked her head, studying him with a clear, direct gaze that cut through any pretense. "I'm not sure that's a good idea."

She was nursing some scars, Pete guessed. Deep ones. Made by whoever had caused those shadows he'd glimpsed in her eyes.

"We're only talking pizza," he said gently.

Randi bit her lip. She'd forgotten how to do this. Her divorce had left her hurt and angry. Her turbulent on-again, off-again relationship with Ty had made her doubly wary of trusting her instincts when it came to men.

Yet Pete was right. They *were* only talking pizza. It wouldn't hurt to spend a few hours with someone outside her circle of friends and associates at the 137th.

"Tell you what. Instead of going out, why don't you bring a pizza up to the house and I'll make a salad."

"Sounds good to me. See you around five-thirty."

He wound things up at the site early and got to Morgan's Falls at five-fifteen. Absol came charging down the drive, barking ferociously until Pete rolled down the window and identified himself. The dog was wearing a brand-new collar and clinking tags. The vet must've given him a clean bill of health.

After a series of joyous leaps, the dog raced back up the hill. Spencer was in the yard, armed with the scooper, which he abandoned when Pete climbed out of the truck hefting two large pizza cartons.

"C'mon, Absol, let's eat."

"Oh, no!" Randi appeared on the porch. "He stays outside until we finish eating." Her expression was more than a little accusing when she turned to Pete. "Someone neglected to teach him table manners."

"Hey, I only had him for a few weeks. Not enough time to teach him anything."

She lifted a brow. "Except to guzzle beer and enjoy an early-morning shower?"

"He already had a taste for both when he found me."

More or less. Pete decided he'd better shift away from dangerous territory.

"I forgot to ask what kind of pizza you like, so I got one plain cheese and one with pepperoni and onions."

"You did fine. Spencer likes his plain, and mine can't have too many onions. Go get washed up," she instructed her son, "then come on down to the kitchen."

She had the table set, the salad ready and a bottle of red wine breathing on the counter. A very fine bottle of wine, Pete noted with a glance at the label.

"My brother-in-law keeps a stash of beer in the fridge if you'd rather have that."

"No, this is great. Shall I pour?"

"Please."

He decanted the wine into tall-stemmed balloon glasses, handed her one and touched her goblet with his. "Here's to the good life. Pizza and a Robert Mondavi Pinot Noir."

Randi sipped appreciatively and eyed him over

the rim of her glass. "Sounds like you know your wines."

"My fiancée was the real connoisseur. She did her best to educate my palate before she gave it—and me—up as hopeless."

He kept the banter light, glossing over the sting and turned the conversation to his project.

"I've got a grad assistant working with the Native American Studies Department at OU to track down possible references to the legend you told me about. If there are any, he'll find them."

Nodding, Randi took another sip of the smooth, mellow red. "So how did it go today at Heavener? Did you finish your site prep?"

"Just about. I want to go back for a few hours tomorrow before I drive down to the Kerr Museum to observe the other stones. We'll be staying there, at the Kerr Conference Center, which makes it—"

The shrill of the phone interrupted him. Randi reached for the cordless instrument and glanced at the caller ID. With a murmured apology for taking the call, she punched the talk button.

"Captain Morgan."

She listened for a moment, a frown gathering. "Yes, sir, I can make it. What's this about?"

Pete carried his glass to the end of the counter for a refill—and to give her privacy. The sound of *her* glass slamming against the scrubbed oak swung him back around.

"What new evidence?" she asked tersely.

The reply turned her face chalk-white. Rigid, she ground out another "Yes, sir," and dropped the phone back in its cradle.

Her breath came fast and shallow. Fists clenched at her sides, she stared stony-eyed at the wall. Whatever news she'd just received had punched her right in the gut.

Setting down his goblet, Pete rounded the counter. "Randi? You okay?"

She jumped, as if the sound of his voice had drawn her from some private hell. "Yes. It's just…I didn't expect…"

She stood stiff as a fence post, her hands still clenched, looking so shell-shocked Pete acted without thinking.

He drew her against him, holding her loosely, wondering who or what had hit her, surprised at the protective urge that swept through him.

Gradually the rigidity left her spine. She leaned against him a moment longer before easing out of his arms.

"I'm sorry. I—I—"

"Got some bad news," he finished when she fumbled for words. "Want to share it?"

She hesitated, and the moment was lost to the sound of sneakers thumping down the stairs.

7

When her son rushed into the kitchen, Randi struggled to hide the shock of the phone call. Spencer's lively presence and incessant questions about the dog helped. So did Pete's good-natured replies.

He was so patient with the boy, listening, explaining, never talking down to him. In the small corner of her brain not stunned by the news she'd just received, Randi appreciated his obvious efforts to divert her son's attention and give her time to recover.

God knew she needed it. That phone call had ripped open the wound of Ty's death and she was bleeding inside again.

As a result, Randi didn't object when Spencer let the dog back into the house without asking permission. She barely registered the fact that he piled up leftover pizza crusts and fed Absol from his own plate. For the next hour the interaction of the three males—one a solid six-three, one a small bundle of energy, one with a goofy grin and perpetual-motion tail—filled the house with enough noise and laughter to cover Randi's silence.

She pretty much had herself in hand by the time she sent a protesting Spencer upstairs to get ready for bed. She was also feeling very grateful to Pete as she walked him to the door. The dog padded along with them as far as the hall, then detoured upstairs to join his new pal. His claws ricocheted off the hardwood stairs like bullets.

"Thanks for the pizza and for keeping Spencer entertained this evening."

"He's a good kid. Amazing how he and Dog have clicked."

That drew a small smile. "Amazing."

He hesitated at the door, searching her face. "I can stay if you need someone to talk to."

She was tempted. She could use another glass of wine and his solid, reassuring presence to keep the ghosts at bay awhile longer. She had to face them sooner or later, though. And she'd have to do it alone.

"It's late, and you've got a long drive back to Norman."

"I'm not driving home. I'm staying over in Heavener."

It would be so easy to take him up on his offer. He was calm and comfortable, a balm to her jangled nerves. Even his touch was soothing when he traced a knuckle down the curve of her cheek.

"I saw what a sucker punch you took earlier, Randi. Everyone needs a shoulder to lean on once in a while. Mine's available."

"Why should you listen to my problems?"

His knuckle made another pass. "I'm a good listener."

That wasn't all he was good at, she discovered when he bent his head. He moved slowly, giving her plenty of time to pull back. She meant to, even started to.

Then his mouth brushed hers and the gentle kiss seduced her. Something deep and hungry stirred as his lips glided over hers. Warm. Smooth. Safe.

Oh, God! The realization that she was comparing his touch to Ty Keane's jerked Randi's head back. She concealed her reaction with a shaky smile.

"Look, Pete, I appreciate the offer of a shoulder to cry on, but I don't need any more complications in my life right now."

"Okay, it's your call. The offer stands, though."

The evening had turned cold. A wind rustled through the trees and sent fallen leaves whispering across the yard. Randi thrust her hands in her pockets and hunched her shoulders against the chill as Pete fished for his keys.

His truck's taillights left red trails in the darkness. When they disappeared down the hill, Randi went back into the house to put Spencer to bed. It took some doing. First they went through the ritual of scrubbing hands and face, brushing teeth and saying prayers. Then there were the usual delaying tactics while he debated which story he wanted read. When she finally got him into bed, he invited Absol to join him, as he'd apparently done last night. Randi nixed that arrangement and banished the dog to the old quilt she'd placed on the floor for him.

Her son's eyes were drooping and the dog's broad, flat head rested on his front paws when she finally went back downstairs and dropped into her grandfather's well-worn Cordova leather recliner. Surrounded by stillness, she resurrected the images she'd tried so hard to put out of her head.

She had to have her facts straight before she met with the 137th commander on Thursday.

She reported to Colonel McLaughlin at 1000 hours, as instructed. A command pilot with more than ten thousand hours in both military and civilian aircraft, McLaughlin had worked his way up through the ranks to take command of the 137th. His incisive knowledge of air guard operations and blunt let's-get-it-done manner inspired universal respect among his troops. His size and fierce dedication inspired more than a little awe.

Randi had flown with the native Oklahoman for almost five years now. The deep crease between his bushy salt-and-pepper brows told her he wasn't any happier about this meeting than she was.

"You wanted to see me, sir?"

"Come in, Randi. Have a seat."

With a nod to the wing vice commander, already seated off to the side, she took one of the chairs in front of the colonel's desk. Like Randi, McLaughlin was wearing his standard duty uniform. The gray-green flight suit stretched across his shoulders as he leaned forward, his big hands clasped.

"I gave you the basics on the phone the other night. Based on evidence that has just come to light, I'm initiating a preliminary inquiry under Rule 303 of the Manual For Courts-Martial to determine if you should be charged in the death of Captain Tyler Keane."

The words stabbed into Randi as viciously now as they had in her bright, cheerful kitchen. Although she'd had all day yesterday to prepare for this moment, she felt her throat tighten and cold sweat break out on her palms.

"I'm not going to read you your rights or discuss the evidence at this point," McLaughlin continued. "The purpose of this meeting is simply to make sure you understand the inquiry process."

Randi understood it, all right. This was different from the Safety Investigation and Accident Investigation Boards that had looked into the incident in Afghanistan. Their findings could have resulted in disciplinary action or the loss of her wings. This investigation could lead to a military court-martial and/or prison.

"Under Rule 303, a commander receiving information that a member of his command has committed or is suspected of committing an offense punishable by court-martial must make a preliminary inquiry into those allegations. That's what we're doing here, Randi."

"Yes, sir."

"I've appointed Major Alex Shores to act as inquiry officer."

Of all the people in the squadron, Shores was the least sociable and the most hard-nosed. McLaughlin couldn't have appointed a fairer—or more ruthless—inquiry officer.

"Captain Mooreman from the Adjutant General's JAG staff has been designated to act as your Area Defense Counsel. We've made you an appointment with him this afternoon to review the allegations and evidence laid against you. Major Shores will contact you within the next few days. He'll take your statement and interview any other persons he thinks may provide insight into this matter. Based on his findings, he'll make a recommendation as to whether there is sufficient evidence to warrant issuing charges against you."

The colonel paused, his shoulders bowed under the Nomex flight suit.

"Do you understand the process, Captain Morgan?"

"Yes, sir."

"Do you have any questions about that process?"

"None right now. But I do have a question about this new evidence."

"I think a discussion of the details had better wait until you've consulted with your attorney."

"I don't want the details. I just want to know how it turned up and where it came from."

Those questions had left Randi sleepless for two nights. The safety and accident boards had interviewed the crews of both C-130s involved, as well as the pilot of the A-10 that had delivered the ordnance to destroy Ty's aircraft. Both boards had reconstructed the scenario minute by minute, picked it apart, studied every phase, pieced it together again. She couldn't imagine any evidence that hadn't already been reviewed by the investigators.

"A copy of the transmitting document has been provided to your attorney," McLaughlin informed her, "but I see no harm in providing you with another."

He slid a letter across the desk. The bold, slashing signature leaped out at Randi even before she picked it up.

Samuel J. Keane.

Her stomach roiling, she stared at the signature. Sam was accusing her of deliberately contributing to his son's death.

The heavy parchment rattled in her shaking hand as she skimmed the brief document.

...argued violently
...accused my son of cheating on her
...refused to acknowledge his paternity claim
...left him to die

Her hand dropped to her lap. It was true. All of it. Except the very last.

The pain erupted then, a vicious spike to the right temple. Randi held her breath until the black spots faded.

"As you see," the colonel was saying, "Mr. Keane chose to address his letter to the governor as ultimate authority for the Oklahoma National Guard in its state role. Since the incident he refers to occurred while you were federalized and on active-duty military status, we're still trying to sort through the jurisdictional lines."

Randi narrowed her eyes. The shock was wearing off, giving way to a gathering fury. "Jurisdictional lines, hell. This is pure politics."

Everyone at the 137th knew Keane was one of the governor's biggest campaign contributors. With a gubernatorial election only months away, Sam was exercising his political muscle with a vengeance.

"It's also pure bullshit," Randi said furiously. "You read the safety and accident board reports, Colonel. You know what happened. Whether Ty and I argued or what we may have argued about has absolutely no bearing on the events of the following day."

"I strongly advise you to say nothing further until you've consulted with your attorney."

That was like a slap to the face. Randi swallowed hard and nodded.

"Yes, sir. Thank you, sir. Is that all?"

"That's all."

Still gripped by fury, Randi marched down the hall of the headquarters building. her first instinct was to call her friend and mentor, General Sanders, and ask how the hell *anyone* could take Sam's allegations seriously.

But Sanders was Colonel McLaughlin's boss, one step above him in the chain of command. She wouldn't undermine his authority by inserting herself into the 303 Inquiry at this point. And she was traveling with the Air Force Chief of Staff, Randi remembered. Would be for some weeks yet.

Fighting a stab of something close to panic, Randi shoved open the glass doors and stepped into the blinding sunlight.

* * *

The JAG appointed as her Area Defense Counsel was young, intense and an assistant district attorney in civilian life. Randi had met John Mooreman many times at wing functions, but had never imagined she'd be sitting across a desk from him in his downtown office, listening while he explained the gravity of the possible charges against her.

"There are two articles of the Uniform Code of Military Justice they could charge you with violating. Article 118, which includes murder, premeditated or otherwise."

Randi's breath hissed out.

"Or Article 119, manslaughter, voluntary or involuntary. The difference between the two lies in the degree of intent and planning."

Frowning, he used two fingers to shove his glasses up onto the bridge of his nose. "The circumstances surrounding Captain Keane's death—the fact that his plane went down, that you went in to rescue him and his crew, that he was running toward your aircraft when he triggered that antipersonnel device—argues against any premeditation on your part. You obviously had no way of knowing what would happen that morning."

Randi had to fight to keep her voice steady. "And manslaughter? How could they prove that?"

"They'd have to show you wanted to kill or inflict great bodily harm on Captain Keane and that, acting from a combination of fear and the heat of sudden passion, you left him to die on that abandoned airstrip."

"Passion," she echoed slowly, "like the anger of a woman who discovered her supposed lover was hitting on another female in the same unit."

"Yes." Mooreman didn't look away. "Involuntary manslaughter would suggest that you killed Captain Keane or contributed to his death, but without provocation and through an act of culpable negligence."

While Randi tried to absorb the distinctions, the attorney shuffled through the file on his desk.

"All they have at this point is the testimony of Technical Sergeant William Bates, who overheard you arguing with Captain Keane behind the mess tent the night before the captain died. And the letter Keane sent his father."

"What letter?"

"The Judge Advocate General's office just faxed me a copy. I haven't had time to study it, but on the surface it's pretty damning."

He took off his glasses and polished them while Randi reeled from her second blow of the day.

Ty had written his father. Told him he'd consoled Randi when her marriage hit the skids, and had been bitterly disappointed when she'd decided to give it one last try. He ended the letter by asking Sam to watch out for Randi if anything happened to him. And for Spencer. The boy could well be Sam's grandson.

"Shit!"

Her stomach lurching, Randi reread the entire letter. Her insides were churning with such dismay, she had to wrench her attention back to her defense attorney.

"As you can see," he was saying, "that letter complicates matters."

"How?"

"It suggests you were involved with Captain Keane on at least one occasion." Her attorney replaced his glasses. "I've read the safety board report and the unclassified portion of the accident investigation."

"Then you know what happened."

"I know what you and the other crew members told the investigators. Do you have anything to add to those statements?"

"No."

Mooreman steepled his fingers and regarded her with a carefully neutral expression. *Here it comes*, Randi thought, bracing herself. The question she'd been dreading since her meeting with Colonel McLaughlin.

"All right. Tell me about this argument you and Captain Keane reportedly had the night before he died."

8

Randi's entire family converged on Morgan's Falls for a war council that same evening. She'd waited until after her meetings with McLaughlin and Mooreman to call them, wanting to know the substance of the possible charges against her before alarming her sisters.

With the kids tucked in upstairs, the adults gathered in a kitchen still spicy from the spaghetti sauce Randi had simmered for supper. She recounted the details of both meetings.

Lissa paced the kitchen. Fury that the air force would conduct even a *preliminary* investigation into these absurd charges showed in the rigid lines of her body. Sarah rubbed her distended stomach and scowled. Cal scratched behind Absol's ears, listening intently as Randi described the incident on that abandoned Russian airfield.

When she finished, he made the same quiet request Mooreman had. "Talk to us about this argument behind the mess tent. Did you really accuse Ty of cheating on you?"

"No!"

Randi rubbed the heel of her hand against her temple, struggling to recall her exact words. The blowup had come so fast, igniting tempers fueled by swirling dust, by heat, by nerves stretched tight.

"In retrospect, though, I guess it could be construed that way."

"Why?" Cal asked patiently.

He'd discarded his suit coat and loosened his tie, leaving the red silk to dangle crookedly around the neck of his button-down blue shirt. His long, clever fingers tugged on the dog's ear.

Absol seemed to sense the tension in the air. His normally quivering body was still, and his head rested quietly against Cal's thigh while Randi tried to find the words to describe her complex relationship with Tyler Keane.

"The reasons for our fight go way back, to the last months before my divorce."

"I'm listening."

They all were. Lissa stopped pacing and sank into a chair. Sarah shifted her bulk and propped her elbows on the kitchen table.

"You all know what a disaster my marriage was," Randi said, dredging up the memories with a grimace. "I fell in love with a skilled surgeon, a man I respected for what he was. He fell in love with a woman he wanted to mold into his idea of the perfect wife."

"Bastard," Lissa spit, her anger at her former brother-in-law undiminished by time. "Handsome as sin, but still a bastard."

"I tried to be what he wanted. I honestly tried."

"We know you did," Sarah said fiercely. "You gave up the active duty air force for him."

"But I couldn't make myself take the last step and give up flying altogether. When Dave told me we were finished if I didn't, I came home for a few weeks to think it all through."

Even now, the memory of those agonizing weeks could shame her. Randi had always been the adventurous one, so eager to spread her wings, so ready to soar with the eagles. Up to that point, she'd accomplished everything she'd set out to do in life. Her inability to hold her marriage together had been a jolt to her self-esteem and her confidence. It had also been a severe reality check.

Her old high school friend had understood, though. All too well.

"When Ty heard I was back, he called and asked me to meet him at the lake house."

Sarah's brows rose. Lissa frowned. Randi had

never told her sisters about that stolen weekend at the Keanes' sprawling lakeside residence. She wasn't proud of what she'd done.

"I was feeling pretty raw then. Not to mention confused and hurt and inadequate. Ty recognized that, and went all out to convince me I could find life after a divorce."

"That was certainly something he'd know about," Sarah drawled. "He'd just dumped, who? Wife number two or three?"

"Two. He met Three after I decided to take a last shot at working things out with David."

She'd had to give it one more try. Her grandparents hadn't raised her to be a quitter. Despite the anger, despite the doubts, she'd owed her marriage one final attempt.

"Six weeks after I returned to D.C. I discovered I was pregnant. I thought the baby would complicate matters. Instead, it made everything so much easier. David walked, and I felt only relief that it was over."

The pregnancy had helped put her life into perspective. Her failed marriage faded into insignificance. Her confusion evaporated. All that had mattered then, the only thing she cared about, was providing a warm, stable, loving home for her child. Something she couldn't have done with David.

Or with Ty Keane. Despite his repeated protestations of everlasting devotion, Ty loved the hunt too much to settle for hearth, home and family.

Cal cleared his throat, breaking the small silence. "Let's go back to the lake house for a moment. Is it possible Ty was Spencer's biological father?"

"It's possible, but unlikely. I got my period shortly after I returned to D.C."

"Oh, sweetie!" Sarah stretched out a hand and squeezed Randi's. "I hate to break it to you, but lots of women have light periods in the early phases of pregnancy. I did with Duncan."

"I know. The question lingered there," Randi said, "at the back of my mind."

"You didn't run any tests?"

"I checked blood types, but both David and Ty were O positive, same as Spencer."

"What about DNA?"

"I thought about requesting a test. Not because I cared *who* had fathered my son, but to know his biological heritage in case of some medical condition or emergency, but, well, it just never became a real issue."

"Ty didn't question you about Spencer?"

"Yes, he did. But I told him about having a period and he let the matter drop."

"It sounds as though that was your intention," Sarah suggested with a keen look.

"I still had the scars from one marriage," Randi admitted, trying not to come across as defensive. "I didn't want to jump into another. And there was the baby to consider. I needed time."

Unfortunately, Ty wasn't any better at waiting as an adult than he'd been as a teen. Absorbed in her new motherhood, Randi couldn't say for sure how many weeks passed before the rumor mill had cranked up and she'd started hearing about his latest conquest. He'd married Wife Number Three less than six months after Randi had given birth and turned down his proposal yet again.

She never doubted that she'd made the right decision. Ty was fun, charming and a tiger in bed, but *not* husband material.

"We stayed friends. We were always friends. We saw each other during drill weekends, flew together occasionally. Then, just before we left for that last rotation in Afghanistan, his third wife filed for divorce."

Facing a bitter court battle over what should've been an airtight prenup, Ty had poured out his feelings to Randi one evening after a lengthy and exhausting mission.

"In a complete reversal of roles, I was the one offering comfort. I assured *him* he could survive this divorce, as he had the others. I..." She released another long breath. "I opened my heart to him, as he had to me."

For a week, maybe two, Randi had almost let herself believe they'd both matured, that the matrimonial fires they'd gone through had tempered their long-standing relationship into something stronger, something cleaner. She'd soon shed that illusion.

"We were so close again for that short time, but things had cooled between us well before we rotated to K-2."

K-2. The armpit of the universe. A former Soviet air base set in the corner of the world where China, India, Pakistan and Afghanistan almost touch. Desert-dry with long, hot summers and high mountain winters.

Only those who'd been there understood what it was like. Living in a tent city. Sweating in the blistering heat of day. Shivering at night. Mouth and nose muffled to keep out the stinging sand. It got into everything, equipment, food, underwear, toothpaste.

"There was no privacy," Randi explained. "My crew and I briefed as a unit, flew together, debriefed, ate and slept in the same tent to maintain crew integrity. Ty's did the same. We'd been in theater almost a month when I started hearing rumors about him and the female loadmaster on his crew."

Like all guardsmen, Debra White had left behind another life to serve her country. In her case it was a dead-end job as a clerk at a convenience store. She'd made no secret of the fact that rich, handsome Captain Keane dazzled her. Randi suspected his rank and authority as crew commander added the additional aphrodisiac of power.

"That's what Ty and I argued about that night. The

possibility that he was screwing a member of his crew."

"And that offended you?" Cal asked, his gaze steady. Sarah and Melissa sat on either side of him. Like a jury, Randi thought. A friendly one at this point, but she could see the doubts beginning to form in their eyes.

"Yes, it offended me. Fraternization happens. Of course it happens. People spend months together in close quarters. The lines blur. But you don't sleep with a member of your own crew in a crowded tent city. There's fraternization, and there's just plain stupidity."

Cal lifted a brow. "Was it your place to take a fellow officer to task?"

"Someone had to, before our detachment commander heard about it. I figured Ty and I could discuss it friend to friend, but he got smart-mouthed and I got mad. Maybe it was the heat. Or the long missions. Or the damned sand. Whatever the reason, we both let fly and said things we'd never said to each other before." She gave the sworn deposition a bitter glance. "It's all there. Or most of it, anyway."

"I want to hear it from you."

Randi tried not to resent her brother-in-law's calm, detached tone. She'd asked his advice and counsel. She needed his unbiased opinion.

"I called Ty a walking dick who couldn't keep his

pants zipped. Among other things. He zinged a few lethal barbs right back at me. Including the reminder that I'd hopped in the sack with him while I was still legally married to David. When he brought up the question of Spencer's parentage, I snarled something to the effect that an asshole like him could never have fathered a terrific kid like Spencer. It wasn't our finest moment."

She caught the look Sarah exchanged with her husband. The communication was lawyer to lawyer and not particularly reassuring. But it was Lissa's stricken expression that almost broke Randi's heart.

"Why didn't you tell me any of this?" she whispered. "Why did you let me go on thinking Ty was such a hero?"

Leaning forward, Randi gripped her sister's arm. "He *was* a hero. He died providing cover fire for his crew. They survived because of him. All this personal stuff—it was just between Ty and me. Or so I thought," she added with a grimace.

Lissa pulled free and shoved away from the table. Randi ached for her, remembering how she'd stalked Ty as a preteen. Remembering, too, how she'd made an all-out play for him after his first divorce. To his credit, Ty had let her down gently by telling her his heart belonged to Randi.

"I can't believe it." Lissa started pacing again, obviously struggling to adjust her mental image of the man who'd figured so large in her life. "After all the years, all you'd been to each other, you hurl these vicious accusations at him and the next day he's blown apart."

Randi flinched, Sarah let out a low hiss and Lissa jolted to a halt. Red flooded into her cheeks.

"Shit! I'm sorry, Randi. I didn't mean that the way it sounded."

"I know."

"It was just an accident, Ty dying like that."

"I know."

Cal gave Absol's ear a last tug and sat forward. "Now all we have to do is convince the investigating officer of that. Do you know who he or she is?"

"Yes. Major Alex Shores."

"What do you know about him?"

Randi gave a short laugh. "He goes by the handle Sledge—short for Sledgehammer. That might give you some idea of his personality."

The war council broke up after 1:00 a.m. The adults woke early the next morning and gathered in the kitchen once again to finalize their plan of attack. The October dawn was cold and gray, matching Randi's mood, but the others brimmed with decision and determination.

Since neither Sarah nor Cal possessed any expertise in military law, their first charge was to research the pertinent sections of the Uniform Code of Military Justice pertaining to the 303 preliminary inquiry process and rules of evidence. To kick off that effort, Cal would schedule a meeting in Oklahoma City with Captain Mooreman, Randi's military defense counsel. Sarah would initiate routine background checks on Technical Sergeant William Bates, Staff Sergeant Debra White and Major Alex Shores.

Lissa announced her intention of spending the next few weeks at Morgan's Falls to give Randi moral support and help take care of Spencer. Her sister's revelations about her tangled relationship with Ty Keane had shaken her, but her loyalty lay first, last and always with Randi. Luckily, Lissa's job as a graphic designer for the Dallas World Trade Center allowed her considerable flexibility.

"I'll zip back down to Dallas this morning to pick up my laptop and a few files. If you don't mind one more boarder," she added with a glance at the animal lolling at Randi's feet. "How did you ever let yourself get talked into such a horse for a house pet?"

"It wasn't my idea. Pete sort of palmed him off on us."

"Pete?"

"Professor Engstrom. He's leading the team from OU I told you about. The one trying to date the runes."

"I forgot about that. How's the project going?"

"It's still in the preliminary stages. The full team's supposed to assemble next week."

"We'll assemble next week, too," Sarah said crisply. "Let's plan on Monday evening, after Cal talks to your defense counsel. Don't agree to a meeting with this inquiry officer until then."

"I may not have that option. Inquiries like this normally have to be completed within a specified period."

"Tell this guy—what's his name again?"

"Alex Shores.

"Aka Sledge," Lissa muttered. The jutting angle of her jaw indicated she'd already placed Major Shores firmly in the enemy camp.

"Tell this Sledge you've retained civilian counsel and need time to consult with them. If he gives you any crap about it, refer him to me." Sarah held up a hand for assistance in levering her bulk out of the chair. "C'mon, Calvin. Let's roust our hoodlums-in-training out of bed and hit the road. We have work to do."

The next hour was spent getting the three kids up and the Howell family on their way. Spencer stuck out his lip when his cousins departed, and clumped out the door to perform morning poop duty, but brightened considerably when he learned his aunt Lis would be staying at Morgan's Falls for a while.

Lissa's presence helped Randi get through Friday and the weekend that followed. Her younger sister entertained Spencer for most of a rainy Saturday and dragged both mother and son out of the house on Sunday for a trip to Tulsa and family dinner at Sarah's.

Monday dawned dark and drizzly. Randi had carpool duty and was corralling Spencer into her Cherokee when a pickup truck turned onto the drive sloping up to the house. Absol took off, barking wildly. Lissa heard the commotion, came outside and sent Randi a questioning glance. "Expecting someone?"

"Looks like Pete Engstrom."

"Your professor? Starts work early, doesn't he?"

To her surprise, Randi felt an unaccustomed flutter just under her ribs. She wouldn't have imagined she'd have room in her head right now for anything except Sam Keane's vicious accusations, but the memory of Pete's lips brushing hers popped in and refused to leave.

She waited beside Lissa while the vehicle crunched to a halt. Pete climbed out, accompanied a moment later by a roly-poly, white-haired companion in a wrinkled business suit. Pete wore a blue-plaid flannel shirt as protection against the chill, with a pair of jeans that soon sported a collection of muddy paw prints.

Randi felt some of her tension ease while Pete laughed and dodged the dog's enthusiastic kisses. Not every part of her life was shaded in tones of gray, she thought. She had Spencer. She had her sisters and Cal and the kids. She had this home, carved out of the wilderness by her ancestors.

She didn't know at this point if what she felt for Pete Engstrom was anything more than physical attraction, but the pull was definitely there and it gave Randi something to think about for a few moments other than the inquiry hanging over her like an axe.

Consequently, a smile slipped out in response to Pete's. His, however, disappeared as he approached. The concerned glance he gave her made Randi wish she'd bothered with more than a few quick strokes with a hairbrush this morning. She knew she looked like hell after her almost sleepless nights. Pete's frown confirmed it.

He didn't comment on the dark circles under her eyes, however, or the lines etched into her face. Instead, he shook hands with Lissa, exchanged a few words with Spencer, and introduced his associate.

"This is Dr. Raynard Jorgenson. He's the curator of the Oslo Museum of Medieval and Viking Heritage."

"I am quite anxious to view your stone," the historian said in heavily accented English. "I have great hopes we can match the runes inscribed on it to others with well-established dates."

"Are you going up to the site now?" Randi asked, eyeing the Norwegian's business suit.

"No, we're headed down to the Kerr Conference Center in Poteau," Pete explained. "The rest of the team assembled there last night, but Dr. Jorgenson's flight was late and just got in."

His smile was back, a slow, sexy rearrangement that crinkled the skin at the corners of his mouth.

"Since you were on the way, we swung by to see if you wanted to ride down to the center with us and watch the first test of the imaging process."

"Sorry, I can't. I have to take Spencer to school."

And wait for the axe to drop.

"I'll drive Spencer in," Lissa offered. "You should go with the professors. You know how much those runes always fascinated you and—" She hesitated for the barest fraction of a second. "You and Ty."

The wound was still raw. For both of them.

"This isn't really a good time, Lis."

"Yes, it is," her sister argued. "We can't do anything more until we hear back from Sarah and Cal. You need to get out, get some color in your cheeks."

What Randi needed was to get this damned investigation over and done with so she could snatch more than a few hours' sleep at a time. Since she didn't appear to have much control over *that* process, she decided to take Pete up on his offer.

"I'll get a jacket."

"Better make it a waterproof one," he advised with an eye to the dark clouds overhead.

With a hug for Spencer and last-minute instructions for Lissa, Randi went back into the house to collect her purse and a hooded jacket. She also hurried into the downstairs bathroom to powder her shiny nose and slap on some lipstick. Her sky-blue turtleneck and matching cardigan were presentable enough, but her brown cord slacks tended to sag at the knees and seat. Not exactly haute couture, she thought wryly.

Pete Engstrom didn't seem to mind. His smile came back as she shut a distinctly unhappy hound in the house and rejoined the physics professor and his visiting Viking historian. With a hand under Randi's elbow that sent a silly thrill fluttering through her veins, he helped her into the pickup.

9

Thunder rumbled ominously during the twenty-minute drive to the conference center just outside Poteau.

With old-world courtesy, Dr. Jorgenson had insisted on riding in the rear seat of the pickup's extended cab. He hung over the front seat, however, full of curiosity about the project and the other members of the team.

Randi angled her body against the door and listened to the lively conversation, but found her glance settling regularly on Pete's profile. His laid-back manner was so different from her surgically precise ex. So different, too, from the supercharged ions Ty Keane used to shoot off almost without trying.

The professors' discussion absorbed her until

they arrived at the Kerr Conference Center and Museum. The sprawling complex featured an enormous central structure of native stone and wood. Two wings fanned out on either side, as if to embrace the hills it overlooked.

The center had once been home to Robert Kerr, one of Oklahoma's most powerful movers and shakers. The oilman had become the state's first native-born governor and later a multiterm U.S. senator. His legacy was seen in educational centers, museums and office complexes all over the state, but nowhere more dramatically than in the magnificent property his heirs had dedicated to the study of Oklahoma's natural resources.

Randi waited in the lobby while Pete helped Dr. Jorgenson unload his gear and check into one of the guest suites. A quick call to Pete's assistant revealed that the rest of the team was just finishing breakfast and eager to get to work.

"I, too, am eager," the Norwegian said, pooh-poohing Pete's suggestion that he might need to rest after his long and much-delayed flight. "I shall meet you in the dining room, yes? All I want is coffee before I examine these runes I have come so far to see."

"The dining room's just down this hall. We'll wait for you there."

Pete's hand went to the small of Randi's back again. She was getting used to the touch, if not the tingle.

"Smart move to make this your headquarters," she commented as they followed the scent of bacon and fresh brewed coffee. "The central location here in Poteau is perfect for viewing these stones, plus the one at Heavener and the one at Morgan's Falls."

"The accommodations aren't bad, either."

"I've never seen the inside of the guest suites, but I know Senator Kerr reportedly entertained presidents, movie stars and astronauts."

"They didn't give any of us the presidential suite, but my room will do nicely. And this dining room sure beats cooking dinner over a fire pit or a portable grill."

"No kidding," Randi murmured, eyeing the mix of wood, wrought iron and flowers that gave the room an air of rustic elegance.

Pete guided her toward a handful of people gathered around a table near the floor-to-ceiling windows. Involved in their conversation, they paid no attention to either their surroundings or the black thunderclouds and lightning just outside the glass. The remains of their breakfast littered the table. The two older members of the group clutched coffee cups and huddled together in deep conversation. A twentysomething kid with a long pony tail and wire-rimmed glasses sipped at what looked like a mug of chocolate and listened with a slight frown. The fourth member of the group was a stunning blonde in hip-hugging jeans and a peach-colored sweater that showed off lush curves. With a toss of her silky, shoulder-length hair, she turned to greet the newcomers.

"There you are." Her glance slid to Randi before shifting back to Pete. "Did you get Dr. Jorgenson settled?"

"We did. He insists he doesn't need to rest and will join us shortly. Miranda, this is my lab assistant, Anne Gillette. She helped develop the imaging process we'll be testing on the runes. Anne, this is Miranda Morgan. I invited her to watch our first run."

"Did you?" The younger woman's smile was friendly enough, but her green eyes were coolly assessing. "I would've thought you'd wait to do that until we set up at her place."

Shrugging the remark aside, Pete introduced Randi to the rest of the team. The two older members were Jack Beasley, a bushy-bearded cryptologist from the University of Chicago, and Pauline Lockwood, a professor of anthropology at OU who had a shock of white hair and a baggy maroon sweatshirt that proudly proclaimed Old Bones Are the Best Bones. The ponytail belonged to a lanky grad student from the history department by the name of Brady White.

"Brady's been researching the legend you told me about," Pete commented, retrieving chairs from one of the other tables for himself and Randi. "He thinks he may have a lead."

Looking disconcerted to find himself in the spotlight, the grad student hunched his shoulders and scooted his chair to one side to make room for the newcomers.

"I found a vague reference in one of the oral histories transcribed back in the fifties. It was buried in an old Quawpaw tale about a drought that caused crops to fail several years in succession. The legend ascribes the drought to various actions that angered the twin thunder gods."

As if to add dramatic emphasis to his report, a bolt of lightning forked down outside the windows. Thunder boomed a second later. Randi's knowledge of her Native American ancestors' beliefs and customs was superficial at best, but she remembered that the crash of thunder meant the twin gods were playing ball in the heavens.

"One of the things that supposedly angered the gods was that a chief's daughter shared her furs with a man not of the People. This woman gave birth to a girl-child with the outsider's strange-colored eyes."

Randi sat back, astonished. Although the legends and folklore her grandfather so delighted in telling had always made an impression, she'd never really taken them seriously. The idea that this particular tale might have its roots in long-held religious beliefs fascinated her.

Pete leaned forward, intent on establishing a link

that would tie the legend to his project. "Does the oral history give a description of this stranger?"

"Unfortunately, no. But it does suggest other disasters befell the People around the time of the girl-child's birth."

Brady tapped a forefinger on the sleek little laptop positioned beside his plate. Randi had the feeling he was never without it.

"I've focused most of my research on oral histories passed down through the tribes currently inhabiting this area. I decided to expand the search to include the early-Mississippian people who populated the western drainage around A.D. 800. Maybe I can find another reference to outsiders with strange-colored eyes."

"Good thinking," Anne Gillette drawled, "particularly since the runes we're trying to date were incised as early as A.D. 750."

The blonde's deliberate sarcasm wasn't lost on her peer. Brady colored up and tugged self-consciously on his ponytail. With a quelling glance at his lab assistant, Pete encouraged the student.

"So what's your plan?"

"I thought I'd drive over to Spiro later today. The folks at the Indian Mound Museum might have some information on pre- or early-Mississippian legends."

The University of Chicago cryptologist looked up at that. "I've heard the Spiro Indian Mounds contained the finest collection of copper incised funeral masks found to date. I'd like to go along with you. If we get through here in time to work in a visit," he added with a glance at his watch.

They were all getting restless, Randi thought. So was Pete, although he controlled his impatience with the same easy manner he controlled his small team. She sensed his relief, though, when Dr. Jorgenson bustled into the restaurant.

Introductions were made, coffee was poured and the team went over the game plan for their first attempt to date the mysterious Oklahoma runes. After her session with Pete up on the bluff, Randi understood the concept of relative dating. She also understood that the team's goal was to capture the characteristics of the Oklahoma runes and—they hoped—match them to other runes with the same or similar characteristics.

The concept became even clearer when the group adjourned to the museum housed in one wing of the conference center. Funded by the Kerr Foundation, the museum displayed artifacts from the nearby Spiro Mounds, exhibits celebrating Choctaw heritage and tableaus portraying early pioneer life.

It also housed the four smaller runestones found in various parts of southeastern Oklahoma over the years. Randi had seen the stones many times during visits to the museum, but caught Pete's infectious enthusiasm as the group clustered in front of the largest stone.

"Look at that!"

The plaque beside the case indicated two schoolboys had uncovered it some years ago in the foothills of Caraval Mountain, outside Poteau. It was a flat piece of shale about the size of a serving platter, broken in two places and refitted together.

Dr. Beasley stroked his beard, eyes bright with excitement as he studied the symbols incised in the shale. "They're old futhark. Most definitely old futhark. Wouldn't you say so, Raynard?"

"Yes, yes. Most definitely. But old futhark was used for more than a thousand years, well into the Viking period. So who cut these runes and when, eh? That is the question we must answer."

That was indeed the question. Eager to get to work, the team hauled in their equipment while the museum curator unlocked the cases to give them access to the precious stones.

Randi had expected to be a mere observer, but was soon put to work. She kept the team members supplied with coffee, helped uncrate equipment and ended up with Pete's laptop on her knees, recording specifics of the silicon casts of incised runes Jorgenson and Beasley had brought with them for comparative purposes.

While Randi labored over that task, Pete and his lab assistant assembled their spectrograph. It sat on a flat platform mounted on a tripod with adjustable legs. The camera itself consisted of two long black lenses positioned at right angles to each other. The lenses included light filters, gratings and calibration devices that took Pete and Anne a good half hour to configure.

"You employ no moving optics," Jack Beasley observed, surveying the setup with a keen eye.

"None," Pete confirmed. "By mounting the lenses on a stable platform like this, we can achieve more precise calibration."

With one eye on the computer screen displaying the settings, he adjusted the right lens angle millimeter by millimeter. The numbers on the screen changed accordingly. Finally, he was ready.

"Okay, Anne, let's shoot the first rune."

Catching her glossed lower lip between her teeth, Gillette sighted the left lens on a jagged *S* that looked much like a lightning bolt. Her computer screen showed blurry gray at first. Slowly, by almost infinitesimal degrees, the blur sharpened and formed a reverse image. When she enlarged the image, the chisel marks around the edges of the letter leapt out in startling detail.

"That's it," Pete said. "That's what we want to see. Make sure you've got the entire rune framed in the notch filter."

Frowning, Gillette tucked a wavy strand behind her ear and performed another minute calibration.

The team seemed to hold its collective breath until the lab assistant glanced up, checked the settings on the computer screen and gave a curt nod.

"I'm fixed."

Edging closer to the rotund Dr. Jorgenson, Randi went up on tiptoe to peer over his head as Pete adjusted his lens. His computer screen fuzzed, then cleared with agonizing slowness. Another view of the chisel marks was painted across the screen like a bold, slashing signature.

"Yes! Okay, let's harness 'em."

Pete clicked in a series of commands. The two images on the screen began to move toward each other. They also seemed to take on a life of their own. Like writhing snakes, the jagged Ss swirled and dipped and flashed every color of the rainbow. Their dance was mesmerizing, almost hypnotic. Randi got dizzy watching the whirling colors and had to blink several times before they finally blended.

The three-dimensional symbol they formed seemed to float on air. It also possessed such stunning depth and clarity that Randi could've sworn it was a solid object instead of a projection.

She wasn't the only one astonished by the holograph. Dr. Jorgenson's jaw dropped. Muttering something in his native tongue, he stretched out a hand to the screen.

Beasley, too, seemed astounded. "Amazing," the Chicagoan murmured. "Simply amazing!"

Hooking his thumbs in his pockets, Pete rocked back on his heels. "It is, isn't it?"

He exchanged a triumphant grin with his lab assistant before hitting the keyboard to save the holograph. He then ran another program to capture its precise characteristics.

"Computerization makes it possible for us to take a cross section at various points," he explained. "We'll measure the width of the cut at surface level and at the base, fix the exact midpoint and determine the incision angles. That data will allow us to build a statistical table describing the characteristics of this rune. It will also allow us to calculate a standard deviation by which to measure it against other, similar runes."

Only when he'd backed up both the image and the data to a hard disk did he and Anne begin the process of repositioning the camera and resetting the lenses.

"We'll repeat this process for each rune on each of the stones." Pete gestured to the other small stones in adjoining cases. "And on the silicon casts of known, dated runes Drs. Beasley and Jorgenson have shipped in. We'll then compare the two sets. If we get a match…"

"Or anything close to a match," Anne put in with the first flash of a genuine smile Randi had seen on her face.

"We'll be one step closer to fixing the origin of the Oklahoma runes."

"Only one step?" Randi asked. "What comes after that?"

"We go to the source of the match and image the original."

Randi's brows lifted. The casts Jorgenson had shipped in had been made from runes incised into rocks in Norway, Sweden, Iceland, Greenland and Newfoundland. Dr. Beasley had contributed models of runes found in Minnesota and northern Illinois.

"If the comparisons between these symbols and the original achieve a diffraction efficiency of eighty percent or more for unpolarized light," Pete continued, "we can postulate that they were incised at relatively the same time using similar tools."

"Ooookay."

Grinning, he rephrased the process in layman's terms. "What we're doing is simply matching cuts and chisel strokes. Pretty mundane and repetitive work, really."

"Right." Randi eyed the group still huddled around the holographs. "I can see that."

"Let me know if you get bored. I'll have Brady drive you home."

"I'm okay."

She was more than okay, Randi realized with a little shock. For over an hour, she'd actually forgotten the inquiry hanging over her. Resolutely, she pushed it to the back of her mind again.

* * *

It stayed there until the team broke for lunch and Randi called to check on Spencer.

"Your neighbor just dropped him off," Lissa said. "She also dropped off her son because the boys wanted to play together. I hope that's okay."

"Sure. Just keep an eye on them. They tend to get physical with things like baseball bats and golf clubs."

"I won't let 'em out of my sight. And Randi..."

"Yes?"

"Major Shores called. I told him you weren't here and wouldn't be back for some time."

Randi managed to swallow the sudden lump in her throat. "You could've given him my cell phone number."

"Why make it easy for the creep?"

"He isn't a creep, just an officer assigned an onerous duty."

"Ha! Anyone investigating my sister qualifies as a class A, numero uno creep in my book."

"Did he leave a number?"

"He did. I told him you'd return his call when you got home."

"I'll be there shortly, Lis."

"No hurry. Like I said, why make it easy for him? Besides, Sarah and Cal want you to wait until you talk to them before you contact Shores, remember? Cal called a while ago, too, saying he'd drive down

around six. You might as well stay at the museum
and keep your mind off things until then."

"You sure you can handle the boys all afternoon?"

"The little monsters and I are getting along just
fine. Or we were," she added at the sound of a crash.
"Way to go, fellas."

"Uh-oh. Any open wounds or spilled blood?"

**"No, but Granddad's spittoon just took a direct
hit."**

The brass spittoon that had performed yeoman
duty in their tobacco-chewing granddad's day now
served as a planter. Lissa issued a brisk order to her
charges to get the broom and ended the call with repeated assurances to her sister that she had everything under control.

Randi stood undecided for long moments after
hanging up. Sledge's phone number burned a hole
in her pocket. She couldn't delay the inevitable for
long. A few more hours at most.

Lissa was right. She might as well spend those
hours here at the museum instead of brooding at
home.

She wasn't quite as successful at putting the inquiry out of her mind during the afternoon as she
had been that morning. The call from Sledge
weighed heavily on her mind, so much so that she
breathed a sigh of relief when Pete finished imag-

ing the third stone and decided the team needed a break.

"Dr. Jorgenson, you look ready to drop."

"Jet lag has caught up with me," the Norwegian admitted, his round cheeks sagging a bit. "I will take a nap, then join you after dinner to image the casts. Maybe we shall make our first match, yes?"

"Maybe."

Although Randi would've liked to see the actual comparisons, the real world was pulling at her.

"I need to get home," she said to Pete. "If Brady's still planning on a drive over to Spiro, he could drop me off."

"I'll tell him you're ready to go."

Collecting her purse and jacket, she said goodbye to the rest of the team.

"Thanks for your help," Pauline Lockwood said, her smile friendly above her Old Bones sweatshirt.

"I enjoyed it."

The short, jolly Jorgenson pumped her hand with real warmth. "We shall see you again when we come to examine the stone on your property, yes?"

"If I'm there."

"I will hope so. I want to hear more of this legend you told Peter about."

Randi made a murmured response and escaped to the hall. Slipping on her jacket, she shoved her hands in the pockets. A slow dread curled in her stomach as she considered the hours ahead.

With her thoughts on the pending war council and the call from Sledge, she let her gaze drift over the photographs lining the walls. The small corner of her mind not consumed with the inquiry registered photos of Senator Kerr with Presidents Kennedy, Johnson and Ford and a host of other celebrities.

Suddenly both her gaze and her thoughts stopped dead. Gulping, Randi focused on a black-and-white shot of two men sharing a private moment at some political rally.

Ty! The blond, square-jawed man on the right was Ty Keane.

She took an involuntary step forward before she realized the clothes and the banners placed the event too early for that to be Ty. It had to be his father.

Randi studied the shot of a younger Sam, one whose face wasn't twisted by grief or hate. Ty had looked just like him at that age. Confident, self-assured, so damned certain life would accommodate itself to his desires.

Without warning, the emotions she'd held at bay suddenly crashed down on her. The guilt, the regret, the fear she'd refused to acknowledge until this moment almost overwhelmed her. Throat tight, spine rigid, she stared blindly at the man who'd become her nemesis.

"You okay?"

The quiet question seemed to come from the far side of the moon. Blinking, Randi turned away from the photo.

"Yes, I…I just…"

She raised a hand to brush back her hair. Embarrassed at the way it shook, she shoved it back in her pocket.

"I just saw a ghost."

Eyes narrowed, Pete examined the photo. He didn't recognize the subjects, but the fine print under the picture identified the one on the right as the man whose generous gift was funding his study.

A sharp kernel of suspicion formed in Pete's gut. His first meeting with Miranda Morgan had left him with the distinct impression that there was more to Keane's generous gift than showed on the surface. Randi's white face and trembling hand now had Pete convinced.

He didn't like the idea of being a used as a pawn in any man's game. Or woman's.

"I changed my mind," he told Brady when the grad student came ambling down the hall. "I'm taking Randi home. Tell the others I'll be back in an hour."

10

Randi made an obvious effort at conversation during the drive. Pete kept up his end until he spotted a roadside rest stop a few miles past Keota. When he pulled in, she frowned and skimmed a glance at the rain-washed picnic table huddled forlornly under two dripping pines.

"Why are we stopping here?"

He killed the truck's engine. "So you can tell me about the ghost you saw back there at the center."

She gave a small, embarrassed shrug. "Sorry. I didn't mean to sound so melodramatic."

What she'd sounded was desperate. And scared. Not qualities Pete would normally associate with a pilot who'd been decorated for courage under fire.

"What's going on, Randi? Why would a photo of Sam Keane give you the shakes?"

"That's my business."

"The hell it is."

She'd deflected him once when he'd offered to help. He wasn't letting her do it again. Not with so much riding on the results of this project.

"Keane is funding the first field test of a process I spent almost a year developing. He made that funding contingent on your cooperation in allowing us access to the stone on your property. What's the connection, Randi? Other than your friendship with Keane's dead son?"

"There isn't any other connection. Not one I can figure out, anyway."

"Bull."

"I'm telling you the truth! Why would I lie?"

"I don't know. But there has to be a reason a photo of Sam Keane can drain the blood from your face."

Her jaw set. "The reason has nothing to do with you."

"That didn't work the first time. It's not going to work now. Talk to me, Miranda."

She shook her head, anger and impatience chasing across her features.

"Talk to me, woman."

Her chin snapped up. Danger flashed in her blue eyes. *"Woman?"*

"This pickup isn't moving until you tell me what's going on."

The atmosphere inside the truck cab grew so thick. Pete could almost see the sparks arcing through the air. He half expected Miranda to tell him exactly where he could park his frigging truck and stomp the few remaining miles to her house through the rain. What he wasn't expecting was the exasperation that pushed through her anger.

"And here I was thinking just this morning how laid-back and comfortable you are to be with."

That hit like a block from a three-hundred-pound tackle. Pete wanted this woman to think of him in any number of ways. Comfortable and laid-back didn't rank anywhere near the top of the list. Feeling as though his manhood had just flunked a midterm exam, he dragged in a breath.

"Looks like we need to get something straight here. What I feel for you is anything but comfortable."

"Excuse me?"

"Why do you suppose I came up with that lame excuse to bring pizza by your place the other night? And practically strong-armed you into coming down to the conference center today? You intrigue me, Miranda. Your refusal to even discuss a problem I suspect involves us both is also beginning to seriously annoy me."

She blinked, obviously surprised by the admission but too irate to cut him any slack. "Sounds like you have a personal problem, Engstrom."

"You're right, Morgan, I do."

Head cocked, she considered that for a moment. Pete used the lull to slide a hand across the back of her seat. She went still when he cupped her neck, and stiffened when he leaned in.

"Unless I'm reading this all wrong," he said, watching her eyes, "I'm not the only one with a problem."

He saw the fight leap into her face, felt the resistance as he drew her closer. For all his need to connect with her on some primitive, male-to-female level, he was prepared to back off.

The fact that she didn't pull away when he brought his mouth down on hers sent something distinctly Neanderthal jolting through him. Pete managed to control the urge to climb over the console, but he was hurting like hell even before her mouth opened under his.

Randi knew this was crazy, knew she had no business letting Engstrom manipulate her like this, but his kiss generated an instant heat. For the first time in longer than she could remember, her blood pulsed and her heart pounded from something other than the adrenaline kick of jockeying an aircraft crammed with forty-six thousand pounds of cargo through an unfriendly sky.

It was Pete who finally lifted his head. Breathing hard, he searched her face. Whatever he saw there put a feral gleam in his eyes.

"Okay, Morgan, I think we've established the attraction is mutual. Here are the options as I see 'em. We can keep this on a purely physical level or we can raise it to a loftier plane and indulge in a little adult conversation before we get naked and sweaty. I'm good to go either way."

So was she, Randi realized with a shock. This man created all sorts of confused feelings in her, not the least of which was plain, old-fashioned lust. Fighting the urge to wrap her arms around his neck and drag his mouth back down to hers, she offered a terse explanation.

"Sam Keane thinks I'm responsible for his son's death."

"Come again?"

"You wanted to know what's going on between Keane and me. That's it. He's accused me of abandoning his son to the enemy. The air force is conducting a preliminary investigation to see if the allegations have merit."

"Jesus!"

When Pete flopped back in his seat, she pasted on a sardonic smile. "A real mood killer, isn't it? I'm guessing you're no longer interested in getting naked and sweaty."

He narrowed his eyes at her jab. Randi knew she was being unfair. Anyone would need a few minutes to regroup after a pronouncement like that—particularly a researcher on the receiving end of Keane's largesse.

"You guessed wrong." With a controlled violence, he twisted the key in the ignition. "Where do you want to take this? Your place, my suite at the conference center, or the nearest motel?"

Perversely, his burst of temper took some of the steam from hers. "Okay, I suppose I deserved that."

"You suppose?"

"Don't push me, Engstrom! That's as close to an apology as I'm capable of right now."

He clenched his hands on the steering wheel and did an obvious mental count to ten. Randi didn't know if she was more relieved or reluctant when he killed the engine once more.

"Tell me why Keane thinks you're responsible for his son's death."

First her area defense counsel, then her family. Now Pete, and soon Sledge. Randi was beginning to feel she'd never be allowed to let the brutal, unrelenting images die.

"Ty Keane and I were lovers in high school and again some years later, after my marriage hit the skids."

The words came out flat and hard. She didn't have to polish the dead man's halo, the way she had for her younger sister. Or watch the carefully neutral reaction of her defense attorney. Fixing her gaze on the metal picnic table and two spindly pines, Randi stripped her tangled relationship with Ty down to the bare, unvarnished facts.

"Ty was part of the reason I came back to Oklahoma after my divorce. Him, and the chance to fly with the 137th. What we had between us turned out to be more heat than substance. The heat burned out, the friendship remained. Then...then came Afghanistan."

She swiped her tongue over dry lips, started, stopped again.

"Tell me," he said quietly.

"It's hard to understand if you haven't been there."

"I wasn't in Afghanistan, but I pulled a hitch in the marines. I was just a grunt," he added when she turned a surprised face his way. "I joined with the specific goal of racking up enough courses and educational benefits to finish my degree, but I learned a helluva lot more than I'd expected to. Tell me."

Randi did. Her breath fogged the windows. The pines blurred. She stared at the steamed glass, seeing flashes of fire in the opaque gray, and related the events on that faraway mountain plateau.

"It started off as a routine mission. We were fragged to perform an ERO—an engine running offload—of munitions for elements of the 82nd Airborne occupying a firebase in the mountains around Mazar-e Sharif. We departed K-2 at oh-six-forty-five in a two-ship formation and flew a low-altitude regime, skimming just a few hundred feet over the peaks, to ingress our drop zone."

The 130s were designed to do just that, come in low to evade radars, drop their loads and get the hell out of Dodge. Unfortunately, low and slow made them ideal targets for ground-launched anti-aircraft systems.

"We'd just overflown an abandoned Russian airfield high in the mountains south of Kunduz when the radar warning receiver lit up, indicating a radar lock."

In a flat tone, she described the controlled chaos that followed. The sudden, heart-stopping shrill of the missile warning system. Her copilot's scramble to activate the infrared countermeasures jammer. The whoosh as the chaff dispenser spit out thousands of bits of foil to deflect the incoming missile.

"I jerked the controls hard left and saw the SAM zing by. Actually spotted it streaking past my starboard wing tip. I was still drenched in sweat when Ty cut in a few moments later. He'd taken a hit and was losing altitude fast.

"We radioed base requesting ground-fire suppression and combat rescue. They advised us there were two A-10s in the area, just twenty minutes away, and that Rescue was launching immediately. I stayed on Captain Keane's tail as he circled back to the Russian airstrip."

The rugged C-130 Hercules were designed for short field and unimproved-terrain landings, but Ty wasn't about to put an aircraft loaded with munitions down on bare dirt. Not in Afghanistan. Ten years of Soviet occupation and warfare had left it the most heavily mined country on earth. An estimated fifteen million explosive devices had been planted in the dry, dun-colored earth.

Despite another twenty years of mine-clearing efforts, more than three hundred Afghanis were still killed or injured every month by land mines. Particularly in the mountainous north, where Americans had learned not to set foot outside cleared areas. The Russian airstrip had been the only option for an emergency landing—a fact not unknown to the bastards who'd launched the SAMs.

They were waiting when the crippled transport circled and came in. Gunfire started popping before Ty put his bird down.

"Ty's Herc went in hard," Randi related, her pulse pounding.

She could see it so vividly. The narrow strip laid straight as a ruler between the crowding mountains. Ty's 130 slamming into the pockmarked concrete and spinning across the runway. The pinpricks of small-arms fire coming from the mountains ringing the airfield.

"They were taking heavy fire. With their load of munitions, the aircraft was a bomb waiting to explode. The crew had to bail."

The cross fire was murderous. Randi had seen Ty's crew throw themselves flat on the runway, had spotted bullets gouging up chunks of concrete all around them. That was when she'd made the decision to go in.

"The A-10s were still ten minutes out, so I circled the airfield and came in from the north to pick up Captain Keane and his crew."

She'd remember the next, horrific moments for the rest of her life. The jarring hit as she landed. Zooming down the runway toward Ty's crippled transport. The turn that took her dangerously close to the edge of the runway. Sending her navigator and flight engineer back to help the loadmaster get Ty and his crew aboard.

She'd kept one eye on the instruments and the other on Ty's crew, running for her bird. She saw Ty lag behind to provide covering fire, heard the A-10s radio that they were almost within range.

Mortar and small-arms fire had rained down. Randi was swimming in sweat inside her flight suit. Hands locked on the controls, boots working the pedals, she kept the engines revved and her aircraft ready to roll.

"We took heavy ground fire. I could hear the bullets pinging into the fuselage. One hit the hydraulics feed line. The gauge dropped like a stone."

Her heart jackhammering against her breastbone, Randi had directed her copilot to test the aileron, elevator and rudder while she threw a frantic glance out the cockpit window to check on Ty.

He was close. So close.

"Ty was running backward, firing as he came. He screamed a frantic order into his radio to the A-10s."

Her hands shook. Clasping them together, Randi continued.

"I can still hear him," she whispered. "Late at night. In my dreams. *Roll in hot*. Those were his words. *Roll in hot*."

"Jesus! He brought in two heavily armed Warthogs with guns blazing while your aircraft was still on the ground?"

"I tried to counter the order, but the transmission got garbled. The A-10s launched their missiles and Ty's plane went up while he was still some yards away from mine. The force of the explosion blew him off the runway. He got up, started toward us again, and then…"

The next sequence was burned in Randi's brain. As if it were yesterday, she saw Ty take a bullet. Spin around. Stumble.

"He triggered a land mine."

His body had disintegrated from the waist down. Randi remembered making some small sound, a raw, animal cry of pain, before turning away from the window. Her plane was in danger of serious collateral damage from the exploding munitions. She had to get out of there and fast, or she might lose everyone aboard.

"I advised my crew that Ty had been killed, told them to close the hatch and started my takeoff roll."

"Did your copilot see Keane go down?"

"No. He was working frantically to compensate for our lost hydraulics."

"What about the other members of you crew?"

"They were all in the cargo hold, helping Ty's crew aboard. The rear hatch was open, but angled away from his position."

"Didn't anyone *hear* the mine explode?"

Randi shook her head. "Mortars were lobbing in all around us, we were being peppered with small-arms fire, and the munitions in the other aircraft were going off like fireworks."

Pete blew out a low whistle. "So you're the only one who saw him die?"

"Yes."

There it was. The crux of the issue. Randi was the only witness, the only one who'd seen Ty go down.

Would Sledge believe her?

Would anyone?

"Neither of the A-10 pilots reported seeing his body," she finished in a hollow voice. "The smoke from the burning plane blanketed that entire end of the runway. By the time the search-and-rescue team arrived, the runway had blown all to hell and the bad guys had departed the scene."

"Taking Keane's body with them."

It was standard practice, claiming the remains of

U.S. soldiers and airmen, dragging them through the streets, displaying the charred corpses like trophies. That might have been the intent in Ty's case, but no gruesome photos had ever surfaced. Captain Tyler Keane had been listed as MIA until an army patrol uncovered his charred remains four months later.

Still staring at the water puddled on the picnic table, Randi added the final postscript.

"Sam refused to believe his son was dead. He hung onto every shred of hope for months, used all his political clout to get the Department of Defense to mount additional search and rescue missions. He even financed a group of private mercenaries to go in and hunt for Ty. Only after the Rangers found the dog tags and bone fragments would Sam finally accept the truth. Then," she added, running her tongue along dry lips, "Sam learned Ty and I had argued violently the night before that last mission."

"What did you argue about?"

"It doesn't matter." She turned toward him, meeting his gaze head-on. "All that matters is that Sam actually believes I would leave a fellow officer to die on the other side of the world. Not just a fellow officer. A friend."

The laughing, golden-haired football star she'd once shared her dreams with.

The companion who'd helped her through the worst period of her life.

The lover who thought he had fathered her child.

"I need to get home," she said wearily, drained now of all emotion. "I shouldn't have skipped out for the whole day like this."

She had to see what Sarah and Cal had turned up, put in a call to her defense attorney, contact Sledge. The stolen hours were over.

As was this crazy interlude with Pete. She'd shocked him, she knew. And given him plenty to chew on. Randi suspected he'd think long and hard before following up on this attraction between them. If word got back to Sam that the professor was in bed with the enemy—literally or figuratively—he could kiss his grant goodbye.

So she wasn't surprised that he spent the short drive to Morgan's Falls in silence. Or that he left the engine running after pulling up to the house.

"Thanks for today," she said, pulling on the door handles. "Good luck with the rest of the test."

Sliding the gearshift into Park, he pushed open his door and rounded the front of the truck. "We should finish up at the Kerr Museum by Wednesday afternoon. Thursday morning at the latest. If the weather clears, I'd like to bring the team onto your property Thursday afternoon."

"I may not be here. I have to meet with the officer conducting the inquiry sometime this week. Can you find your way up to the site on your own?"

"I should be able to."

"I'll try to get up there and mark the turnoff before you come."

"Don't worry about that. I'll find the trail. Just keep your focus on this investigation."

Nodding, she started to turn away. He caught her arm, swung her back and shattered any illusion that her grim recital had killed his interest.

The kiss was hard and hungry and entirely too brief. There was promise in it, though, and in his blunt admission.

"What you told me doesn't change how I feel. I'm ready to take whatever this is between us to the next level anytime you say the word."

Surprise rippled through her. Hunger followed fast and sharp. Randi couldn't act coy if her life depended on it. But the best she could manage at the moment was a gulp and a mumbled, "I'll think about it."

Pete's mouth curved into a sardonic grin. "So will I. A lot."

He drove off then, and Randi turned to find a threesome observing the proceedings from the front window. Absol woofed ecstatically at Randi's return. Spencer appeared confused. Lissa's face was tight and unreadable.

Randi's heart sank. She wasn't up to explaining that moment in Pete's arms, but she braced herself for the inevitable inquisition.

Spencer fired first. Scowling, he demanded an explanation. "Were you just *kissing* Pete?"

"Yes."

"Why?"

Why indeed? Need? Desperation? Lust? She settled for the simplest explanation.

"I like him."

Her son considered that, and to her relief, the scowl lifted. "I guess that's okay. I like him, too."

Her sister kept silent until Randi suggested Spencer play upstairs until dinner. When his lip jutted out, Lissa preempted his protest with uncharacteristic sharpness.

"Upstairs, bud. I need to talk to your mom."

The brief glow from Pete's kisses faded. Randi prepared for a more detailed grilling, but her sister didn't ask the expected questions. Drawing an arm through Randi's, she pulled her into the den.

"I just heard a trailer for the six o'clock news. I think we'd better watch."

11

Pete spent the short drive back to Poteau trying to digest the grim details Randi had shared with him.

He'd joined the marines right out of high school. Like all grunts, he'd trained for combat but had served during the decade between the two major conflicts in the Middle East. He'd never fired his weapon in battle. Had never gone in, heart hammering, to rescue a squad of fellow soldiers pinned down by enemy fire. Had never watched a buddy get blown away.

And Ty Keane had been a whole lot more than a buddy to Randi. She'd made that clear.

A completely irrational jealousy stirred in Pete's gut as he recalled the TV image of the slick, handsome Captain Tyler Keane in full dress uniform.

Christ! He was jealous of a dead man! He had it

worse for Miranda Morgan than he'd realized. That thought sobered Pete almost as much as Randi's grim revelations.

He was still trying to sort out everything he'd learned in the past hour when he parked at the conference center and entered the guest wing. Anne had left the door to her room partially open and had evidently been waiting for his return. The thud of Pete's footsteps on the parquet flooring brought her into the hall.

"About time you got back." A disapproving frown marred her perfect features. "I thought we were going to shoot some of the samples after dinner."

"We are," he confirmed, slipping his key card into the lock. "Where are the others?"

"Professor Jorgenson's still zoned out in his room. Brad and Beasley are in Spiro. Dr. Lockwood is in the museum, preparing the samples."

"Tell her I'll be there in five minutes."

Anne ignored the instruction and followed Pete into his room. "Did you by any chance happen to catch the news on the radio?"

"No, why? Did they air something about our project?"

"No, but they did do a story about the Morgan woman. Seems the air force is investigating her in connection with an accident that resulted in the death of a fellow pilot."

"Hell! That was on the news?"

"You knew about it?"

"Randi just told me, on the drive home."

"I only caught the tail end of the story. I didn't hear the details. Who's she supposed to have killed?"

"Sam Keane's son."

Anne's brows soared. "The same Sam Keane who's funding our test?"

"The same one."

She pursed her lips, obviously not pleased. "Looks to me as though you've gotten pretty chummy with the Morgan woman these past few days. That's not going to sit well with our benefactor if he hears about it."

"First, her name's Miranda. Not 'the Morgan woman.' Second, my friendship with Randi is none of Sam Keane's business."

"That's bullshit, Pete. The man put up big bucks for this study with the specific condition that we date the stone on Morgan property. There has to be some reason for that condition. Judging by this business about the investigation into his son's death, I'd say the reason doesn't bode well for Ms. Miranda." Her cat's eyes narrowed to slits. "Or for us, if you start screwing around with her."

Pete allowed his assistant considerable latitude because of her formidable intelligence and up-at-dawn diligence. There was a line between instructor and student, however, and she'd just crossed it.

"Watch yourself, Gillette. My personal life isn't any of your business, either."

"It is if it affects our work."

"This discussion is over. Tell Dr. Lockwood I'll be there in five minutes."

Anne was as unused to hearing that icy tone from him as he was to using it. Frowning, she tucked a strand of silky hair behind her ear and tried to recover.

"I'm sorry. It's just that we're so damned close to validating the process we've worked on for so long. I hate to see anything jeopardize the test."

Pete relented. He knew Anne had grown up in a dirt-poor farming family. She'd completed four years of undergraduate work on full scholarship and depended on her meager income from the lab assistantship to make ends meet. He also knew she was hoping to cash in big-time if—when—they validated the improved imaging process.

"I don't want to see anything jeopardize the test, either. Just trust me to know what I'm doing."

When she nodded and departed, Pete blew out a long breath. Talk was cheap, he thought wryly. But *did* he really know what he was doing?

Here he was, up to his ass in a project that could boost his professional reputation, add considerably to his financial standing and unlock mysteries that had remained unsolved for decades. Yet his mind refused to focus on incision depths and chisel angles. All he could see right now was Randi's stony face when she'd stared at that photo of Sam Keane and the bleakness in her blue eyes when she'd described the desperate rescue attempt in the mountains of Afghanistan.

Then there was the small problem of how his body reacted every time he got within ten yards of her. He hadn't ached so much—or so long—since junior high school, for God's sake! Although he'd made a joke of it, his parting shot had been dead serious. He wanted Randi Morgan any way he could get her.

"Smart, Engstrom. Real smart."

Chucking his jacket onto a chair, he made a quick detour to the bathroom before heading down to the museum.

Pete didn't hear from Randi at all on Tuesday. He called her home that evening and left a message that went unanswered until Wednesday morning.

"I'm sorry I couldn't get back to you," she said, her voice tight. "It's been hell around here. The phone rang incessantly all day yesterday and I've got reporters camped almost on my doorstep."

Pete could imagine. The other networks had picked up the story and run repeated clips from Ty Keane's funeral, as well as a formal statement read by his father's attorney. The charges had also made the front page of the local paper. Randi had issued a statement saying she had complete confidence this informal inquiry would *once again* show she'd exercised sound judgment in an extremely hostile situation. She'd refused all requests for interviews but the media circus continued unabated.

"I can't talk now," she said. "I have an appointment with my lawyer today. I'm on my way out the door."

"Okay. I just wanted you to know…"

What? That she was in his head and he couldn't get her out? That he'd spent as much time thinking about her as he had his damned study during the past week?

"The shoulder's still there if and when you need it."

Some of the stiffness left her voice. "Thanks. I may have to take you up on that offer."

"Anytime."

"Do you still intend to bring your team to Morgan's Falls tomorrow?" she asked after a moment.

"That's the plan."

"As I said, I don't know if I'll be here. I've got to meet with the investigating officer in Oklahoma City tomorrow afternoon. But I marked the turnoff to the runestone site with a bright red ribbon. You can't miss it."

That she'd attend to this small task in the midst of the firestorm that had broken over her both surprised and touched Pete. Something stirred inside him, something he'd have to think about later.

"Give 'em hell, Morgan."

"I'll do my best."

By noon on Wednesday, Pete and his team had imaged every rune on the five stones housed in the Kerr Museum. They'd also imaged the silicon casts shipped in by Raynard Jorgenson and Jack Beasley. Although several of the cuts had similar angles and depths, none of the holographs matched closely enough to satisfy Pete.

Disappointed but refusing to give up, Anne clicked the keys of the master computer. "I think we should take another look at these."

The team members crowded around her as she pulled up a side-by-side of two colorful holographs. They were the third letter of the old futhark alphabet, a pointed *P* that carried a "th" value. One image had been lifted from a stone in the Kerr Museum, the other from the cast of an ancient Danish rune.

Chewing on her lower lip, Anne selected one letter and manipulated it over the other, then altered the input values.

"If we adjust for temperature sensitivity and geometric changes in wavelength, we come up with a 250nm-width spectral window."

The images blurred, sharpened, seemed to merge.

Raynard let out a small hiss. Jack Beasley's eyes widened. Brady gave a grudging nod. He obviously still smarted from Anne's cutting remarks the first day the team had assembled.

"She's right," he muttered. "The spatial resolution is much finer at that width."

"But not fine enough," Pete countered. "I won't accept less than 400nm."

"We've only achieved that in laboratory conditions," Anne argued, "with clean samples."

"Unfortunately, we're not working with either here."

"Yes, but—"

"No buts. We've got too much riding on this test to alter the parameters. We're going to do it right."

"An admirable sentiment."

The comment came from the doorway and everyone swung around. Pete recognized the newcomer from the recent news coverage of his son's funeral—and from the photo here in the museum that had drained the blood from Randi's face.

Sam Keane was dressed head to toe in black. Black cowboy boots with scuffed stacked heels and lethally pointed toes. Black jeans, black shirt, black tailored sport coat with western-style detailing. His string tie had a clasp with a silver nugget the size of a goose egg. Above the tie his face was like a hawk's, with skin stretched tight over the bones, penetrating dark eyes and a shock of wavy white hair.

Randi had cause to be worried, Pete thought as

he crossed the room. Sam Keane looked as though he'd make a formidable enemy. Fighting a sense of disloyalty, Pete offered his hand to the man whose millions were funding his test.

"Hello, Mr. Keane. I'm Pete Engstrom. I'm heading the team attempting to determine the age of the runes."

Regardless of Pete's own loyalties, the man had suffered a devastating loss. Common courtesy dictated an expression of sympathy.

"May I say, sir, how sorry I am..." He encompassed the rest of the team with a sweep of his arm. "How sorry we all are about your son's death."

"Thank you." Those dark, brooding eyes took Pete's measure. "Dr. Bruhn, the head of your department, told me about the technique you've developed. I thought I'd stop by to see how the first test is going. Not well, judging by what I just heard."

"We didn't expect to hit the ball out of the park first time up at bat," Pete replied easily, refusing to let Keane put him on the defensive. "Why don't I introduce you to the rest of the team and explain what we're trying to do before you form an opinion?"

Keane acknowledged the slight reproach with a sardonic nod. Pete knew damn well the old buzzard hadn't racked up his billions by jumping to hasty conclusions. Nor could he have all that much interest in symbols incised in stone. The conviction that

Keane was working out some private agenda was stronger than ever.

Pete put the feeling aside as he introduced his small cadre. Keane had obviously read the bona fides on each member of the team. He shared memories of a long-ago visit to Oslo with Jorgenson and complimented Beasley on his recent award from the International Society of Cryptologists. Pauline's Old Bones sweatshirt produced a smile, but Brady's pigtail earned the grad student a quick handshake and a quelling glance. Anne received a warm, two-handed grip and the admiration due her stunning looks.

"Times have changed since my one semester at OU," Keane murmured, keeping her hand in his. "If more women like you had attended college in my day, I might've hung around campus instead of dropping out to work in the oilfields."

"But then you wouldn't be the man you are today."

"That's true."

Never shy about employing her assets to her best advantage, Anne angled her head in a move Pete recognized all too well. When her hair played peek-aboo with her cheek, part of him cringed at the blatantly provocative gesture. Another, less noble, part said *what the hell*. If Anne could charm Keane into keeping an open mind, why object?

With every evidence of regret, Keane let her hand

slide free of his and turned his attention to Pete. "I read the study proposal, but you could've written it in Greek for all the sense it made to me. Tell me about this relative chronology business."

Despite his professed lack of higher education, Keane had a mind that cut through detail like a broadsword, and an oil rigger's affinity for machinery. He grasped the concept, if not the more esoteric optical laws associated with holographic imaging, and peered intently at the three-dimensional letter Pete pulled up on the screen.

"This is one of the runes we've imaged here at the museum. And this…"

As Anne had a few moments ago, Pete brought up an image made from one of the silicon casts.

"…is a copy of one incised in a stone in Denmark. Archeologists also found various tools at the site that were forged using iron-smelting techniques dating to A.D. 1000, although there's evidence the village was occupied well before that."

"Those same iron-working techniques weren't employed by Native Americans until after the Spaniards introduced them in the late 1500s," Pauline Lockwood put in. "Thus, if we find a match between the Oklahoma runes and one like this from Scandinavia, we can postulate they were made with similar implements at roughly equivalent times."

"But I just heard you say you didn't have a match."

"Not with this one."

Pete overlapped the images and clicked the mouse to highlight the areas that didn't intersect. With another click he zoomed in on one of those sections.

"As you can see, these runes contain cuts of approximately the same depth and angle, but there are just enough differences to counter the supposition that they were incised using the same types of implements."

The oilman leaned in to study the superimposed images. When he straightened, he'd raised one bushy white eyebrow. "I guess it's all in the eye of the beholder. They look almost identical to me."

"*Almost* doesn't stand the test," Pete said with a smile. "Not for me."

"So I gather."

He was damned if he could tell whether Keane intended that as a compliment or a condemnation. Not that it mattered. Pete wasn't about to jeopardize his reputation or the integrity of his process by applying anything less than the most rigorous parameters, even for the man funding the study.

Those hooded eyes shifted from him to Anne and lingered on her before making a slow circle back to Pete.

"Maybe you'll find a better match with this."

With studied casualness, Keane reached into his pocket and withdrew a flat plastic case. Inside was a jagged piece of shale the size of a half-dollar. A rawhide thong was threaded through a hole punched at the top of the stone. Below the hole was a single rune—two pointed *P*s touching nose to nose. The letter *M* in the old futhark alphabet.

The same letter was repeated in both the Heavener runestone and the one on the Morgan property. Excitement licking at his veins, Pete accepted the plastic case and tipped it to the light.

"Where did you get this?"

"It belongs to a friend of a friend of a friend. I first heard about it some years ago, but didn't pay much heed to the man's story until I read your proposal."

"Story?"

"He claims the amulet's been in his family for generations, a sort of good luck talisman passed from father to son for hundreds of years. He also claims his family immigrated to this area from Canada."

Pete's heart gave another quick bump. "Where in Canada?"

"Newfoundland."

A chorus of exclamations greeted the announcement. The 1962 finds at L'Anse aux Meadows in Newfoundland had opened a whole new chapter in the history of the Vikings in North America. Current theory suggested the Norsemen had used that site as a base for explorations further south.

The possibility that this rune might match the other one of the Oklahoma runes and provide the link they'd been searching for galvanized Pete's imagination—until he noticed Keane observing them with the sly smile of a magician who's just produced a rabbit out of a hat.

Reality hit like a mailed fist. This contribution to the study was too pat, too convenient. The sense that he was being jerked around came rushing back. Pete didn't like it any better this time around than he had a few days ago. Jaw tight, he cut through the babble of voices.

"I'd like to talk to you, Mr. Keane. In private."

"Certainly. First, let me just assure you and your colleagues that I have in my possession a certificate of authenticity, sworn to by the man who owns the amulet and witnessed by two attorneys. I'll make it available after my attorney verifies the signatures."

When they found a quiet anteroom near the entrance to the museum, Pete's simmering anger rose to the surface.

"What the hell's going on here?"

Keane didn't so much as blink at the curt demand. "Exactly what you proposed, Dr. Engstrom. A scientific attempt to determine the age and authenticity of the Oklahoma runes."

"Why do I get the feeling you're not particularly interested in solving the riddle of the Oklahoma runes? Only the ones on Morgan property."

"I'd like to see them all dated."

"Then why did you make the study contingent on including the Morgan stone?"

"That's my business."

"And mine, when it impacts the test."

"It *doesn't* impact your test."

That was bullshit and they both knew it.

"You're hoping for some finding, some result, you can use to your advantage."

"You're right, I am. But I'm not asking you to compromise your study in any way to achieve those results. Just do what I'm paying you to do, Engstrom."

Pete's mind churned out a dozen different scenarios. Only one made any sense. "You've bought into the theory that the runes constitute boundary markers, haven't you?"

"Maybe. Maybe not."

Pete sorted through various options like a dealer shuffling a slick new deck. "You're looking for a link between the Heavener stone, the one on Morgan property and this amulet. You're hoping they all tie together to support some sort of property claim."

The man's thin, bloodless lips pulled back in a smile. "I repeat, my reasons for funding this study are my business."

"What are you going to do if we make a match? Back the owner of the amulet? Get him to take Randi to court and challenge her ownership of Morgan's Falls?"

"Randi?" Keane's smile evaporated. "I wasn't aware you were on a first-name basis with the bitch who left my son to die."

The venom came fast and deadly, like the strike of an adder. Pete managed not to flinch, but the skin on the back of his neck crawled.

"I met Ms. Morgan when I went up to her property to conduct the initial site survey. We've spoken several times since."

They'd done more than talk. And if Pete had his way, they'd do a *whole* lot more.

"I'm telling you here and now, Mr. Keane, I won't be a party to your personal vendetta against anyone, Randi included."

Randi especially.

The old man's gaze burned with the fiery ice of a laser. Pete thought for a moment that they were going to take off the gloves and go at it bare-knuckled, but Keane clenched his jaw and made an obvious effort to get his emotions in check.

"I'll tell you this much about my motivation, Dr. Engstrom, and this much only. I funded this study in my son's memory. The Oklahoma runes always intrigued Ty. If you solve the mystery of their origin, I'll consider it a lasting memorial to my son. If you don't feel you can continue the test with absolute objectivity, however, we'll terminate it right here, right now."

Well, hell! Damned if the bastard hadn't turned

things around and put Pete's professional integrity at issue instead of his own motivation. Before he could formulate a response, Anne answered for him.

"Sorry if I'm interrupting." She marched into the anteroom with a snap to her step. "I couldn't help overhearing your last comment, Mr. Keane. I know my opinion doesn't carry as much weight as the President of OU or the head of the physics department, but we all agree Dr. Engstrom is not only brilliant, he exercises absolute scientific objectivity in every project, every experiment. I wouldn't work with him otherwise."

Pete was moved by her fierce defense. "Thanks for the endorsement, Anne, but this matter is between Mr. Keane and me."

"I beg to differ. I have a vested interest in this test. I don't want to see it terminated." Her flashing glance encompassed both men. "By either of you."

Keane acknowledged the hit with a stiff nod. "Your loyalty does credit to you and to Dr. Engstrom, Ms. Gillette."

His hawk's gaze swung back to Pete. The two men contemplated each other for a long moment before Keane broke the stark silence.

"What's it going to be, Engstrom? Are you going to continue your study or not?"

Pete held on to his temper while he weighed the pros and cons. He knew what ten million dollars could do in terms of facilities and scholarships. He also knew the immeasurable value to the state, perhaps the country, of solving the riddle of the runes.

Then there was the process he'd spent almost a year developing. Was he willing to lose this chance to validate it because he was falling for a woman who might—or might not—be falling for him? Neither he nor Randi had had time to explore the welter of feelings they aroused in each other.

He'd talk to her. Tell her what was going on. Tell her, as well, that he'd shut down the operation in a heartbeat if he discovered that Sam intended to use its results in a very personal, very private war.

"I'll continue," he said coolly. "For now."

Keane nodded, murmured a goodbye to Anne and left. When his spare frame disappeared from view, the lab assistant rounded on her mentor. The loyalty she'd displayed just moments ago was overturned by irritation.

"Jesus, Pete! What the hell was *that* all about? You looked like you were ready to shove our whole project down the man's throat and out his ass."

"How much of the conversation with Keane did you overhear?"

"I heard him refer to Randi Morgan as the bitch who left his son to die. What's the deal here? How does our study figure in Keane's grudge against her?"

"He wouldn't say and I'm only guessing, but I

think he's planning to use the runes as proof of a prior claim to her property by whoever supplied that amulet."

"You're kidding! I can't imagine that a claim based on such flimsy evidence would stand up in court."

"It doesn't have to stand up," Pete replied, thinking aloud. "But it could tie her up in legal battles for months or even years."

Anne whistled softly. "First he lays charges against her with the air force. Now, maybe, he goes after her land. He must really have it in for her."

"No shit."

"And we're right in the middle of it."

More than she knew, Pete thought grimly.

"You still want to image the runes on Morgan property tomorrow?"

Hell, no. Not until he'd talked to Randi. He'd camp out on her doorstep until he did.

"I need to brief the rest of the team on my conversation with Keane. I also want to image this amulet and find out about its owner. We'll decide the next phase then."

Pete set the team to work again and tried to reach Randi, both at home and via her cell phone. Each time her voice mail kicked in with a request to leave a message.

He checked his watch, remembering that she'd

mentioned a meeting with the inquiry officer appointed to investigate the charges against her sometime this afternoon. He hated the idea of hitting her with his suspicions about Keane hard on the heels of an official inquiry. He didn't see any way around it, though. She needed to know. More to the point, Pete needed to tell her. He couldn't take his team onto her property without advising her of the situation first.

He also needed to advise his boss about the agreement he'd just struck with Sam Keane. Grimacing, he made the call. As he'd expected, Bruhn got nervous as hell when Pete related the gist of his conversation, and oozed relief when informed that Keane had agreed not to pull the plug on the ten million. For the time being, at least.

"So you're going forward with the study?"

"For now."

"Keep me posted."

Pete gave a noncommittal grunt, cut the connection and punched in Randi's cell phone number once again. Her crisp voice came on asking him to leave a message. Swallowing an oath, he complied.

"It's Pete. Call me."

He snapped his cell phone shut. He had a mental image of Randi in full dress uniform, facing the officer appointed to investigate the charges Keane had leveled against her.

She'd hold her own. Any pilot who could put

her plane down amid a hail of ground fire to rescue a stranded crew could handle herself during an official inquiry.

12

Randi sat across the table from Major Alex Shores and the administrative assistant recording the interview. It was being conducted in the 137th Wing Headquarters conference center. Like her, Sledge had donned his blues for the occasion. Row upon row of ribbons marched up his right shoulder, crowding his silver command pilot wings.

Randi's defense attorney, John Mooreman, flanked her on one side. Her sister and brother-in-law sat on the other. Sarah had no business being in Oklahoma City. According to Cal, she'd bolted awake in the middle of the night with what turned out to be false labor. But she'd turned a deaf ear to her husband's arguments that she stay in Tulsa, close to her obstetrician, and insisted on attending the proceedings.

Lissa was here, too. She and Spencer had driven over with Randi. Spencer didn't understand the full ramifications of what was happening, but he'd heard the phone ringing with reporters asking for interviews and seen the stream of news vans that had converged on Morgan's Falls. Randi absolutely refused to leave him at home.

So here she was, with Lissa entertaining Spencer in the break room down the hall while his mother faced the officer appointed to decide whether she should be charged and with murder or manslaughter.

They'd been at it for almost an hour now. Sledge had opened the session by reading Randi her rights. That alone was enough to unnerve anyone. He'd followed with an explanation of the Rule 303 inquiry process, reminding her that this was just a preliminary investigation to determine if her commander should lay formal charges against her.

Stone-jawed, his eyes like flint, Sledge had listened while she described that last, fatal flight, from crew prebrief to takeoff to the wheels-up emergency landing at K-2. It helped that he'd been in country, that he'd chewed on gritty sand with every meal, slept fully clothed on a narrow cot, and shared a latrine and shower with thirty other crew members.

He didn't speak, didn't interrupt Randi's recitation, but did take copious notes on ruled notebook paper. When she'd finished, he flipped back the pages and zeroed in on the issues he wanted clarified.

"Did you see the surface-to-air missile hit Captain Keane's aircraft?"

Conscious of the advice pressed on her by Sarah, Cal and Captain Mooreman, Randi kept her answer short and precise. "No, I did not."

"Were you in communication with Keane the entire time he and his crew were on the ground?"

"Not every minute. He switched frequencies to talk to base and to the Warthog pilots."

"Right." Sledge's gray eyes lasered into hers. "You stated that the A-10s were still ten minutes out when you made the decision to go in and pick up the downed aircrew."

Sweat pooled on Randi's palms. She'd relived that decision a thousand times in her dreams. She knew she'd made the right choice. Ty's crew agreed, wholeheartedly.

It was one thing to make a life-or-death assessment in the heat of battle. Another altogether to defend it in a conference room half a world away from the scene, with every word being recorded.

Sledge flipped to a clean page and shoved notebook and pen across the table. "Show me the position of both aircraft."

She wiped her hand on her uniform slacks and

willed it not to shake when she picked up the pen. Two quick lines outlined the runway. Short, slashing strokes depicted the jagged peaks surrounding the abandoned base.

The diagram looked so clean on the pristine white paper, so damned antiseptic.

"Captain Keane's aircraft had hit hard coming in and skidded to a stop here, at the north end of the runway." Randi marked a spot near the edge. "Another few feet, and he would've gone off the concrete. I came in from the south, rolled up to his aircraft and executed a sharp left break."

"Then all hell broke loose," Sledge said softly.

Randi gave him a careful look across the polished surface of the conference table. He knew. He understood.

It didn't let her off the hook, by any means, but that hint of perception in his otherwise stony face somehow gave Randi the strength to nod.

"Then all hell broke loose."

When she didn't elaborate, Captain Mooreman spoke up. "As my client has already stated, she kept her aircraft positioned while Captain Keane's crew boarded, then saw him detonate an antipersonnel device."

Sledge didn't take his eyes off Randi. "You saw the explosion? You saw him go down?"

"I saw what was left of him go down." She swallowed again, painfully. "And then I ordered my crew to close the hatch, revved up to full power and initiated my takeoff roll."

"Describe the exact damage to your aircraft for me."

"As I said, our hydraulics were shot all to hell and number-three engine blew a gasket. After we landed, maintenance counted thirty-seven ruptures in the outer fuselage. Mostly from bullet holes, although fragmentation from the munitions in Captain Keane's aircraft did serious damage to our tail section."

Sledge leaned forward, his gray eyes intent. "What about damage from the land mine? If it was powerful enough to kill and not simply maim Captain Keane, secondary fragmentation from the mine casing or mechanism must have struck your aircraft."

Randi's brows drew together. She immediately understood the reason for his question. She was the only one who'd witnessed the mine go off. None of the others had seen the blast, nor had they heard it. The sound of its detonation had been lost in the concussive shock of the munitions load on Ty's plane exploding. If Randi needed proof that Ty was dead when she left him beside that deserted airstrip, physical evidence from the land mine would certainly back up her statement.

Maintenance had documented the damage to her aircraft in reams of reports. They'd photographed the bullet holes, measured the gaping tears in the fuselage and entered every hit into a database before reskinning the wounded 130. But as far as she knew, they hadn't broken down the specific types of fragmentation that had caused the damage. She wasn't sure such detailed analytical capability had existed at Bagram.

"Pieces of the damaged fuselage and tail sections were shipped back to the C-130 depot for metallurgical and explosive analysis," she said slowly. "I haven't seen the final results."

"I have." Sledge's stare drilled into her. "The experts identified four sources of fragmentation that ripped into your aircraft. Shards of metal from Captain Keane's aircraft caused two. One came from the casing of a 50-caliber shell, presumably part of the cargo his aircraft was carrying. The fourth from a jagged piece of rock."

Ice formed in Randi's veins. Below the surface of the conference table, her hands locked in a death grip.

"So none came from any metal known to be used in Soviet or Afghani land mines?"

"None of those four. There were several other tears in the skin of your aircraft, however. The experts at the depot couldn't verify the source of that damage."

With a small grunt, Sarah squirmed forward in her seat and stabbed a finger at Sledge. "We want a copy of those analyses, Major Shores."

"I made a copy for you."

He drew a couple of pages from the stack in his briefcase and slid them across the table.

An idea began to form in the back of Randi's mind. She started to ask Sledge what the tests had entailed, but before she could get the words out, Sarah shoved back her chair, and pushed to her feet. Her face was white as she faced the investigating officer.

"We'll continue the interview after we review these test reports, Major Shores."

"Wait a minute," Randi protested. "I want to ask—"

"I'm advising you to terminate this interview, Captain Morgan." Her sister gave another small grunt and gritted her teeth. "Now."

Small beads of sweat had popped out on her brow. Alarmed, Randi scrambled to her feet. "Sarah! Are you all right?"

"On the record, yes. Off the record…"

"Hell!" The normally calm, steady Cal shot out of his seat. "Are you having contractions?"

His wife's lips stretched in a grimace. "Like you wouldn't believe!"

Cursing herself for not noticing her sister's strained face earlier, Randi whipped around. "Sorry, Sledge. The interview's over."

"I'll get the car," Cal announced, cramming papers into his briefcase. Captain Mooreman looked to Randi for guidance before doing the same.

Randi took her sister's arm to help her up. After a startled moment, Sledge came around the table to take her other arm. Once in the hallway, Randi let out a bellow.

"Lissa! Spencer!"

The two emerged from the break room at the end of the hall.

"Sarah's in labor," Randi informed them. "Cal went to get the car. I'll drive to the hospital with them. You can follow in my car. Here, take this."

She thrust her briefcase at her sister while Sarah smiled at a bewildered and somewhat frightened Spencer.

"It's okay, bud. We're just having a baby."

The boy's eyes rounded. "Are we having it *now?*"

"Pretty quick."

Randi heard a strangled sound coming from Sledge and urged her sister toward the front door. While they waited for Cal to drive up, Sarah aimed a rueful smile at her broad-shouldered escort. "Thanks, Major Shores."

"Major?" Eyes narrowing, Lissa took in the name tag pinned to the chest full of ribbons. She opened her mouth, bit back whatever she intended to say and then muttered something that sounded like *what the hell.* Rounding on Sledge, she let loose with both barrels.

"I know this is out of line, but I'm here to tell you my sister did *not* leave Tyler Keane to die in Afghanistan."

"You're right," he agreed. "You're out of line."

"I don't give a rat's ass." Her blood up, Lissa poked a finger at his acre or so of chest. "Randi loved him. So did I."

"Lissa…"

She ignored Randi's low warning. The unquestioned loyalty that had always bound the Morgan sisters held her in its grip.

"Ty was always there, always part of our family. Maybe I sensed… Okay, I knew he was two-thirds flash and one third pure sex. But that was part of his charm. Don't take my word for it," she snapped when the major didn't respond. "Just ask his ex-wives. Or the sergeant on his crew he was screwing."

"I intend to interview everyone involved."

The cool response clearly wasn't acceptable to Lissa. Despite another low warning from Randi, she jabbed her finger at his chest again.

"Just make sure you get the truth out of them."

"I will, Ms. Morgan. It is Morgan, isn't it?"

"What? Oh. Yes, I'm Randi's sister."

"You look like her." His glance cut to Randi, then back to Lissa. "Same hair. Same mouth. Different eyes."

"I'm like her in more than just looks. We Morgans protect our own." She leaned in for emphasis, five-six of fiercely determined female. "If your inquiry doesn't get to the truth, I swear I'll hunt you down and…and hurt you."

A dent appeared in one of his cheeks. In anyone else, that small crease might have been mistaken for the beginnings of a smile.

"I'll watch my six, Ms. Morgan."

"You do that."

When Cal screeched to a halt at the Southwest Medical Center E.R., Randi raced inside to get a wheelchair. Twenty-two minutes later, Elizabeth Morgan Howell made her debut.

Elated and smug at having produced such utter perfection, Sarah nestled the swaddled infant in the crook of her arm and brushed a fingertip over her swirls of dark, feathery hair.

"She's definitely got the Morgan mane," Randi said, smiling at the newest addition to the family.

Remembering the intense emotions that had swept her the first time she'd held her son, she placed an arm around Spencer's shoulders. She knew she could never articulate the joy that came with having this demanding, wondrous being in her life.

"Her face is all scrunched up," Spencer announced on a less than admiring note. "You should call her Raisin 'stead of 'Lisabeth, Aunt Sarah."

"Think so?" Smiling, Sarah played with the downy curls. "Okay, Raisin it is. You're going to have to tell her sister and brother how she got that nickname, though."

"Speaking of whom..." Cal pushed off his perch on the edge of his wife's bed. "I'd better drive over to Tulsa and collect them from the babysitter. They're going to be disappointed that they missed the big event."

"You stay with Sarah," Lissa instructed him. "I'll fetch the kids."

"Thanks."

"Want to keep me company on the drive, bud?"

Uncharacteristically, Spencer shrank back against Randi's thigh. Hers wasn't the only world that had been turned upside down in the past few weeks, she acknowledged with a pang.

"We'd better get home," she answered for both of them. "Who knows what havoc Absol has wreaked in our absence."

Lissa nodded. "I'll spend the night here in Oklahoma City with Cal and Sarah and the kids, then.

I want to hear more about what happened at the hearing."

"Yeah," her brother-in-law drawled. "And I want to hear more about this exchange you had with Major Shores."

Sarah looked up from her daughter's fuzzy black crown. "I can't believe you took him on like that, Lis."

"Hey, someone goes after my sister—either of my sisters—he'd better know he's going to answer for it."

Randi suspected the threat hadn't intimidated Sledge in the least, but gave Lissa a hug for wading into the fray.

"I need that analysis of the damage to my aircraft, Cal. I want to read through it tonight."

"Sure." He retrieved the report he'd stuffed into his briefcase. His gaze held hers as he passed her the crumpled papers. "Fax me a copy when you get home, will you? I want to read it, too. I'm thinking our case might well turn on the results of these analyses."

Randi's stomach knotted. She remembered the question in Sledge's eyes as he'd reviewed the position of her aircraft relative to the land mine she insisted Ty had triggered.

"I'm thinking the same thing," she agreed.

"We might need to get an outside opinion. A metals engineer trained in structural failure analysis. I've worked with several experts on vehicular accident cases. I don't know any in the aviation industry, but I'll ask around."

"Thanks, Cal."

13

Randi drove home through the darkness with Spencer dozing in the backseat. She was almost at Morgan's Falls before she thought to check her cell phone for messages.

She listened to almost a dozen, mostly from friends offering their support, some from enterprising reporters who'd somehow obtained her cell phone number. There were also three calls from Pete. The urgency of the last one yanked her mind from the events of the day and had her punching the redial button.

"Pete? It's Randi."

"I need to talk to you. Where are you?"

"About ten miles from home."

"I'll drive up there. A half hour okay?"

She couldn't envision anything less okay. Her

nerves were still humming from the interview with Sledge. The rush to get Sarah to the E.R. hadn't exactly made a calm finish to the day, either.

"Make it an hour," she heard herself saying. "I need to put Spencer to bed."

"I'll be there."

Getting Spencer undressed and into bed proved more of a chore than usual. Sleepy and cranky and more than a little confused by the disruption in his life, he squirted toothpaste all over the bathroom floor and batted away Randi's hands when she squatted down to help him.

"I kin do it."

She sat back on her heels while Absol slurped Crest off the tiles and her son took aim at his toothbrush again.

He was growing so fast. And so tall. She could remember holding him for the first time, gazing down at him with utter joy. The same joy Sarah had shown when she'd looked at Elizabeth today. A joy touched with absolute panic at the thought of being responsible for another human being.

How in the world had she managed to produce such a bright, eager child? And where had she learned the skills to cope with potty training, chicken pox, skinned knees and loose teeth?

Thank God for her sisters and her brother-in-law. They'd coached her through the joys and secret terrors of motherhood. More importantly, they'd made Spencer feel safe and secure during the long months Randi had been deployed. She couldn't have left him otherwise, couldn't have continued flying.

Now his world was threatened once more, and whether Randi would ever fly air force transports again remained in question. Sighing, she resisted the urge to stroke his hair while he attacked his teeth. Finally, he was done.

"Come on, baby. Let's get you into bed."

"I'm not a baby," he muttered, still irritable.

"You're right. My mistake."

Twenty minutes later he was tucked in, read to and drifting off. Changing out of her uniform, Randi pulled on jeans, a fuzzy red sweatshirt and the floppy slippers Spencer had given her last Christmas before going downstairs to brew a fresh pot of coffee. Absol came down while the pot was still perking. Now that his buddy was in bed and asleep, he wanted his dinner.

Randi fed him, then carried her coffee into the den. The fresh-brewed decaf cooled on the coffee table while she pored through the report Sledge had provided. Absol joined her on the second read.

The damage to her aircraft had been meticulously diagramed and photographed. The objects that caused the damage had been imaged as well. A variety of bullets dating from the days of Soviet occupation. The 50-caliber shell fragment Sledge had mentioned. Shards of metal from Ty's aircraft. A jagged piece of rock.

Then there was the damage that hadn't been explained. A slashing gap in the right rear section of the fuselage. A dent in the right stabilizer. The perforated section of skin that maintenance had recovered and mounted on a slab of marble for her.

Frowning, Randi retrieved the grim memento from the kitchen and lined it up next to the report. She'd always assumed a bullet had ripped through that particular piece of metal. Now she had to wonder exactly what had left those twisted, jagged edges.

She was still studying the piece when Absol lifted his head. A rumble started low in his massive chest and worked its way into a full-blown growl at the sound of a car door slamming. Anticipating the din that would ensue when the doorbell rang, Randi scrambled to her feet.

"Quiet! Don't wake Spencer!"

She managed to keep him shushed and beat him to the door, but restraining the dog after he caught sight of his old friend was beyond her capabilities. Absol did most of his barking outside, thankfully, and was reduced to a state of tail-thumping delight when Randi stood aside to let him back in.

Pete followed, bringing with him a rush of frigid night air and a sense of purposeful determination. He said nothing, however, until he'd wrapped an arm around her waist, dragged her against him and dropped a cold, fast kiss on her mouth.

"Hello, beautiful."

The compliment got to her almost as much as the kiss. She felt like hell and probably looked worse. He, on the other hand, looked good enough to swallow whole. His jacket hung open, exposing a gray OU sweatshirt and jeans that molded his tall, muscled frame.

"Hello to you, too."

Randi leaned back in his loose hold, wondering how she could experience such a ridiculous rush of pleasure from his touch. With everything else piling up on her, she should be numb to any feeling even vaguely sexual.

"So you had a rough day," he said, those keen, clever eyes of his all too perceptive.

"It was mixed," she admitted on a shaky laugh. "I had my first interview with the officer conducting the inquiry and my sister had a baby."

Pulling out of his arms, Randi led him into the den. "Sarah's an attorney. She and her husband both. They accompanied me to the hearing this afternoon, and Sarah went into labor after an hour or so."

"I'll bet that was a first for the investigating officer."

"Yeah, he seemed a little surprised."

"How'd it go otherwise?"

"I don't know. Okay, I think, but it's not over."

Shuffling the papers into a neat pile, Randi stacked them on the coffee table. "Do you want something to drink? Coffee? A beer?"

"I'm good, thanks."

Nodding, she curled up in a corner of the couch. Pete shed his jacket and took the other end.

"What did you need to talk to me about?" she asked. "You sounded so serious on the phone."

"We had a visitor today. Sam Keane."

It was as if a cold wind had blown through the room.

"I guess that's not surprising. Sam's funding your operation, after all."

"I think I know why, Randi. He's hoping to use it to get at you."

"I suspected that right from the beginning. I just can't figure out how."

"He's located another rune. A single symbol on a jagged piece of shale. It's the same letter *M* that's on your stone and the stone at Heavener."

"Where the heck did he come up with that?"

"He says it belongs to a friend of a friend of a friend. A sort of good luck charm that's been in the man's family for generations."

"I don't get it. How does this good luck charm affect me?"

"There are several different interpretations of the Oklahoma runes. The most prevalent is that they constitute boundary markers."

"Right. Some scholars think they spell out 'Glome's Valley.' So?"

"If this friend of a friend's story is true and he's descended from some ancient explorer, it's conceivable that he could try to claim all or part of the land designated by those boundary markers."

Randi bolted upright, startling Absol out of a half doze. "That's absurd! We've got deeds going back as far as 1820 granting various Morgans title to this land."

"What if we succeed in dating the runes to several centuries before that?" Pete said slowly.

"No court would entertain a claim based on a single letter carved in stone!"

"Maybe not, but Keane could tie you up with expensive suits and countersuits for years. It wouldn't hurt to have your lawyers do a little preemptory damage control and check out those deeds you mentioned."

"My God!"

Too agitated to sit, she untangled her legs and jumped off the sofa. Whatever sympathy Randi had felt for the grieving father was gone now. Whirling, she faced Pete across the coffee table still littered with weapons in her current battle.

"So are you going to include Sam's rune in your study?"

"Yes."

That hurt. More than she would've thought.

Shoving both hands in the front pockets of her jeans, she lifted her chin.

"Okay. Sure. I understand. Sam's paying the fiddler, you dance to his tune."

"Not completely. I informed Keane I wouldn't be a party to his personal vendetta."

"Yeah, right."

Temper flared in his eyes, but he controlled it. "I told him and I'm telling you, Randi. I'll shut down operations if I believe the findings will result in deliberate harm to anyone, you included."

"And Sam agreed to that?"

"He didn't have a whole lot of choice."

She waited a few beats, still suspicious, still wary. "You admitted the first time we met how much you have invested in this imaging process. Why would you risk it—not to mention the ten million dollars for OU—by taking Sam on like this?"

"I've been asking myself the same question," Pete said, running a hand through his hair. "Some of it has to do with a distinct aversion to being jerked around. Most of it has to do with what we talked about the other day."

"What? Wanting me naked?"

"Yeah, well, that's how it started out. Now I pretty much want you any way I can get you."

Randi ached to believe him. He was the one good thing that had happened since her world had begun to spin out of control. But she was feeling gutshot at the moment, and too damned wounded to accept anything at face value.

"I can't get involved right now, Pete. With you. With anyone."

"Think I haven't told myself that? I'd be a total asshole to push you right now. I can wait until you're ready."

He moved closer and brushed a knuckle down her cheek.

"I can wait, Randi. I didn't come here tonight hoping to score. I wouldn't do it with your son sleeping upstairs, in any case. I just wanted you to know about this business with Keane.

Shaken as much by his touch as by what he'd told her, she nodded. "Thanks. For both."

"You need to talk to your sister and brother-in-law. Get their take on the possibility of a claim to your land if this new rune matches the one on your stone."

"I will. Thank God they're giving me a family discount for all the business I'm sending their way."

His startled expression drew a weak chuckle.

"I'm kidding."

Mostly. Despite Sarah and Cal's vigorous protests, Randi had insisted on paying at least a nominal rate for the work they were putting into her defense. Since Randi was a silent partner in their law firm, as Sarah and Lissa were in Morgan Corporation's cattle, wheat and timber operations, it pretty well amounted to a paperwork transfer of assets.

Thinking of the latest business she'd handed Cal and Sarah, Randi sighed and let her gaze drift to the twisted bit of metal occupying center stage on her coffee table.

"You don't happen to know any engineers trained in aviation structural failure analysis, do you?"

"Yeah, I do."

When she blinked at the unexpected answer, he shrugged.

"I've been talking to one of the accident investigators at the FAA about imaging aircraft skin to calculate the probability of catastrophic failure."

She kept her jaw from dropping. Barely. "Are you serious?"

"As a heart attack. There are endless possible applications for the process as I've refined it. Metal fatigue and stress analysis are just two of them. Why?"

"Alex Shores—the officer detailed to investigate Sam Keane's allegations—obtained a copy of the aircraft damage assessment. The investigators documented perforations from enemy fire, collateral damage from Ty's plane and a large tear in the fuselage they attributed to a jagged rock. They couldn't pinpoint what caused several other tears, though. Nor," she added, "did they find any fragmentation that might have been projected from an exploding land mine."

Pete picked up on the significance of that immediately. "So you have no physical evidence to prove Captain Keane triggered the mine that killed him."

"None."

Frowning, he bent and scooped up the memento from Ty's crew. "What about this? What does the accident report attribute this to?"

"That's one of the unexplained penetrations."

He turned the scrap of twisted metal around in his hand, studying it from all angles. "What section of the aircraft did this come from?"

"The right aft portion of the fuselage."

"How close was that section to the explosion that killed Captain Keane?"

"Forty, maybe forty-five yards."

"So it's possible that fragmentation from the mine ripped this hole?"

"It's possible."

She stared at the grisly memento, sick at the thought of shrapnel ripping through Ty with the same force it had torn through her aircraft.

"I could image this, Randi. Run a comparative analysis for you."

Her head whipped up. "And compare it to what?"

"I'd need another section of pierced aircraft skin," he said slowly. "One where the damage is known to have been caused by fragmentation from an antipersonnel device similar to the one that killed Captain Keane."

"I don't have any idea what kind it was. The Soviets reportedly laid millions of mines during their occupation. The Afghanis planted almost as many in their struggle to oust the Russians."

"The Explosive Ordnance folks responsible for clearing the areas around U.S. bases might be able to help with that."

"Good God, you're right."

Randi's mind raced, recalling the briefings she and other aircrew members had attended.

"When we first arrived in the country, EOD talked to us about the various types of mines to watch out for."

They'd also shown slide after slide detailing the lethal results of triggering one. The photos of charred trucks and aircraft riddled with holes were bad enough. Those of the men, women and children who'd lost limbs—and lives—had brought home with awful clarity the danger of wandering outside designated clear zones.

"I can check with our EOD folks at the base," Randi said. "Have them contact their counterparts at K-2 to see if they have samples of fragmentation damage to C-130 aircraft skin."

She fought down the lump that rose in her throat, hating the idea that she had to prove Ty had been ripped apart by a mine in order to refute Sam's charges.

"Do you really think this would work?"

"Hell, yes, it would work. Holographic imaging is already employed in a variety of military and commercial applications. The techniques I've developed merely take those applications to a higher level. And comparing metal shards is far more likely to return statistically significant results than comparing bits of aged, weathered rock."

The possibilities tumbled through her head but came to a screeching halt a few seconds later.

"What am I thinking? I can't ask you to do this."

"Why not?"

"It would put you in direct conflict with Sam Keane."

"I'm already there. I told you, Keane and I agreed to disagree and cut a deal."

"One that includes keeping him advised on your results. If it leaks that you're helping me, using the same process he's funding, he'll consider that a breach of your deal."

"I fully intend to keep Keane informed on the runestone project. What I do on *other* projects is my business."

"But you'd be using university equipment, maybe their lab. If Sam finds out…"

"That's my problem, Randi. You just work on tracking down a sample we can use for comparison."

How could she let him risk his job, his career, his reputation?

"You'd better think about this, Pete. You cross Sam and he'll get you fired."

"That wouldn't break my heart. The politics of academia wear pretty thin at times." He picked up the shattered metal, already working out the logistics in his mind. "We've finished at the museum. I can shoot this piece tomorrow, after we set up operations here. Assuming you still want me to go ahead with imaging your runes, that is."

Randi raked a hand through her hair. Talk about your basic damned-if-you-do, damned-if-you-don't situation.

If she withdrew her permission for Pete's team to access her property, Sam wouldn't hesitate to kill the funding for the project. If she let the team image the runes up on the bluff, he might use the results to back an outsider's claim to Morgan land.

Now there was a new factor that skewered the equation. Unlocking the mystery of the runes would help validate the process Pete had developed. That, in turn, would add weight to any findings that might result from applying his comparative imaging process to the damaged aircraft skin.

Her own dilemma aside, there was Pete to consider. He was laying so much on the line for her. She could hardly do less for him.

"Yes, I want you to press ahead. I'll talk to Sarah

and Cal tomorrow about a possible claim against our land. I can't imagine it would mean anything in court, but…" She struggled to keep the bitterness out of her voice. "Sam wields a lot of political clout. It wouldn't surprise me if he exercised some behind-the-scenes muscle with a judge or two."

God, what a mess! She felt like she was trying to find her way out of a maze blindfolded and alone.

No, not alone. Lissa and Sarah and Cal had stood beside her from the beginning of this nightmare, providing advice and support and unquestioned loyalty.

And now Pete.

Gratitude and guilt over what he was risking got all mixed up together until she walked him to the door and he pulled her into his arms again.

"See you tomorrow," he murmured against her mouth.

14

The possibility of employing his imaging techniques to support Randi's case occupied Pete's mind during the drive back to the conference center. When he walked through the door to the guest wing, Anne practically pounced on him.

"Finally! Where the hell have you been?"

"Out. Why, what's up?"

Her cat's eyes narrowed at the noncommittal reply, but she was too keyed up to take exception to it. Excitement lit her from the inside out, adding a flush of heat to her flawless complexion.

"We've got a match!"

"What?"

"I ran the new rune Keane gave us against the casts Dr. Beasley shipped in. At 400nm it mirrors a character incised in one of the stones from L'Anse aux Meadows almost stroke for stroke."

Pete's heart slammed against his ribs. He made an instant detour away from his room and walked toward hers. Her laptop sat on the scrubbed pine desk, its high-definition screen glowing with dual images. A computer-generated label identified the one on the right as Rune 27, provided by Samuel Keane, source as yet unverified. The image on the left was labeled Rune 3, fire pit stone, L'Anse aux Meadows, Newfoundland.

Elbowing Pete aside, Anne used the pointer to scroll the screen. "Here they are, superimposed. With adjustments for hardness of the stone and the variations in surface silica, we get a ninety-three percent correlation on the depth of the cuts. Eightnine on the angles."

"Jesus!"

Blood pumping, Pete stared at the slowly rotating three-dimensional images. They might have been twin zygotes sharing the same glowing green womb.

"What aperture ratios did you use for the comparisons?"

"I set the f-stop at 1.6 for this shot. I also imaged it at 1.8."

Shrugging out of his jacket, he threw it on Anne's bed and grabbed the desk chair.

"Let's take a look."

***

It was almost 2:00 a.m. before they quit. Tipping the chair onto its back legs, Pete dragged a palm across the bristles on his chin.

"I think you're right, Anne. We have a match."

She thumped him on the shoulder. "Told you!"

Whooping, she did a high-stepping jig around the small room. Her antics woke Brady, who occupied the room next to hers. Bare-chested, his baggy jeans riding dangerously low on skinny hips, he shuffled through the open door.

"What's all the noise about?"

"The Keane rune is a fit with one from Newfoundland," Anne announced gleefully.

"No shit?" His lanky body jolted as if stung with a Taser. "Show me!"

Jack Beasley appeared a few moments later, followed in short order by Jorgenson and Lockwood. Pete turned the computer over to Anne to let her demonstrate the results of her efforts. As expected, they produced a chorus of excited exclamations.

"We should be toasting this," Anne pronounced after the tumult had died down. "I don't suppose anyone has any champagne stashed away?"

"I've got some beer," Brady volunteered.

"Bring it on!"

Much as he hated to put a damper on their enthusiasm, Pete felt it was time for a reality check.

"We're only halfway home, folks. What we have

is a correlation between a silicon cast and a rune of as-yet-unproven origin. I suggest we hold off on the celebrations until we verify the source of Keane's rune and compare it to the original. And…" he added when Anne seemed ready to protest, "we still haven't linked either to the Oklahoma runes. Our charter is to date those, remember?"

"We will," she insisted, gesturing to the screen. "This same letter appears on both the Morgan stone and the one at Heavener. One of them's going to fit right into this spatial profile. I feel it in my bones!"

That was what Pete had hoped for, what he'd envisioned when he'd proposed this study. However, Sam Keane's vendetta against Randi had altered the picture considerably. Now Pete wasn't sure whether he wanted to solve the riddle of the damned runes or not.

Some of his indecision must have shown on his face. Anne eyed him with a gathering frown and signaled for him to wait until after the others downed their beer and dispersed.

"I expected you to be turning cartwheels, Pete. Why the lukewarm response?"

"I'm too old for cartwheels," he said with a smile. "You did good, though. Damned good. As I said, we're halfway there."

"Is this about Randi Morgan? It is, isn't it?" Thoroughly exasperated, she threw herself down on the bed. "What's going on with you two? And what the *heck* am I sitting on?"

Hiking up one leg, she felt beneath her thigh and pulled out Pete's jacket. Searching the pockets, she found the jagged shard of metal mounted on the square marble base. Brows knit, Anne read the inscription on the small brass plaque.

"To Captain Morgan, from the crew. Thanks for bringing us home…" Her head shot up. "What is this?"

"A segment of skin from a C-130 Hercules."

"A segment of skin from *Morgan's* 130, I gather. Why is it in your pocket?"

"I want to image it." Striding across the room, Pete scooped up the sample and his jacket. "It's late, Anne. I'll see you in the morning."

He should've known that wouldn't end it. She trailed him through the door and into the hall.

"Why do you want to image that piece of metal? Oh, Christ! It has something to do with Sam Keane's allegations that Morgan abandoned his son, doesn't it?"

She whipped around in front of him. Fury infused her face, stripping it of beauty and leaving an ugly mask.

"Dammit, Pete, you can't do this! You're putting everything we've worked for, everything we're doing here, at risk."

He'd had enough. "That's it, Anne. I don't owe

you an explanation of my actions. And I won't have you repeatedly challenging my decisions. Cross the line one more time and you're off this project."

She curled her hands and struggled visibly with her temper. "You're right," she said after a long, tense moment. "I've gotten so wrapped up in what we're trying to accomplish, I've lost a little perspective. I'm sorry."

"Apology accepted, but the warning stands. I'll see you in the morning."

Pete got his team assembled and on the road a little past nine the next morning. As they drove to Morgan's Falls, a bright sun burned off the glittering ground frost and gilded the still-colorful leaves. The perfect day acted like a spur to the team's spirits, already high from the night before. Even Anne, who'd greeted Pete with a cool nod, had thawed by the time the small convoy rattled over the cattle guard and drove up the hill to the house.

Absol charged down the sloping drive to greet them. Barking wildly, he went at the vehicles with fangs bared until Pete rolled down the window and identified himself.

Randi probably wouldn't admit it, but Pete had done her a favor by foisting the animal off on her. He doubted there were many reporters brave enough to climb out of a van when Absol flattened his ears and rolled back his lips to expose those black gums.

The dog raced up the drive and ran circles around the pickup until Pete climbed out and endured a wet, sloppy reunion. Only then did the rest of the team leave the safety of their vehicles. Tucking her hands in the pockets of her denim jacket, Anne took in the two-story house with its commanding view of the river, the barns, the horse paddocks and orchards beyond.

"Nice place. Looks like the Morgans have done well for themselves." Her glance slid to Pete. "I suspect Randi would fight tooth and nail if anyone tried to steal this from her. I know I would."

"Why don't you help the others unload the gear? I'll see if she's home."

While Anne supervised the unloading of the equipment and the ATVs she'd rented in Poteau, Pete took the steps to the front porch. He found a note wedged in the screen, along with the key to the rusty lock on the shield protecting the runes. The note explained that Randi had a line on a possible sample of land mine damage to another C-130 aircraft and had driven into Tulsa to check it out. She, Spencer and her sister would be back later today.

In the meantime, Pete and his team were welcome to use the ATVs she'd left parked by the barn. Also the orange vests she'd stacked beside the vehicles. Hunting season still had a week to go.

Disappointed that he'd missed her, Pete stuffed the note in the back pocket of his jeans and distributed the vests to his team. "Better put these on. The woods are really thick up where we're headed."

"Yeah," Brady muttered. Thrusting his arms into a vest, he tugged his ponytail free. "We don't want some Bambi-killer taking potshots at us."

"You've got the thing on backward," Anne pointed out with a touch of acid. "And you wouldn't be so quick to put down hunters if you'd grown up the second youngest of nine kids. We pretty well made it through the winter on the wild turkey and venison my dad bagged."

Pete intervened to keep the peace between the two grad students. "Equipment loaded? Let's power up and circle the yard a few times to test our driver skills before we head up to the bluff."

Absol had apparently decided that going in circles was great fun. His booming barks echoed on the crisp air as he chased the ATVs around the yard. After the third or fourth attempt, Pete gave up trying to convince him to stay put. He figured Randi would have shut him in the house or the barn if she hadn't wanted him to jog along. Besides, the recent frost would've killed off most of the fleas and ticks.

Thankful he'd made the initial scouting trip with Randi, Pete took the lead. Once across the stubbled fields, they picked up the old logging road. As before, the going was fairly easy for twenty minutes or so. The dog followed for the first part of those twenty minutes, but eventually turned back. His guard duties called to him, Pete guessed.

The going got a whole lot rougher after they located the red ribbon Randi had tied to a tree trunk and took the steep path to the ridge. When the team chugged up the last twisting turn and drove onto the bluff overlooking the Arkansas River, the stunning vista hit the first-timers with the same wallop it had Pete.

They fanned out on the ridge, drinking in the spectacle of searing blue skies and slopes forested in dark pine and blazing oak, all watched by keen-eyed hawks floating and dipping on air currents.

"It is so beautiful." Raynard Jorgenson cupped his palms and huffed warm air into them. "This place reminds me of Stören, where I was born. It, too, has green forests and steep hills cut by the Gaula River, which feeds into the fjord by Trondheim."

"One of the great Viking capitals," Jack Beasley commented. "Who knows? Perhaps some intrepid soul sailed from Stören or Trondheim to Newfoundland, and then to this very place deep in the heart of Oklahoma."

The idea that they could be standing on the same spot as some long-ago Viking infused the team with eagerness to see the runes that voyager might have carved. Pete led them to the overhanging ledge and maneuvered the key into the rusty hasp. Seconds later, he swung aside the plastic shield Randi's grandfather had constructed to give them their first good look at runes in their natural setting.

"Ahh." Jack Beasley stooped under the ledge to get a closer view. Almost quivering with excitement, the cryptologist pointed to the symbol comprising two pointed *P*s facing each other. "Look, it's the old futhark *M*. The same as on the amulet. We should image this letter first!"

An image of Sam Keane's gaunt face filled Pete's mind. The old man hadn't owned up to his motivation for funding this study, but Pete knew damned well he wanted to do more than advance knowledge. Torn between the hungry urge to see that rune swirling on his computer screen and reluctance to aid Keane in his blood feud against Randi, Pete opted for sticking to the established protocol.

"We'll work them in order. Let's get set up."

By late afternoon, they'd imaged and made silicon casts of the first two runes. The *M* called to them like a siren, but the sun had sunk to an angle that blanketed the grooves in shadow. There was also a chill in the air. Pete knew they should start down the steep trail before the early-fall dusk made travel too dangerous.

"We'll finish here tomorrow, then shift operations to the Heavener stone."

"We still have an hour of light," Anne protested. "I vote we shoot the *M*."

When Pete sent her a sharp look. Last night's warning was evidently still fresh in her mind. "You're right," she said quickly. "That steep track would be treacherous in the dark. We'd better get packed up."

They made it to the logging road without mishap. When they drove across the stubbled fields, Absol streaked out to welcome them. The house was still shuttered, Pete saw, and the circular drive empty.

He'd been hoping Randi would be home, maybe invite the team in for coffee. Shelving his disappointment, he got the equipment loaded into the trucks and his small convoy rolling down the drive.

His pulse jumped when a dusty SUV turned off the road and rumbled across the cattle guard. With a honk and a wave, Pete halted his pickup.

Randi pulled alongside and rolled down her window. "All finished?"

"For the day. We should wrap things up tomorrow morning, then head for Heavener."

Her glance slid to his passenger, then back to Pete. He saw a simmering excitement in her eyes.

"Maybe we'll get a chance to talk before you go up to the site tomorrow."

"We can talk now. I'll drive to the house with you. Anne, how about you ride to the conference center with Raynard or Brady?"

"We really need to run the comparative analyses on the images we shot today, Pete."

"You start the runs. I'll check when I get back to the center."

She knew better than to argue this time. Shrugging, she slid out of the cab and hiked over to Brady's beat-up Camaro.

When Pete parked in the drive and joined Randi, the excitement inside her had bubbled to the surface. Her blue eyes were alive above cheeks pinked by the rapidly advancing chill.

"You were right!" she said, fending off Absol's ecstatic greeting. "Our EOD chief just rotated home from K-2. He says they shipped over a whole slew of samples—C-130 aircraft skin damaged by exploding ordnance, including a belly section hit by fragmentation from a blast-type land mine."

"Where did they ship the samples?"

"Warner Robbins Air Base, just outside Atlanta. It's the air force's C-130 Depot Overhaul Facility."

"Atlanta, huh?" Pete was already juggling his schedule to squeeze in a trip to Georgia. "Think you can get me access to the depot?"

"I can do better than that. We have a crew flying out to Warner Robbins the day after tomorrow to pick up a cargo of spare parts. I've called Sledge—

the officer conducting the inquiry—and told him
what we want to do. He's agreed to contact the
depot folks and arrange for them to send the damaged skin section back to Oklahoma City with the
spare parts."

"That makes it a lot easier."

"Sledge wants to observe the tests," Randi
warned. "He also asked me to e-mail him your credentials. Guess he wants to make sure my 'outside
expert' is as much of an expert as I billed him."

"Told him I was Einstein reincarnate, did you?"

She didn't rise to the teasing comment. Instead,
the sparkle left her eyes and she caught her lower
lip between her teeth.

"I told him you were the best," she said after a
moment, "and I'm beginning to think that qualifies
as the understatement of the year. I don't know how
I can thank you for helping me like this."

Several ways leaped instantly to mind. Most involved the lip she'd just chewed on.

"We'll work something out. In the meantime,
why don't we go inside? I'll call up my resumé on
your computer so you can zap it off to this Hammer
guy."

"Sledge."

"Right. Sledge."

With Absol at his heels, Pete followed her up the
front steps. She'd put the key in the front door before he thought to ask about her son's whereabouts.

"Spencer wanted to play with his cousins in Tulsa. Lissa's bringing him home later."

"How much later?"

The sudden rasp in his voice must have alerted her. That, or the loud thumping in his chest.

She stared up at him, comprehension dawning in those indigo eyes, and Pete's voice dropped to a hungry growl.

"How much later, Randi?"

"I, uh, talked to her about ten minutes ago. She said she'd start home around six."

Pete looked at his watch and factored in driving time from Tulsa. "That gives us two hours. Plenty of time to—" with a wicked grin, he bent and brushed her lips with his "—call up my resumé."

15

Pete fully intended to take things slow. Miranda Morgan wasn't the kind of woman a man should rush. As he drew her against him, he envisioned a sweet seduction, a gradual rush to frenzy.

One taste of her, just one taste, shot his half-formed plans all to hell. With her breasts flatted against his chest and her hips bumping his, he went from hungry to aching in what felt like a single heartbeat. He managed to keep from tumbling her to the floor. With a fervent prayer of thanks that the leather sofa in her den was man-size, he opted for its soft cushions instead.

They had just sunk into the leather when Absol decided he wanted in on this new game, whatever it was. One wet slurp was enough for Pete to detach himself, lure the dog out of the den and slam the door in his face.

Randi was wedged in the corner when he returned, her black hair falling around her shoulders. He didn't remember unbuttoning the top two buttons of her sweater, but the creamy swell of her breasts shoved the breath back down his throat.

"You're so beautiful." Propping a knee on a cushion, he framed her face between his palms. "Now where were we? Oh, yeah. Right about…here."

The small interruption might never have occurred. In moments, she'd gone from husky to hot and Pete was damned near doubled over with wanting her.

"You know this is crazy," she panted.

"Idiotic," he agreed, fumbling with the rest of the buttons on her sweater.

"I can't… I shouldn't… Oh, hell! Why not?"

It didn't exactly qualify as a romantic declaration, but was all the encouragement Pete needed. This flushed, aroused woman had dominated his thoughts since the day he'd met her. The primitive urge to take her shredded every vestige of control.

His urgency ignited Randi's. She was on fire before he yanked off her sweater, and panting with need when his hands went to the snap on her jeans. The insanity of what she was doing struck her again as she attacked the buttons on his shirt.

Then she planed her palms over the broad expanse of T-shirt-covered chest and gave up any attempt at reason. The hardness of muscle and bone under the soft cotton called to everything that was female in her.

Somehow they got rid of most of their clothes. Randi explored him with hands and teeth and tongue, gasping while he did the same. A brief jolt of sanity returned only when he slid his knee between hers and parted her thighs.

"Wait! I hope you brought something! I'm not... I don't have..."

"I stocked up a couple of days ago." His grin was pure wickedness. "Don't move."

As if she could! His weight pinned her to the leather, already slick from their exertions. She felt an answering grin on her lips as he reached for his jeans.

When he rolled upright and dug a condom out of his wallet, Randi gulped in some air. They hadn't bothered to turn on any lamps. Dusk dimmed the room, leaving just enough light to make out the broad planes and seductive hollows of Pete's back.

Once again she was struck by the differences between this man and the two others who'd figured so large in her life. Unlike her ex, Pete was so easy to be with, even easier to talk to. And God knew he didn't shoot off the same testosterone-charged bullets Ty had around any and all persons of the female persuasion.

Yet the thrill that raced through her as she trailed

a fingertip down his spine was more electric than any Randi had experienced before.

She welcomed his weight with eager hands and mouth. So arousing, she wouldn't let him ease into her. She wanted him, all of him, with a greed that shocked her.

The first time was hard and fast, the second lazy and slow. So slow, they were only half-dressed when a series of booming barks erupted in the hall. Moments later, they heard the sound of a car driving up to the house.

"Oh, Lord! That's probably Spencer and Lissa."

Feeling every bit as guilty as a teenager caught making out, Randi scrambled into the rest of her clothes. While Pete got dressed, she dashed to the downstairs powder room and finger-combed her hair, but there wasn't anything she could do about the whisker burn on the left side of her jaw.

Brushing her fingertips against the reddened spot, she wondered again if she'd lost her mind. With everything else coming down on her, she had to be insane to get this serious about any man right now.

Instantly, she backed up and corrected herself. Pete Engstrom wasn't just *any* man. She stroked the tender spot on her jaw, trying to categorize the reactions he evoked in her. Comfort, although he hadn't been thrilled when she'd told him so. Curiosity about him, about his work, about the rune-stone project that now involved them both. Gratitude for his willingness to help her.

There was more, though. Emotions she wasn't ready to examine too deeply. Feelings she couldn't think about until she'd put this damned inquiry behind her. Flicking off the light, she went to greet her sister and son.

As expected, she took second billing to Absol. When dog and boy had joyously reunited, however, Spencer's attention went not to his mother, but to her visitor.

"Hi, Pete! I didn't know you were here."

"I stopped by to see your mother."

"Oh. Did you kiss her again?"

"Yeah, I did." Pete hunkered down to his eye level. "Is that okay with you?"

"I guess so," Spencer replied with a careless shrug. "Mom said she likes it when you kiss her."

"That's good, as I plan to do a lot of it."

"Yuck." Losing interest in the subject, Spencer aimed for the kitchen. "C'mon, Aunt Lis. Let's eat. I'm hungry."

"I stopped at Rick's Chicken Shack and picked up a bucket of crunch-fried," Lissa said. "Rick always packs enough in his buckets to feed a small army," she added casually. "Care to join us, Pete? From those whisker burns on my sister's chin, I'd say you two worked up an appetite."

The bland observation sent heat crawling up Randi's neck, but Pete merely grinned. "Crunch-fried chicken sounds good. Count me in. We still need to pull up my credentials," he reminded Randi as they walked to the kitchen. "For this guy, Sledge. Interesting name, by the way. Does his personality fit him?"

"Like a glove," Lissa muttered.

"You've met him once, Lis, and then only for a few minutes."

Randi had no idea why she was defending her in-quisitor. An innate sense of fairness, she guessed. She just hoped to God Sledge felt impelled to exer-cise the same quality.

"Once was enough." Lissa thumped the blue-and-white chicken bucket on the kitchen counter. "The man looked like his face would break if he smiled. I feel sorry for his wife, living with someone that up-tight."

"He lost his wife three years ago in a car acci-dent."

"Oh. Well, I suppose that puts him in a different light. He's still not someone I'd want to get up close and personal with."

"I'm not too keen on finding myself in that posi-tion, either," Randi admitted. "Let's get dinner on the table. I'm starved."

The two males made themselves useful by set-ting the table while Lissa unpacked the bucket and

Randi prepared lettuce and vegetables for a salad. Table set, Pete filled glasses with milk for Spencer, iced tea for the adults.

"Smart *and* domesticated," Lissa murmured to Randi. "Now if only he's good in the sack…"

Hissing at her sister to hush, Randi tore at the lettuce. Lissa's speculative gaze stayed on Pete as he returned the milk carton to the fridge and ambled back to the table with a raw egg in his hand.

"Want to see a magic trick?" he asked Spencer.

"Sure."

Smiling, he put the egg on the table and sent it into a spin, then touched it briefly with a fingertip to stop it. When he took his finger away it began to twirl again.

"Hey!" Wide-eyed, Spencer tracked the egg's wobbly progress across the tabletop. "How'd you *do* that?"

"I didn't. Inertia did. Do you know what inertia is?"

"Nope."

"It's the tendency of an object to remain at rest or in motion unless acted on by an outside force." He set the egg twirling once more. "See, I can stop the shell with my finger. But the liquid inside is still sloshing around. So when I take my finger away, the inside movement starts the egg spinning again."

"Cool!"

"Here, you try it."

His bright gold curls brushing Pete's shoulder,

Spencer made several unsuccessful attempts to repeat the trick. One particularly energetic spin sent the egg off the edge of the table. Pete caught it before it splattered on the tiles.

"Spin it a little slower. That's it. Now touch it lightly."

His patience with her son started a little ache just under Randi's ribs. The welter of emotions Pete stirred in her came rushing back. Against all reason, almost against her will, she could put a name to another one now. She was pretty sure she was falling in love with the man.

The ache spread at Spencer's triumphant hoot when he performed the magic trick. "Look, Aunt Lis! Look, Mommy! I did it!"

"I see."

"This is *soooo* cool. Wait till I show the kids at school. What's that thing that makes it spin again, Pete? Initials?"

"Inertia."

"You know any other neat tricks?"

"A few. Ever collapse a soda can using nothing but hot air?"

"No."

"I'll teach you that one next visit." Grinning, he ruffled the boy's hair. "By the time you hit first grade, we'll have you acing science and math."

"Speaking of science," Lissa said as she joined them at the table, "how's the runestone project going?"

"We think we might have a match with one of the Poteau runes and the amulet Sam Keane supplied."

"Randi told me about that." Pursing her lips, Lissa dished out the chicken. "She also told me the same letter's carved into our rock."

"That's right. We're going to image it tomorrow morning. Why don't you and Randi come up and watch?"

"We just might do that. Not that we're worried about its being a match," Lissa said. "Our brother-in-law, Cal, thinks there isn't a chance in hell any court would—"

"You're not supposed to say hell," Spencer chirped. "Or shit or—"

"You're right. Sorry 'bout that. Cal thinks there isn't *any* chance a court would back a claim to Morgan land based on a single symbol carved in stone."

But Randi knew that Sam could tie them up in a long legal battle, as Pete had said. Cal, too, had warned her about the possibility. So had Sarah, who was not only ready but eager to take Sam on in court. She swore she'd pay him back for what he'd put Randi through, and then some.

Randi just wanted the whole mess to be over. Shoving Sam and his machinations to the back of her mind, she encouraged Pete to explain his efforts to date the runes. Her heart warmed when he did so in terms even a child could understand.

Spencer soaked it up like a sponge. He particularly liked the idea that the symbols might have been carved by Vikings who rowed up the Mississippi and Arkansas rivers.

"Vikings? You mean those guys with the swords and funny hats with horns?"

"Those are the dudes, although I'm told the horned hats are a matter of historical debate."

"Wow!"

Spencer turned his wide blue eyes on his mother. The excitement in his face started another ache inside Randi. He was as fascinated by the mysterious runes as Ty Keane had been as a boy.

"Kin I go up with you 'n Aunt Lissa to watch Pete, Mom? Please?"

"You've got school tomorrow. You've already missed two days."

His lower lip jutted out. "I want to go with you 'n Aunt Lis."

"Spencer..."

At her low warning, the stubbornness Lissa always swore he'd inherited from his mother produced a scowl. Pete intervened before the boy could work his way into a full temper.

"Tell you what," he said smoothly. "We'll be at Heavener for at least a week. Maybe your mom can bring you over there after school one day? If you ask her nicely."

That clearly wasn't what Spencer wanted, but

a warning glance from Pete put the lid on a potential tantrum.

"Please, Mom."

"Depending on how…"

"Please, please, *please!*"

"Depending on how things go," she finished, "we should be able to fit in a visit."

"Can I bring Absol, like I did last time?"

"Spencer…"

"Can I, Pete?"

"If it's okay with your mom."

When Pete was on his way back to the conference center, Randi put Spencer to bed. Lissa was feasting on a bowl of ice cream when Randi came downstairs.

"So what's the deal with you and the professor? And don't try to tell me you two just indulged in some heavy necking earlier this evening. You were wearing the expression of a *very* satisfied woman when Spencer and I walked into the house."

Randi settled at the table and plucked the spoon from her sister's hand. Digging into the chocolate fudge ripple, she helped herself.

"I don't know *what* the deal is. I shouldn't have room for anything in my head right now but this damned inquiry. Yet every time I turn around, Pete's there." Brows furrowed, she let the ice cream slide down her throat. "I'm coming to depend on him, and I'm not sure that's smart."

"Depend on him for what?"

"For help and for... Oh, hell. I don't know. Distraction."

Snorting, Lissa snatched back her spoon. "Is that how you're labeling hot, raunchy sex these days? Distraction?"

"Well..."

"It *was* hot and raunchy, wasn't it? The professor looks like he's got all the right equipment and knows how to use it."

"He knows how to use it," Randi conceded, laughing. "He most certainly knows how to use it!"

"So what's the problem here? He obviously has the hots for you and he's wonderful to Spencer. What's more, you light up around him in a way you haven't with any man in a long, long time."

Randi's laughter died. "The problem is, I have this inquiry poised above me like a sword. I can't make any plans, I can't let myself think about the future, until we refute Sam's allegations."

"And that's all they are. The allegations of a wounded mind. Hang in there, Randi. This will all be behind you in a few weeks. Then you can get your life back on track and explore this chemistry you seem to have with Pete."

"God, I hope so!"

* * *

Pete felt pretty damned good about himself, about Randi, and about the world in general during the drive back to the conference center.

His mood dimmed a few degrees when he spotted light spilling through an open door halfway down the hall in the guest wing. Anne was waiting for him. Jaw tight, he prepared for another confrontation with his lab assistant. His *last* confrontation, he vowed.

The thud of his footsteps brought her to the door. Her lips were set in a thin line and the skin across her high cheekbones had stretched taut. What Pete took for disapproval of his growing involvement with Randi, however, turned out to be something else entirely.

"I got a call from my mom a few minutes ago," she said with a catch to her voice. "She thinks my dad's had a stroke."

"Oh, Christ. I'm sorry, Anne. How bad was it?"

"Mom says his speech is slurred, but he hasn't lost mobility. I need to go home and get him to a doctor, Pete."

"Of course."

"I'll return as soon as I can. I'm sorry to leave you shorthanded like this."

"Randi said she'd go up to the site with us tomorrow. We'll press her into service. You take care of your dad."

"Thanks."

Pete didn't want to step on her pride, but he was well aware of her financial situation.

"I know you don't get paid until the end of the month." Pulling out his wallet, he emptied it. "You'd better take this. Let me know if you need more. I'll call my bank and have them do a wire transfer."

Her fist closed around the folded notes. Eyes as bleak as frost-dead moss, she nodded.

16

To Lissa's disappointment, she couldn't join the small expedition headed back up to the runestone the next morning. Her boss called with an urgent project he needed done and online by noon. It involved incorporating a new mirror-art wholesaler into the Dallas World Trade Center's merchant directory, store layout and interactive product inventory. Pretty much a no-brainer for someone with Lissa's skills, but time-consuming.

She wasn't the only member of the expedition to bail, she and Randi learned when Pete arrived with his team. His lab assistant had some kind of family emergency and he'd sent two other folks ahead to the Heavener site to start setting up equipment. Shoulders hunched against the bite of a north wind, Lissa greeted the jolly Norwegian she'd met a few days ago and was introduced to a bushy-bearded cryptologist from the University of Chicago.

She didn't miss the flush that warmed Randi's face when she helped Pete into a bright orange hunting vest. The look that passed between them suggested the professor might just be able to force the ugliness of the inquiry out of Randi's mind for an hour or two. Whatever happened between her sister and the physicist, Lissa would always be grateful to him for that much, at least.

With a wave to Lissa, Randi gunned the engine on her ATV. The others trailed after her, but narrowly avoided disaster when Absol charged in front of their ATVs. Exasperated, Randi banned the wildly cavorting hound from the expedition.

"Take him in the house, will you, Lis? And keep him there!"

That proved easier said than done. Using both hands and all her strength, Lissa dragged the protesting animal up the front steps. Crushed at being left out of the fun, the dog howled mournfully until Lissa shushed him with two raisin-filled cinnamon buns. She downed the third herself, then settled in front of her laptop.

Updating the center's merchant listing and three-dimensional floor plans was easy. The interactive product inventory, however, turned out to be a real bitch. For some reason, the HTML code the dealer had used on his site wouldn't interface with the

Center's. Each time Lissa thought she'd fixed the problem and attempted to run the merchant's clear-streaming video, his images came through fractured.

Muttering, she reopened the subdirectory files and searched screen after screen of code. Again. Two cups of coffee and a string of obscenities later, she found the glitch. One small string of code prefaced by a right > instead of a left.

She made the switch, hit view to scan the results and was just congratulating herself for pinpointing the problem when the dog let loose with an ear-splitting woof.

Lissa jumped half out of her chair. "What?"

Absol shot across the room and plastered his nose against the front window. The barking rose to a frenzy. Abandoning the desk, Lissa joined him at the window.

"What is it? What do you—?"

She broke off, tensing as she spotted a shadow of movement in the woods beyond the bare fields. Her first thought was poachers out to bag more than their limit on deer-rich private property. Her second, another damned reporter hoping to score a shot of Randi with a telephoto lens. She was all set to march to the front door and sic Absol on the intruder when an antlered buck bolted out of the woods. He was magnificent, carrying a rack that must have had twelve or fourteen points.

The dog, of course, went crazy at the sight.

"No way, fella! You're not chasing after him."

Lissa had to listen to his wild barking while she tried to see what, if anything, had startled the stag. When the buck disappeared into the woods and the dog's howls degenerated into long, mournful whines, she gave up the search and went back to work.

Consequently, she was less than pleased when Absol erupted again twenty minutes later. Grimacing at the noise, Lissa checked out the low-slung muscle car coming up the sloping drive.

She was at the front door when the cherry-red Camaro pulled up and the driver emerged. She didn't recognize him at first. A battered Stetson sat low on his forehead. Aviator sunglasses hid his eyes.

The granite jaw gave her the first clue. The military set to his shoulders when he turned in her direction cinched the matter. Setting her own jaw, Lissa slammed the front door on Absol and stomped down the steps.

"What do you want?"

Major Alex Shores peeled off his sunglasses. Squint lines creased the skin at the corners of his gray eyes as he met her unfriendly glare. "Your sister was going to e-mail me the credentials of this outside expert she's hired."

"She sent them to you last night."

"I didn't get them," he said with a frown. "My spam filter must've blocked the e-mail."

"So you drove all the way over from Oklahoma City to pick up a copy?"

"I live in McAlester and had some other business to attend to close by."

Last night Randi had mentioned that the man had lost his wife to a car accident. Now Lissa knew he lived less than an hour from Morgan's Falls. Practically a neighbor. These bits of information were making Sledge a little too human for Lissa to sustain her animosity toward him. She gave it a genuine effort, though.

"Is this an official visit, Major? If so, why aren't you in uniform?"

"I'm not going into the base until this afternoon." Impatience and a touch of exasperation colored his deep baritone. "Is your sister here, Ms. Morgan? I'd like to get a copy of those credentials. And a phone number for this analyst she's hired. I need to talk to him about testing the samples I'm having shipped in."

The reminder that he'd personally contacted the depot outside Atlanta and arranged to have a section of damaged aircraft skin shipped to Oklahoma took a little more of the edge off Lissa's belligerence.

"Sorry, Randi's not here. If you want to come inside, I'll try to find a hard copy of the information she sent you."

* * *

Hell, yes, Sledge wanted to come inside. This inquiry was one of the most disagreeable tasks he'd had to perform as an air force officer. He hated having to investigate a fellow pilot, particularly one he admired and respected as much as he did Randi Morgan.

Sledge had spent the past two days interviewing the crews who'd flown with Randi and with Ty Keane on their last mission. He'd also interviewed the sergeant who'd overheard the two pilots arguing the night before. He understood his job was to separate innuendo from fact, but the human emotions tangled up in this case didn't make for easy separating.

He was still sifting through the facts, but he was close to making a determination as to the substance of the allegations. Hopefully, these additional tests would answer the remaining questions.

The outside expert Randi had tagged could play a pivotal role in that. Assuming the guy's credentials checked out. That dominated Sledge's thoughts as he followed Randi's sister into the house.

Melissa Morgan came damned close to crowding it out, though. The woman looked as good from the rear as she did from the front, and her front was certainly impressive.

She'd caught Sledge's attention that day at the base in more ways than one. So had her sister the lawyer, he remembered wryly as he paused to let a monster of a dog sniff his hands.

"How's your sister? The one who went into labor?"

"Sarah made it to the hospital. Without a moment to spare."

"What did she have, a boy or girl?"

"A girl. With the cutest little pug nose you ever saw."

A smile softened the lines of her face as she rummaged through the papers on an antique rolltop desk. The massive piece had been fitted with a power strip and hideaway keyboard tray. A perfect blend of new and old.

Which also described the rest of the Morgan homestead, Sledge decided. Hat in hand, he let his gaze roam over comfortable leather furniture, brass-fitted tables and what looked like a genuine Tiffany lamp in glowing jewel tones. The den he now stood in had probably once served as the main parlor. The mantel above the fireplace was hand carved and the oak floorboards wore the dark patina of age. In contrast, the wide Pella windows framing a view of the river and valley beyond were new and double-paned to block the winds that could knife through these hills.

"I don't see anything here."

Lips pursed, Lissa powered up Randi's com-

puter. When she couldn't find what she was looking for, she blew out a frustrated breath.

"I *know* Randi sent those credentials. I can try to
reach her on the cell phone and find out where she
filed her copy."

"That's okay. They're probably waiting for me at
the base. I just figured I'd check this guy out while
I had a few hours to spare."

"Actually, Dr. Engstrom is here today."

"Here?"

"He's up at the bluffs. He and his team are working on a special project to date the rock carvings here
and at Heavener State Park. Randi's with him."

Thoughtfully, Sledge circled his Stetson in his
hands. Like most natives of southeastern Oklahoma, he'd visited Heavener at one time or another
to view the mysterious carvings. He'd also heard
about this latest attempt to date the runes. He
wasn't aware that the man heading the study was
the expert Randi had hired to analyze the damage
to her aircraft.

He couldn't quite make the leap between rock
carvings and explosive ordnance fragmentation. He
tried to put the two together as his hat made another
slow circle.

"You say this Dr. Engstrom is up at the bluffs?"

"He and his team spent most of yesterday there.
Pete—Dr. Engstrom—said they'll finish this morn-

ing." She glanced her watch. "They should be down anytime now."

"Mind if I wait? I'd like to talk to him."

He could see she wasn't particularly thrilled at the prospect of entertaining the enemy. A crease formed between her black brows as she folded her arms and leaned against the desk.

"Did you know that Sam Keane funded Professor Engstrom's project?"

Sledge's hands stilled. "No."

"Sam made the ten-million-dollar gift he gave OU contingent on Dr. Engstrom and his team having access to the runes on Morgan property. We're not sure why, although we suspect Sam intends to use the study to punish Randi in some way for his son's death." Her eyes met his. "Just like he's using you."

Sledge had no intention of justifying himself or the inquiry. But his gut told him it was no coincidence that the runestone project had kicked off at almost the same time as the investigation into the allegations made by Sam Keane.

"Where do you want me to wait, Ms. Morgan? Here or in my car?"

The blunt question stiffened her back. Sledge half expected her to throw him out of the house, but she issued a grudging invitation.

"Have a seat. And my name's Melissa. Lissa to my friends. Which don't include you, by the way."

Her offer of coffee was even more reluctant.

Sledge accepted, tossed his hat onto one chair and took a seat in another. The dog hunkered down beside him and plopped a massive paw in his lap.

Sledge caught it just in time to keep his balls from taking a direct hit. Shoving the paw aside, he settled in to wait for Miranda Morgan and her so-called expert.

High on the bluff overlooking the Arkansas, Randi gritted her teeth and tried to ignore the pain spiking into her left temple.

It had started small, just a dull ache hovering above her ear when she'd woken up this morning. Nothing she couldn't manage under ordinary circumstances. But the bone-jarring ride up to the slope had sent little knives into her head, and almost two hours of intense concentration had fired the blades to white-hot. Wishing she hadn't volunteered to man the computer set up on a folding aluminum camp table, Randi squinted at the blurred image on the screen.

Thank God Pete was almost done. Only one more image of the last rune. Unfortunately, it was proving difficult to shoot with the sun almost directly overhead and the overhanging ledge throwing the symbol into deep shadow.

"I need direct light on that *M*, Raynard." Bent over the right lens of the spectrograph, Pete adjusted the settings. "Can you get in closer?"

Nodding, Professor Jorgenson wedged his body further into the stone cavity and angled a high-intensity light at the symbol.

"Good. Good. Jack, do you have the letter framed in your notch filter?"

"Got it. Christ, look at the depth of those chisel marks."

"Whoever hacked into this stone exercised some serious muscle," Pete agreed. "He must've had one heck of an arm."

"Strong Arm!"

Professor Jorgenson jerked upright, banging his head on the ledge in the process.

"Bjorn Strong Arm!"

The name captured Jack Beasley's attention instantly. "Good God! Could it be?"

"Could it be what?" Pete wanted to know.

"Not *what!*" Jorgenson yelped. "Who!"

Almost dancing with excitement, he whacked his head again and backed out from under the rock butt first.

"There is a wood stick. It was found on the isle of Kingigtorssuaq, in Greenland. The stick is engraved on three sides."

"With old futhark runes like these," Beasley put in, abandoning the spectrograph to join his colleague.

"One inscription reads Bibrau is the name of the girl who sits in the blue," Jorgenson announced. "The second says Ingibjorg's grave."

The Norwegian's accent grew thicker with every syllable. Between that and the jackhammer at work in her skull, Randi had to strain to follow his words.

"There is considerable debate over the inscription on the third side, but some scholars have translated it to mean Letveig, mother to Bjorn of the Strong Arm, who—"

"—sailed to far places," Beasley finished on a rush. "Isn't there another inscription that mentions him?"

"Ja, ja! He is included on a stone erected by Harald Bluetooth, King of Denmark and Norway, sometime between A.D. 965 and 985. Harald describes him as a great warrior with pale hair and eyes the color of a summer sky."

"Just like in the legend," Randi murmured, recalling the tale that had been handed down through her family for generations.

"Ja!"

Jorgenson's whoop drove another spike into her head.

"Just like in your legend!" he exclaimed. "It all comes together. I feel it in my bones."

Randi was feeling it in her bones, too. So much so, she was dangerously close to throwing up.

"You okay?"

The quiet question came at her through a fog of misery. She saw the concern in Pete's face and dredged up a smile.

"I've got a headache. Nothing a couple of aspirin won't fix. Do you happen to have any on you?"

Pete didn't, but Jack Beasley produced a bottle of industrial-strength Tylenol. "For my arthritis," he explained while Pete fetched a bottle of water.

The directions called for a max of two capsules every eight hours, but Randi quickly swallowed three. This killer wasn't going to respond to anything less.

"You sit here and let those pills work," Pete said. "Jack, you take over the computer."

"You need Jack on the second lens and Raynard to hold the light," she countered. "Just feed me the numbers and I'll enter them."

"You sure you're up to it?"

"I'm sure."

"Okay, folks, let's get this last shot and pack up."

Pete and Jack Beasley bent over the lenses set at right angles to each other. Jorgenson burrowed under the ledge with his high-intensity light. Randi willed the capsules to get to work and concentrated on the blurred image filling the screen.

"Read me the settings, Randi."

Squinting, she recited the numbers on the grid as the image occupying the center screen began to dance. She hoped to hell it was Pete adjusting the lenses and not her head making the symbol swirl.

The mesmerizing blur of color and movement drew Randi in. Slowly, the blur sharpened. Grooves appeared, became defined.

Pete left his post and peered over her shoulder.

"Perfect! Randi, when I give you the word, just hit control-f to shoot a second image through Jack's lens."

Repositioned at the platform holding the spectrograph, he had her verify the settings.

"Okay, we're good to go. Shoot it, Randi."

She hit the control and f keys, holding her breath until a second image appeared beside the first. Blurry at first, it soon spread across the screen in bold, slashing strokes.

"I've got it, Pete."

"Good. Now hit control-g."

The process of merging the two symbols into a three-dimensional holographic image took only seconds, but seemed to Randi to go on forever. The letters swirled and spun into a dozen different colors. Her head swirled and spun with them.

The images whirled faster. Bright lights seemed to jump from the screen. A figure took shape amid the blinding colors, indistinct at first, then with violent clarity.

A man. Bare chested. Heavily muscled. Rushing toward her through the vortex.

Pain and dizziness combined to raise bitter-tasting bile in Randi's throat. She gulped it back, tried to look away, but her brain seemed to have short-circuited.

The brute bared his teeth. Lifted his arm. Swung his sword.

Sword?

Dear God, she was hallucinating! Stress, tension, lack of sleep, the damned inquiry, all this talk of Vikings—everything had come together and fried her brain.

She'd barely formed that thought when the computer-generated image seemed to lunge from the screen and Randi's feeble attempt at reason fled.

This was real!

He was real!

Blind with pain and a sudden animal terror, she rocked back at the same instant a sharp crack pierced the roaring in her ears.

The screen shattered. The laptop flew off the camp table and smashed to the ground a good ten yards away.

Instantly, the swirling colors disintegrated.

The image vanished.

Unable to move, unable to think, Randi stood frozen as Pete and the others rushed out from under the ledge.

"What the hell?"

His shout jerked her out of her trance. Reason returned, and with it a gut-clenching awareness of what she'd just heard.

"Get down!" she yelled, diving for cover. "That was a rifle shot!"

17

Randi's immediate impulse was to hit the ground. But even before she connected with hard rock, training and instincts bred into her by generations of warriors and adventurers sent her into a roll.

Someone shot at her, she shot back.

Scrambling to her feet, she dropped into a crouch and raced for the hard-sided rifle case attached to her ATV.

"Stay down!" she shouted at the others.

Raynard and Jack kept their faces planted in the dirt, arms and legs splayed, but Pete was already up and running. Closer to the parked ATVs by at least six yards, he got to the vehicles first and ripped open the rifle case. When Randi reached him, he had her grandfather's Winchester under his arm and was snapping back the bolt with an expertise that told her he'd picked up a few lethal skills in the marines.

"Where are the cartridges?"

"Side pocket of the case!"

Pete plunged a hand into the zippered pocket, grabbed the box of shells and abandoned the dubious protection of the gasoline-powered vehicles for a short, scrubby pine. Randi ducked behind the tree next to his.

While he loaded the Winchester, she searched the direction the shot had come from. The ridge was rocky and thinly wooded for twenty yards or so. Beyond that were impenetrable stands of pine and spruce.

"See anything?" Pete asked over the snick of rounds being chambered.

"Nothing."

"Goddamned hunters!"

Pointing the rifle skyward, he pumped out three quick rounds. The warning shots split the air and reverberated across the bluffs. The percussive waves hammered at Randi's ears as she continued to scan the woods.

She saw nothing. Heard nothing except the pounding of her heart.

"Hey!" Pete's furious shout boomed into the ensuing silence. "In case you didn't understand that message, there are people working here!"

Still nothing. No ripple of movement. No apologetic answering shout.

Seconds went by. Minutes.

"Stupid bastard. I'm going after him. Stay here."

Randi didn't bother to argue with that piece of idiocy. This was her land. Her special place. She knew every gnarled tree, every slippery slope.

"You take the path to the right," she said tersely, ducking under the branches. "I'll go left. Cover me until I get to the rocks."

"Randi, wait!"

She ignored him and darted for the edge of the bluff. Cursing, Pete whipped the rifle to his shoulder. After she'd gained the safety of the protruding rocks, he took off running.

They gave up the hunt after twenty minutes of searching the still, silent woods. Once back at the runestone, Pete calmed his thoroughly shaken colleagues while Randi got on her cell phone.

Her first call went to the county sheriff, her second to Lissa. Her sister's reaction to the news that they'd been shot at mirrored Pete's.

"We've got No Trespassing signs posted all over the place. Damn poachers ought to be strung up by their balls! Shit, I may have spotted one earlier."

"When?"

"An hour or so ago. Absol set up a racket like you wouldn't believe. When I went to the window to see what had him so excited, I noticed some movement in the woods behind the orchard. A stag bolted out a few moments later."

"Something must have startled him," Randi said.

"Or someone."

"Sheriff Jefferies should be there in ten, fifteen minutes." She rubbed the heel of her hand across her forehead. Now that the adrenaline surge had passed, her headache had returned with a vengeance. "Tell him what you just told me, then point him in the direction of the logging road, will you? One of us will drive down to meet him and escort him up to the site. In the meantime, I need you to pick up Spencer."

"Will do. By the way, you have a visitor. He showed up about an hour ago."

"Who?"

"Major Shores."

"Sledge is at the house? Why?"

"He wanted a copy of the professor's credentials. I couldn't find the file you e-mailed him, so he decided to wait and talk to Pete himself."

"God, I can't handle Sledge right now! Get rid of him, will you?"

"With pleasure." She paused a beat or two. "Just be careful up there, sis."

Sheriff Jared Jefferies had played poker with Randi's grandfather the third Tuesday night of every month. He'd also busted Sarah several times for speeding, had removed a fishhook from Lissa's right ear and had once driven Randi home in the back of his squad car after catching her skinny-dipping with Ty Keane.

Masses of wrinkled skin hung in loose folds from his jowls and surrounded his droopy, hound-dog eyes. Concave-chested and stoop-shouldered, he looked lost in his tan-and-black uniform. But no one who'd ever gotten crosswise of him, Randi included, was fooled by his appearance.

A handful of citizens had expressed concern during the last election that Jefferies was well past retirement age. A few unenlightened others had suggested he wasn't as up on modern investigative techniques and forensics as he could be. The rest of the county returned him to office with a resounding majority. Around these parts, experience, instinct and common sense still trumped technology any day.

Rolling the toothpick that was never out of his mouth from one corner to the other, Jefferies hooked his thumbs in his belt. His sad eyes surveyed the scene while the deputy he'd brought with him snapped Polaroid photos.

The camp table was toppled onto its side. The shattered computer lay where it had hit the rocky ground. Thoughtfully, the sheriff drew a visual line from the laptop to the trees and back.

"You say the bullet came from behind you?"

Randi nodded. "Behind and a little to the left."

Ambling over to the metal table, he righted it. "Show me where you were standing."

She took up her position.

"You sure that's where you were?" Jefferies asked, studying the distance between her and the woods. "The bullet would've had to pass right through you to send the computer flying across the rock like that."

"I got a little dizzy," Randi admitted, "and stumbled a step or two to the side just before the bullet hit."

"You did, huh?" The toothpick made a shift to the opposite corner. "Still havin' those headaches?"

"Some. Not as much as before." She resisted the urge to dig her fingertips into her temple and grind at the pain. "The symbols on the computer screen were swirling and the colors were so bright, my head started to swim."

It had started swimming well before Pete's holographic images lit up the screen. Those gyrating symbols had only made her headache worse. Not to mention the phantom Viking she'd conjured up.

He'd leapt straight for her. Sword held high. Eyes glowing like fierce blue flames.

Randi's throat closed. She could see him, almost feel the air around her vibrate with the swipe of that vicious broadsword.

"Why didn't you tell me you were in such pain?"

Once again, Pete's voice jerked her from a near-trance.

"What?"

"Why didn't you tell me—" He broke off, his eyes narrowing on her face. "You're *still* hurting, aren't you?"

"I'm okay."

"The hell you are." With an impatient sound, he addressed the sheriff. "You need us anymore? If not, I'll take my team down the bluff and Randi back to the house."

"You folks go ahead. Deputy Hoffman here and I will nose around a bit, see what we can find. Randi, you know how to contact these gentlemen if I have questions for them?"

"Yes."

"Good enough."

Pete sent Raynard and Jack ahead to Heavener State Park, but refused to leave Morgan's Falls himself until Sheriff Jefferies was finished at the site.

He was at the house when Lissa returned from picking up Spencer. Joining forces, Lissa and Pete pressured Randi into popping a couple of her prescription pain pills and going upstairs to lie down. She was still asleep when Jefferies appeared and made his report.

"We found a shell casing in the woods," he told

Pete and Lissa. "A 7mm Remington Magnum boat-tail. Be interesting to see if it matches the bullet embedded in your computer."

"Very." Frowning, Pete searched his memory. "Best I can recall, the 7 Mag has a fairly flat trajectory and high ballistic coefficient."

"Been hunting a few times, have you?"

"Once or twice. In the Corps."

Nodding, Jefferies worked his toothpick. "A spire-point boattail like this one can bring down a mule deer at six hundred yards. Make a clean kill at three hundred."

"Depending on the shooter. He'd have to be a helluva marksman to hit a target at six hundred yards. Where'd you find the casing?"

"'Bout two hundred yards up from your site. It was in a small clearing with a partially obstructed view of the ridge where you were working."

Partially obstructed. That left the door open. It *could* have been a hunter getting a jump on gun season with a blind shot at a deer. Then again...

"Did you find anything else? Footprints? Gum wrappers? Cigarette butts?"

"No sir, only the shell casing. We'll send it up to the state lab to see if the wizards in white coats can lift a print or DNA. We'll also send 'em your computer, or what's left of it."

Pete winced. He'd made backups of everything but the last few images of the *M*. That data was locked in the chewed-up guts of the laptop. He'd have to go back up to the ridge and reshoot.

Later, he decided. After the team finished at Heavener and the sheriff had concluded his investigation.

He soon discovered Jefferies wasn't anywhere near done. Accepting Lissa's offer of coffee, the lawman shed his jacket, hitched his Sam Browne belt higher on skinny hips and straddled a kitchen chair.

"You want to tell me about this project of yours, Doc?"

Before Pete could comply with the laconic request, Lissa thumped two mugs down on the table. "Sam Keane funded it. What does *that* tell you?"

The sheriff's salt-and-pepper brows inched upward. "Well now, missy, it tells me there's more behind the professor's study than an attempt to date the hen-scratchings on a pile of rocks."

The air in the kitchen took on a different feel. Thicker. Heavier. Pete didn't understand why until Lissa locked eyes with Jefferies.

"We both know Sam's the biggest contributor to your war chest come election time. Is that going to create a problem with your investigation?"

Instead of taking offense, the sheriff heaved a long sigh. "I don't know how many times I told your granddad he should've taught you girls to keep a rein on your tongue."

"Is it going to be a problem, Jared?"

Pete had to admire her dogged determination, if not her tact. Like her sister, Melissa Morgan packed a core of solid steel under all that lustrous black hair and soft, dewy skin.

Evidently the sheriff had gone head-to-head with the Morgan sisters before. Seemingly unperturbed, he promised to drive over and have a chat with Sam Keane after he left Morgan's Falls.

"When you do," Lissa said, "you might ask him if he hunts with 7mm Remington Magnums."

"You telling me how to do my job, missy?"

Jefferies didn't alter his voice or his comfortable slump against the back of the chair, but Pete heard the warning buried in the genial response. So did Lissa. Flushing, she pulled up short.

"No, sir."

"Good. Now maybe you'll let the professor here explain just what he and Randi were doing up on that bluff."

Pete was halfway through the intricacies of the imaging process and the politics behind his project when Randi made a belated appearance. The tight lines at the corners of her eyes suggested she hadn't completely conquered her pain, but her face had regained its color and her movements were brisk. Pouring herself some coffee, she joined the enclave at the table.

She said nothing until Pete finished his explanation of the runestone project and Jefferies turned his coon-dog eyes in her direction.

"I've been following the news stories 'bout this investigation, Randi. I've heard Sam's side of things. You want to tell me yours?"

She didn't flinch, didn't look away.

"I can't, Jared. My attorneys have advised me not to discuss the inquiry with anyone outside my chain of command or my immediate family."

"All you need to know," Lissa put in fiercely, "is that Sam's allegations are absurd!"

The sheriff didn't argue the point. "Guess I've got enough to work with for now. I'll get back to you."

Lissa showed him out, then reclaimed her seat at the kitchen table. Pete noted the glance the two sisters exchanged and waited for one of them to voice the suspicion on their minds.

Randi was the first to break. "I can't believe Sam took that shot, Lissa. I *don't* believe it."

"He's been hunting since before we were born. And not just here in Oklahoma. How many African safaris has he been on? How many hunting trips did he and Ty take to Alaska? You should see the trophies in his den," she flung in Pete's direction. "In his prime, Sam Keane kept taxidermists in three states employed full-time."

Randi shook her head, a touch of desperation in her face. "I still don't believe he'd try to kill me."

"I don't want to believe it, either, but we both

know he's out to hurt you any way he can. If he didn't fire that shot himself, he could've hired someone to do it for him."

"It doesn't make any sense. Why now? Why not wait until Pete completes his study and Sledge wraps up the inquiry? Sam initiated both for a reason. Why not play out those hands?"

"Could be the shooter wasn't trying to kill anyone," Pete commented. "We can't rule out a careless hunter. Or the possibility that someone wanted to give Randi a helluva scare."

"He certainly accomplished that! Between the shot and the Viking, I just about died."

Pete's brows snapped together. "Viking?"

Instantly, Randi regretted the slip. She had yet to deal with the fact that she'd spaced out for a few seconds up there on the bluff.

She'd have to tell the flight surgeon about that weird hallucination. She couldn't return to flight status and take up an aircraft or crew knowing she'd blanked, however briefly. The docs would run more tests. Probably another MRI. Discouraged and depressed by the prospect, she shrugged.

"My head was hurting. The swirling symbols and bright colors on the computer screen made me dizzy. For a crazy moment everything seemed to come together to form the image of a man. A warrior. Complete with sword and leather helmet. He was big," she added, thoroughly embarrassed. "Buff. And gold-bearded."

Lissa reached over and squeezed her arm. "Oh, Randi! The headaches have gotten worse instead of better. You won't be climbing back in the cockpit for a while."

"Yeah, I've pretty well figured that out. The strange thing was…"

She glanced at Pete, saw him watching her with an expression that combined worry, doubt and a reluctant curiosity.

"The strange thing was," she continued, "this warrior lunged straight at me. All I could think was that he was going to jump off the screen and skewer me."

"Understandable." Pete's shoulders relaxed as he came up with a logical explanation for her descent into the world of fantasy. "We'd just been talking about…what did Raynard call him?"

"Bjorn Strong Arm."

"A fierce warrior, according to King Harald."

"I know, I know. But…"

"But what, Randi?"

Creasing her forehead, she tried to recreate those few chaotic seconds. The shock, the ferocity, the pulse-pounding terror surged back with a violence that made her palms sweat.

Something else came with those gut-wrenching memories. Something that hadn't really registered until she'd had a chance to think about it.

"At the time, I thought he was attacking me. Now it almost seems as though he was trying to warn me."

Lissa made a strangled noise. Pete kept silent.

Fully aware of how delusional she sounded, Randi plowed ahead. "If he hadn't leapt at me like that, if I hadn't jerked away, that bullet would've gone right through me."

Before Pete left, Randi contacted Sledge. She reached him at the base, assured him she was okay and confirmed that she'd sent him another e-mail detailing Pete's credentials.

She also confirmed that the sections of damaged C-130 skin had arrived from the Air Logistics Center in Georgia. Acting as a go-between, she negotiated a time on Saturday afternoon to bring Pete and his imaging equipment out to the base.

As anxious as she was to move forward with the inquiry, she realized what an inconvenience this would be for Pete.

"I'm sorry to screw with your schedule," she said as he pulled on his plaid wool jacket and prepared to rejoin his team. "You'll barely have started imaging the Heavener runes before you have to shut down and crate your equipment again."

"Not a problem. The team can use a few hours off. They've been hard at it nonstop for a week now."

His mind had obviously moved ahead to the

metals test. "Depending on the size of the sample, I'll have to shoot from a number of angles. It might take a while without Anne there to help."

Randi knew better than to offer her assistance. The test could hardly be considered objective or impartial if she participated in it.

"Are you sure you want to do this?" she asked as she walked him to the front door. "It's going to get you crosswise of Sam. Big-time."

"I'm sure."

That rifle shot this morning had shattered more than Pete's computer. It had also blown away any lingering doubts about conflict of interest.

Like Randi, he couldn't believe Sam Keane would take his vendetta so far as to try to physically harm her. Until Sheriff Jefferies ruled out that possibility, though, there was no question about where his loyalties lay.

"What time do you want me to pick you up on Saturday?"

"Better make it around noon."

"See you then."

He dropped a swift kiss on her lips. When he raised his head, concern added a gruff edge to his voice.

"Try to get some sleep tonight."

"I will."

Sleep proved all too elusive. The shooting dominated Randi's thoughts for the rest of the afternoon and well into the night. She lay awake in the darkness as the muted bong of the grandfather clock in the downstairs hall marked the hours. Outside, branches now almost denuded of leaves scratched against the house.

The familiar sounds had always soothed her. Tonight, she hardly heard them. Dismay knotted in her stomach whenever her mind strayed to those few seconds of alternate reality up there on the bluff. She couldn't just shrug off the incident. Or simply blame it on the stress of the inquiry and Sam's apparently relentless campaign.

She'd have to call Doc Russell tomorrow and tell him about the incident. She'd been a pilot too long to risk her safety and that of her crew by ignoring the episode. Suppose she blacked out again? Suppose it happened while she was at the controls?

Suppose it had happened before?

The knot in her stomach twisted tighter. The possibility that she'd flatly refused to give shape or credence to all day now pushed everything else aside and stomped around in her head.

What if it had happened high in the mountains of Afghanistan?

She clenched her fists under the covers. Sweat beaded her forehead as she relived those moments of sheer terror when she'd swooped in to pick up Ty and his crew, when small-arms fire and mortars were digging up big chunks of concrete and the emergency alerts on her console had lit up like Christmas lights.

What if she'd only *imagined* seeing Ty take a bullet? What if he'd never stumbled off the runway? Oh, God! What if he hadn't really triggered a land mine and been blown apart before her eyes?

Nausea rose in Randi's throat, hot and sour. Gagging, she leaped out of bed and dropped to her knees on the bathroom tiles. As sick at heart as she was to her stomach, she hugged the toilet and vomited until her throat was raw and she had nothing left to lose.

Except, she thought bleakly as she sank back on her heels, the last threads of her sanity.

18

Randi kept the fear that she was losing her grip on reality to herself as she got Spencer up and off to school Friday morning. She didn't even want to talk about it with Lissa, but her sister commented several times on the shadows under her eyes and offered her own interpretation of what had happened up on the bluff.

"You're just stressed. Who wouldn't be, after everything you went through in Afghanistan? Now this business with Sam…"

She followed Randi into the den and leaned against the corner of the desk while her sister searched through her Rolodex for the 137th's flight surgeon's phone number.

"Then there's Pete," Lissa pointed out. "You've gotten so involved with the professor and his project, you're probably seeing runic inscriptions on bathroom walls."

No, Randi countered silently. She'd seen her future on the bathroom wall and it had scared the crap out of her.

"You *want* Pete to date the runes," her sister continued with dogged determination. "You *want* him to accomplish what no one else has been able to. You want it so badly that you conjured up an image of the voyager who might've carved those symbols."

"He was real, Lis. Too real."

"C'mon, Randi! You and Ty used to go up to the bluff. I'll bet you both sketched pictures of Vikings in your heads." Her eyes widened with a sudden memory. "Didn't he once draw a picture of the ship they might've rowed up the Arkansas?"

"I don't remember that."

"I do! It had a tall, curving prow, a fat keel and rows of long oars." Her mind obviously churning, she poured out her ideas. "You said this image, this fierce warrior who leapt out at you, had blue eyes. *Ty* had blue eyes! Maybe you just got the two all mixed up in your head."

Wearily, Randi slumped back in her chair. "This character didn't look anything like Ty. His eyes were pale blue, almost pewter. This guys's were deeper, more like indigo. And they glowered at me as though...as though they were lit with blue fire."

"Like yours when you're royally pissed about something."

"Yeah, like mine."

"That just proves my point," Lissa insisted. "Everything's wrapped up together inside your head. You, Ty, Sam, Pete, the runestones, what happened in Afghanistan. They're all interwoven in your mind."

A mind that had short-circuited.

Maybe more than once.

Sick all over again at the possibility, Randi left a message for Doc Russell saying she'd be out at the base on Saturday afternoon and needed to talk to him if he was available.

With her stomach and her future in such turmoil, Randi had completely forgotten her vague promise to take Spencer on a visit to the Heavener site.

Unfortunately her son hadn't forgotten. The proposed excursion was the first thing that popped out of his mouth when Randi picked him and his best friend up at noon.

"Kin Joey go with us?" he asked as the boys scrambled into the backseat and buckled their seat belts.

"Go with us where?"

"To see Pete. 'Member? Pete said we should come watch him."

"We can't go this afternoon, Spencer."

"But Pete *wants* us to."

"I've got too much to do. Maybe next week."

Spencer didn't trust such vague promises. "You always say that. I want to go today."

The prospect of seeing those symbols start to swirl on a computer screen again made Randi's breath go shallow. She sent her son a firm glance via the rearview mirror.

"Next week. I promise."

"Joey wants to go today." A sneakered foot thumped the back of her seat. "I want to go!"

"Spencer…"

At the second thump, Randi's hands clenched on the steering wheel. "Kick my seat one more time, bud, and you'll be sorry."

"I bet Aunt Lis would take us. Kin I use your cell phone 'n ask her?"

"No."

"Why *not*?"

The whining scraped Randi's nerves raw. She could hardly explain her worry that one of the team might say something about yesterday's shooting. And she sure as hell wasn't going to tell a couple of impressionable four-year-olds about her out-of-body experience. Frazzled and frustrated, she resorted to the age-old response of harried parents.

"Because I said so!"

Spencer sulked until after they dropped Joey off at his house. Randi managed to coax him out of his bad mood with the shameless promise of a new video game. He jumped out of the car eagerly at Wal-Mart and picked the one he wanted. He was planning his conquest of Megazoid monsters when Randi drove them across the South Canadian.

Her gaze went to the stream spilling down the tumble of rocks that gave Morgan's Falls its name, then lifted to the house set high on the riverbank. She could see the shape of the original structure—the two-story rectangle, the flanking single-story wings. Added to and expanded over the years by successive generations of Morgans, the house commanded a sweeping view of the river and the rolling hills beyond.

Her family's home.

Her family's land.

Did Sam really intend to use Pete's study to back a bogus claim to either? He must know he couldn't win. Any more than he could make these allegations against her stick. Not with Sarah and Cal arguing her case. Not as long as Randi had a breath left to fight him.

Rounding the bend, she slowed for the entrance to the drive. The sight of a nondescript gray sedan parked by the mailbox generated a frown.

"Who's that?" Spencer asked, leaning forward to peer over the seat at the vehicle.

"I don't know."

She hoped to hell it wasn't another reporter. She

and Lissa had plastered No Trespassing signs all over the gate and fence to keep them out. Several white news vans had lingered for a day or so on the side of the state road, hoping to catch Randi coming or going.

The idea that some persistent reporter had returned to stake out her home riled Randi enough to bring her vehicle to a skidding halt.

"Wait here," she instructed her son.

As Randi strode toward the sedan, the driver squeezed out. Short and unbelievably squat, she had to weigh close to three hundred pounds, with frizzy blond hair and a roll of chins that jiggled when she waddled forward.

"Ms. Morgan?"

"Yes."

"Ms. Miranda Morgan?"

"What do you want?"

"I have a delivery for you." She held up a buff-colored envelope and a pen. "If you'll just sign here, indicating receipt...."

Frowning, Randi glanced at the official-looking envelope. It bore a return address of the Haskell County Courthouse.

"What is this?"

"It's a summons to a judicial hearing. I'm a process server appointed by the court to deliver it. Sign here, please."

Sam! It had to be Sam, launching his attack on her

property. He'd sworn he would bring her down, one way or another. Maybe that shot yesterday had been a warning, the opening round in a skirmish that was about to turn deadly.

If so, the man was in for the fight of his life!

Fury coiling in her gut, Randi snatched the pen and scribbled her name. The process server thanked her politely, handed her a copy of the receipt and wedged herself back in the car.

Randi ripped open the envelope and unfolded the single page it contained. The headers made no sense to her the first time she skimmed them.

Keane vs. Morgan. Family Court docket 763. Preliminary custody hearing scheduled for November 20th.

"Custody? Custody of what?"

Two lines later, shock jolted her back on her heels.

Her son! Sam was suing her for custody of her son!

Stunned, disbelieving, she read the justification Keane had cited in his petition to the court.

Abandonment occasioned by Captain Morgan's long absences in performance of her military duties. Her recent head trauma and accompanying incapacity. Sam's rights as a grandparent.

And there, in the last paragraph, a request for Captain Morgan to provide the court with a DNA sample of the minor child to confirm the claim put forth by Samuel H. Keane as to his legal rights over said Spencer Morgan.

"Son of a bitch!"

Randi crumpled the document in her fist. Fury exploded inside her, swift and all-consuming. Her grief for Ty, her guilt, her worry about the damned inquiry... Everything she'd carried inside her all these weeks went up in a searing fire burst of rage.

"You arrogant, malevolent son of a bitch!"

Three strides took her to her vehicle. Her entire body shaking with wrath, she shoved the key in the ignition and gunned the engine.

"What did that lady want?" Spencer asked as they rattled over the cattle guard and rocketed up the drive.

The question was scared and it penetrated Randi's seething fury. Her son's world had been turned upside down these past weeks, too. Not as violently as hers, but enough for him to know something was wrong.

Something *was* wrong, and she'd waited too damned long to put it right.

"That lady delivered a letter that made me angry," she admitted. She'd never lied to her son. The likes of Sam Keane weren't going to make her start now. "Very angry."

"Are you mad at me?"

"No, baby! No!"

She tore her eyes from the gravel drive and met his worried gaze in the rearview mirror. The uncertainty in his small face ripped a hole in her heart.

"I could never be mad at you. Irritated, maybe. Once in a while."

"Like when I kicked your seat?"

"Like when you kicked my seat."

"I'm sorry I did that."

"And I'm sorry I snapped at you."

She pulled up in front of the house, forcing herself to brake slowly, forcing her voice to suggest a calm she was nowhere close to feeling.

"I'll leave you here with Aunt Lissa while I go straighten the matter out. Then I won't be mad at anyone anymore. Okay?"

"Okay."

She left the car running while he hopped out, then followed him into the house. Absol was waiting to greet them, his body one ecstatic wag.

"Randi?" Lissa called from upstairs. "Is that you?"

"It's me."

"I'll be down in a few minutes. I'm putting some highlights in my hair."

"I have to go out for a little while, Lis. I'm leaving Spencer here with you."

She waded past boy and dog on her way to the front door again. Halfway there, she swung back.

"Go upstairs, Spencer. You and Absol. Show Aunt Lis your new video game. Maybe you can talk her into taking you on when she finishes her hair."

Impelled by the prospect of a no-holds-barred

battle, her son darted up the stairs. He was pleading with his aunt when Randi yanked her grandfather's brass-topped cane from the umbrella stand. He'd carved it himself from a knobby length of oak. It wasn't as lethal as the Winchester, but it packed a helluva punch.

She was at the front door when her sister appeared at the top of the stairs. A plastic cap covered her scalp. Long, glistening black strands poked through the plastic at closely spaced intervals.

"Hey, sis! Doc Russell returned your call. He's pulling a duty day tomorrow and can see you then if—" She stopped, staring at the cane Randi held like a club. "Where are you going with that?"

"To pay Sam Keane a visit. I figure it'll get his attention."

"Shit!" Her body taut with alarm, Lissa clattered down the stairs. "What's going on?"

"You're not s'posed to say shit," Spencer sang out from his room.

Randi yanked the crumpled letter from her pocket and tossed it to her sister. "This is what's going on."

She didn't wait for Lissa to read the document. Her fury was a cold, steady flame that left no room for reason, no time for arguments.

Sam maintained two residences, a sprawling pile of brick and marble columns on the shores of Kerr

Lake and the original family homestead up by oil-rich Bartlesville, near the border with Kansas. He also owned rental and investment properties scattered around the state, including a luxury golf villa in the ultra-exclusive Gallardia Country Club complex in north Oklahoma City.

Randi was fully prepared to hunt him from house to homestead to villa if necessary. The scattering of vehicles parked in the circular drive fronting the lake house told her she'd flushed her prey on the first attempt.

Barreling through the brick pillars framing the driveway entrance, she skidded to a stop. Once out of the driver's seat, she leaned through the open door and planted her fist on the horn.

The raucous blare brought a tall, spare woman in her mid-sixties out onto the columned portico. Sam's new housekeeper, Randi guessed, the latest in a long string hired after his wife passed away almost fifteen years ago. As Ty had often joked, his father paid his employees extremely well. He had to, to keep them in his employ for more than a month.

"Stop that noise!"

Randi let up on the horn and issued a terse order. "Tell Sam that Miranda Morgan wants to talk to him."

"You should've called for an appointment. Mr. Keane is in a meeting and—"

"Tell him!"

She slammed her fist back down and kept it on the horn. The housekeeper dithered for a moment, as if unsure whether to notify Sam or call the police, before retreating into the house.

When the front door opened again, a spear of pity pierced Randi's fury. Sam had lost a good ten or fifteen pounds in the weeks since Ty's funeral. Gaunt and haggard then, he now looked skeletal. His clothes hung loosely on a stooped frame that had once bristled with energy. His silver-tipped string tie circled a shirt collar that seemed several sizes too large.

The bitter tragedy of this confrontation ate at Randi's soul. She couldn't count the times this man had invited her to join him and Ty for lazy weekends on the water or jaunts up to Tulsa or Oklahoma City. She'd eaten so many meals in his home, turned to him for support and guidance when she lost her grandparents.

Randi should've been with him these past weeks. She should've wrapped her arms around his thin frame, held him tight, offered what solace she could as he struggled to deal with the death of his son. Instead she faced him across a gravel drive in a deadly duel for *her* son.

"You can't have him, Sam."

He didn't pretend to misunderstand her. "The hell I can't."

"I won't let you take him."

His lips curled back in a thin, bloodless smile. "You don't have the time, the money or the political savvy to stop me."

"Maybe not, but I have this."

She slid the knobby cane off the seat. Moving away from the door, she let him see it.

His death-head's smile didn't alter. "You swing that at me, Miranda, and you lose more than your boy."

"Maybe. Maybe not. Someone fired a shot at me yesterday."

"Jefferies told me. You think it was me?"

"I think Ty's death has pushed you over the edge," she returned with brutal honesty. "So when I come to see you, I carry something to protect myself."

"Something to use on me, you mean. You figure you can get away with killing me *and* my son?"

The viciousness of it hit Randi like a backhand to the face. She knew she couldn't reason with him, knew he was past heeding anything she said, but she had to make one final attempt.

"Listen to me, Sam. I loved Ty. All those years we went our separate ways and married the wrong people, I never stopped loving him. We both knew it wouldn't have worked between us, but that didn't change how we felt. Yes, we fought. Yes, we tore into each other the night before he died. Yet I risked the lives of my crew to go in after him."

"You left him." Hate bled through every syllable. "You left him to die."

"He was already dead when I left him, Sam. There's nothing you or I can do to bring him back. And I'm telling you to your face, I won't let you take my son and make him a substitute for the one you lost."

"Then you'd better raise that club and bash my head in, because that's just what I intend to do."

Randi's grip tightened on the heavy cane. The last remnants of reason battled with the blind, atavistic instincts of a mother protecting her child.

Always after, she would wonder how the showdown between her and Sam might have ended if a pickup hadn't careened past the brick pillars at that moment and screeched to a halt less than a yard away.

19

ϵ∞∞ϵ

Pete's pulse pounded as he slewed his pickup to a stop. It had been hammering in his ears ever since he'd flipped open his cell phone and heard Melissa Morgan's frantic voice.

Randi was on her way to Sam's place. The bastard was trying to take Spencer from her and she was out for blood.

She'd have to follow Route 9 west, then head north on 59. If Pete put his foot to the floor and raced up from Heavener, he might catch her before she reached Keane's lakeside residence. Lissa was bundling Spencer over to a neighbor's house and would follow.

Abandoning his startled team, Pete had barreled through the Oklahoma countryside and taken the turn onto the drive leading to Keane's place on two wheels. Relief had poured through him when he'd spotted Randi and her tormentor facing each other in the drive. Then he caught the gleam of brass glinting in afternoon sun.

His heart hammering against his ribs, he yanked at the door handle. Everything in him screamed that he should leap out and beat the shit out of Keane, but Randi came first. He had to make sure he didn't jump in with both feet and strike a spark that would ignite a dangerous situation.

Forcing himself to move with careful deliberation, he took the few steps necessary to put himself between Randi and Keane.

"Lissa called and told me you were headed this way."

A muscle quivered in the side of her jaw. "Did she tell you why?"

"Yes, she did."

Keeping himself squarely between the two combatants, Pete turned to face the hawk-faced oil magnate. Whatever pity he'd felt for the man's loss had long since evaporated.

"I'm terminating the runestone project, Keane. Right here, right now."

"The hell you say!"

"I told you I wouldn't be part of a vendetta against Randi."

Blood rushed into the old man's face. "You'd better think about what you're doing, Engstrom. Your bosses at OU won't appreciate hearing that you pissed a ten-million-dollar grant down the toilet."

No, they wouldn't. But all Pete had to do was look into Keane's hate-filled features to know he couldn't in good conscience continue. He'd scrape together another source of funding eventually. The riddle of the runes would have to wait until then.

"It's my project," he said curtly. "My process, my decision."

"You sure about that? I checked you out before I funded your study. You *and* your imaging process. You used university facilities to develop it. And I seem to recall yours isn't the only name on the provisional patent you filed to protect it. Ms. Gillette might have something to say about terminating the study."

Pete refused to argue. Right now, his number one priority was to get Randi off the premises before the situation went from bad to worse.

"It's my decision," he repeated flatly.

The red in Keane's face shaded to purple. Obviously, the billionaire wasn't used to having his wishes thwarted by lowly college professors.

"You're going to regret this, Engstrom." He threw Randi a look of loathing. "You *and* the bitch who has you thinking with your dick instead of your head. She's using you, Engstrom, just like she used my son."

"Fuck you, Sam!"

Randi's snarl provoked harsh laughter from Keane. "You won't have any idea what fucked is until I get done with you."

With another vicious glance in her direction, he spun on his boot heel and stalked into his house. Pete didn't unkink his muscles until the door banged shut.

"That was smart, Morgan. Real smart." Whirling, he grabbed the club from her slackened hold. "Get in your car."

"It isn't over between Sam and me."

"Get in your car."

Her blood was still up. Digging in, she refused to move.

"I'm telling you this isn't over! It won't end as long as Sam believes I left his son to die."

"And threatening him is going to convince him otherwise?"

The retort raised red flags in her cheeks.

"Okay, maybe I wasn't thinking straight by coming here like this, but—"

"You weren't thinking at all." Taking her elbow, he pulled her with him. "Now get in the car before Keane has you arrested for trespassing or attempted assault with a deadly weapon. Think how *that* would help your case."

The biting sarcasm got through to her. Or maybe the bruising grip on her arm. At this point, Pete didn't care which. Once in the driver's seat, she jerked the seat belt into place with an angry snap.

"Grief has twisted Sam's mind until there's nothing in it but hate."

"Yeah, I got that impression."

She stretched out a hand for the keys dangling from the ignition but didn't turn the engine over. Her gaze went to the columned portico a few yards away.

"He's tearing my life apart. Piece by piece."

The fire died, replaced by a fear she didn't try to disguise as she swung a tight, desperate face back to Pete. "Now he wants my son."

"No way is that going to happen, Randi."

"You don't know him! You don't know the kind of power he wields."

The anguish in her voice softened his. "I've had a good taste of it."

"I won't let him take Spencer. I'll do whatever's necessary to stop him."

"Christ! Don't say that around anyone else."

That she'd say it even to him made Pete realize just how close she was to falling apart.

"You need to talk to your sister and brother-in-law about this. Move over. I'll drive you home."

Shuddering, she made an effort to pull herself together. "I'm okay. You don't need to—"

"Move over!"

They spotted a Range Rover tearing toward them just a few miles from Sam's place.

"That's Lissa."

Pete slowed the Cherokee and flashed the lights to get the other driver's attention. Stomping on the brakes, Lissa stopped her car in midlane and whirred down the window.

She was wearing a plastic cap sprouting long strands several shades lighter than the rest of her hair. When she spotted her sister, relief spread across her face. In the next instant, fury replaced it.

"Dammit all to hell, Randi, you scared the crap out of me! Are you all right? Is she all right?" she fired at Pete when her sister didn't respond fast enough.

"She's okay."

"What about Sam Keane?"

"He's still alive."

"Well, thank God for that. Not that I wouldn't be thrilled to hear he'd keeled over from a heart attack, you understand. I just don't want Randi to be blamed for precipitating it."

"You and me both," Pete said tersely.

"So what happened?"

"We'll give you the details at the house. When we get there, by the way, one of you needs to contact your other sister and lawyer-in-law and advise them about the summons Randi got."

"Already done. Sarah can't take the baby out yet, but Cal's burning up the turnpike as we speak." She pulled out her cell phone and flipped up the cover. "I'll let him know he doesn't have to break the sound barrier to get here."

Randi leaned across Pete, her voice taut with worry. "Where's Spencer?"

"I dropped him off at Joey's. He's spending the night."

"I want him home. With me."

Pete figured that was probably a good idea. He was just beginning to understand the depths of Sam Keane's vindictiveness.

"We'll pick him up on the way back to Morgan's Falls," he said.

He put the Cherokee in gear again. Phone jammed to her ear, Lissa executed a U-turn and stayed on their bumper until the turnoff that led to Randi's nearest neighbor.

When Randi went into the house to collect her son, Pete put in a call to Jack Beasley. Jack wasn't happy about the team chief's sudden disappearance. Even less happy when Pete asked him to tell the rest of the crew that he was shutting down the project.

"Why, for God's sake?"

"I'll explain when I get back to the conference center. Just pack things up, will you? I'll meet you there."

Lissa and Absol met Randi and Pete at the door when they returned with Spencer a half hour later.

The plastic cap was gone. The overbleached strands weren't.

Eyes wide, Spencer forgot his vocal disappointment at being hauled away from a sleepover with his friend. "You look like a zebra, Aunt Lis."

"Thanks. That's exactly the effect I was trying for."

"Can you put stripes in my hair, too?"

"Sure."

"Over my dead body," Randi muttered as Absol barged into the hall to welcome Spencer home.

Boy and dog collapsed to the floor with a maximum of noise and a minimum of concern for inanimate objects in their immediate vicinity. Their antics relieved some of the tension gripping Pete and the two women.

It returned full force when Randi's brother-in-law stormed into the house. He banked his obvious anger, tossing his nephew into the air until the kid shrieked with delight, but let Randi have it with both barrels once she'd sent Spencer and Absol upstairs.

"Have you lost your mind?"

"Cal—"

"You must have, to charge into Keane's lair like that. What were you planning to do? Beat some sense into the old man?"

Conveniently ignoring the fact that she'd expressed exactly the same disgusted sentiments a short time ago, Lissa leaped to her sister's defense.

"Hey! Let's not forget someone took a potshot at Randi. That someone might've been Sam. She couldn't confront him without a little insurance."

"She shouldn't have confronted him at all!"

Cal's exasperated bellow boomed through the den. By contrast, Randi's response was flat and unrepentant.

"He's going after Spencer, Cal. I wanted to tell him in person that he's not getting him."

"Let me see the summons."

Taking off his cashmere overcoat, he turned to throw it across a chair and saw Pete for the first time.

"Who the hell are you?"

"Pete Engstrom."

"Randi's professor?"

"That's me."

Crossing the room, Pete held out his hand. The attorney gripped it, making an obvious effort to control his anger.

"Cal Howell," he said, giving Pete a thorough once-over. "Aren't you and your team supposed to be at Heavener? How did you get dragged into this?"

"Lissa called me."

"Heavener's only a few miles from Sam's place," she explained, "so I asked him to, uh, provide backup for Randi until I could get there."

"Backup?" Howell shook his head. "Christ!"

Both his expression and his attitude altered considerably as he skimmed the crumpled document Randi shoved into his hand.

"The sick, twisted son of a bitch!"

"Is that your considered legal opinion?" Lissa asked with a snide smirk. "Or do you now understand why Randi reacted the way she did?"

"Okay, okay. We can argue that she had more than sufficient justification for wanting to address this issue personally with Keane. We can also argue that she felt the club was necessary for self-protection."

"Forget the club." Randi's skin was stretched across her cheeks. "What about Sam's petition for custody?"

Howell's glance shot to Pete. Picking up on the unspoken question, Randi made a small, impatient motion with one hand.

"Pete knows about Ty and me. Just tell me, Cal! Does Sam have a chance in hell of getting custody of Spencer?"

"I didn't have time to do much research after Lissa's frantic call, you understand, but no, I don't think he has a chance in hell of getting custody of your son."

Randi closed her eyes. Lissa let her shoulders slump. Pete would've relaxed his rigid stance, too, if he hadn't noticed Howell's guarded expression.

"I don't know about you three, but I could use a

drink," the other man said. "How about you break out your granddad's favorite scotch, Lis, and we all sit down so we can talk our way through this."

Lissa rummaged around in the antique sideboard that served as a liquor cabinet and produced a dusty bottle. Pete recognized the black-and-gold label with a kick of anticipation. After the showdown at Keane's place, he could use a good, stiff wallop.

His first sip of single malt went down smooth and smoky. It also cleared his sinuses. Howell knocked back a long swallow and cut right to the chase.

"Most states, Oklahoma included, have enacted legislation that embodies strong preference for children to be presumed legitimate."

"Spencer *is* legitimate!" Randi said angrily. "I was married to Dave when I got pregnant. The fact that David never cared enough about his son to send even a birthday card doesn't alter that."

"Exactly. The law states that if a child is born to a married couple or within ten months of the end of a marriage by death or divorce, the child is presumed to be a product of that union. The statute goes on to say that if the child is raised by the husband and wife as the legitimate product of their marriage for a period of two years without either disputing the legitimacy, no one else can dispute it."

"David never questioned the fact that Spencer's his son."

"He didn't have any reason to," Lissa said. "Maybe because you never asked him for so much as a penny in child support. He was content to let you assume full responsibility for Spencer."

Randi waved that aside as unimportant, all her attention on her brother-in-law. "Sam must know what the law says."

"Of course he does. He also knows that the only people who can dispute the paternity of the child within that two-year period are the husband, the wife and the putative father or their descendants."

"Descendants?" She picked up on the significance of that immediately. "Not parents?"

"Right. The law allows for possible estate claims by the children themselves, but for obvious reasons that provision is rarely exercised."

"So Sam has no legal basis for this custody suit?" Randi hunched forward, her knuckles white as she clamped her hands around the heavy crystal highball glass. "This petition is just another form of harassment?"

Howell's eyes met hers across the coffee table. "I'm guessing that he's basing his suit on that damned letter. Since Ty expressed a wish that his father look after you and Spencer, Sam could claim it was his son's de facto attempt to assert his paternity."

"But he didn't do it within the first two years."

"That, of course, will be our main argument.

There's plenty of case law to back us up. This other business, though..."

Frowning, he smoothed out the summons.

"This charge of abandonment and neglect pursuant to your military duties is way outside my area of expertise. I'll have to research your rights under the law while performing military service."

"Start with the Soldiers and Sailors Civil Relief Act," Pete suggested, his eyes on Randi's tight, angry face.

"I'm familiar with the basic provisions of the SSCRA," Howell said slowly, "but I'm not sure how it applies in this instance."

"I'm not sure, either," Pete admitted. "I do know a buddy of mine in the Corps got slapped with a divorce petition while we were pulling a six-month Med cruise aboard the *USS Eisenhower.* The JAG helped him frame a response, citing the Soldiers and Sailors Civil Relief Act as reason to delay in civil court proceedings until he could be present to defend himself. According to the JAG, it's a pretty powerful piece of legislation."

"He's right," Randi said. "The act protects all active-duty military personnel and members of the national guard when we're activated for federal service."

"Protects you how?"

"I'm only familiar with certain provisions. Reduced interest rates on debts if we're called up for extended periods and lose our civilian income. Cancellation of leases. Guaranteed job reinstatement. Things like that."

A savage determination replaced the desperation in her blue eyes.

"But I have a friend, another female officer at the 137th. Janice got into a knockdown drag-out with her former husband for custody of their kids a few years back. I'll bet she could provide plenty of ammunition for us."

"I'll take any help I can get. I'll also take this back to Tulsa with me." Folding the summons, Cal tucked it in his suit pocket and shifted gears. "You're all set for the test at the base tomorrow, right?"

"We're set," Pete confirmed.

Rising, Cal thrust out his hand again. "Call or fax me with the results as soon as you have them."

He hugged both sisters-in-law and gave Randi a last piece of advice.

"For God's sake, don't go off half-cocked again! Sarah and I have enough on our plate right now without defending you against a charge of communicating a threat."

She grimaced but made no promises. Noting that omission, Pete formulated a swift change of plans.

"How about you drive me back to pick up my truck?" he asked Lissa.

"Sure. I'll get a jacket."

In her absence, he announced his intentions to Randi. "I have to tell my team what's happened. Then I'll be back."

"I'm okay. There's no need for you to make another trip to Morgan's Falls."

"Yeah, there is. I'm camping out here tonight. Tomorrow, we'll drive over to Oklahoma City together."

"Are you appointing yourself my bodyguard? Or are you worried I'll do something stupid? *Another* something stupid," she amended with a wry smile.

He could only imagine what that wobbly grin cost her. She was under attack from all sides. She faced losing everything she held dear, including her son. Anyone else would have cracked under the pressure.

Aching for this tough, resilient woman, he cradled her face in his hands. "Let's just say I'm hoping we find some time to *both* do something stupid."

20

Pete found his team huddled over coffee mugs in the conference center's rustic dining room. Raynard and Pauline Lockwood watched his approach with expressions that hovered between disappointment and disapproval. Slouched in the chair opposite a scowling Jack Beasley, Brady played with the ends of his hair.

Anne wasn't back yet, Pete saw. He'd have to call her after he contacted his boss. He didn't look forward to either conversation.

Beasley spoke up first. Tugging angrily on his beard, he glowered at Pete. "What the hell's going on? Why did you shut us down?"

"I met with Sam Keane this afternoon. Turns out he and I have a fundamental disagreement over his reasons for funding this project."

"What difference does it make *why* he funded it? The point is, we're on the verge of something really important here, something that'll contribute immeasurably to scientific and historical knowledge."

"I won't allow anyone to use me or my work to cause harm, which is what Keane intends. I'm sorry, folks, but this project is finished. You'll be fully recompensed for your time and travel expenses."

Raynard puffed out his chubby cheeks. "This is too bad, Peter. We have collected so much data." Shrugging, he tried to make the best of things. "Ah, well, I have had a visit to your beautiful Oklahoma, *ja?* And we can write up our findings to date. Publish them in the journals."

Beasley snorted. "What findings? We matched one rune. One. To an amulet we haven't yet authenticated."

"Then we must authenticate it," Raynard insisted. "Or image the last rune up on the bluff to see if it is also a match, as we suspect."

His accent thickening, the Norwegian made an urgent appeal to Pete. "You could image it. You and Miranda, since the rest of the team is disbanding. She knows what we do. She would assist you."

"She would, if I asked her. But I won't. She's got more serious matters on her mind right now."

"Later, then, after these matters are resolved. And when you image that symbol and run it against the others, you will share the results with us, *ja?*"

"Of course." Pete drew a hand through his hair, hating to pull the rug out from under them. "Look, I'm sorry about this. Really sorry. I've got to let my boss know we've shut down, then I'll get back to you about travel arrangements."

"I'll take care of my own arrangements," Beasley snapped. "I'll be on a flight back to Chicago tomorrow morning."

It was a sad breakup for a team that had come together with such enthusiasm. Pete left them stewing about the abrupt termination and went to give his boss the bad news.

Dr. Bruhn's secretary informed him the head of the physics department had already departed for the weekend.

"His niece in California is getting married tomorrow. He should be somewhere in the air over Arizona right now."

"When he calls in, tell him I need to speak with him."

"Will do, Dr. Engstrom."

Unlike Bruhn, Anne was immediately available. She answered her cell phone on the first ring and recognized from caller ID who was on the other end.

"Hi, Pete."

"Hi, Anne. How's your dad?"

"Good. Fine, in fact. He did have a stroke, but not nearly as bad as we'd feared. I'm loading up to drive back as we speak."

"No need to rush."

"Of course there is! This project is as important to me as it is to you."

"I've shut the project down."

"*What?*"

"I saw Sam Keane this afternoon. It wasn't a friendly meeting."

A stark silence stretched for several seconds. Anne broke it with a short, vicious curse.

"Where are you?" she demanded.

"At the conference center."

"I'll be there in less than an hour."

"I won't be here. I'm checking out. I'll pack up most of the equipment and take it with me. Brady can take the rest back to OU."

Pete had already made a mental inventory of what he'd need at the base tomorrow. The platform-mounted cameras, certainly. His backup computer. The disk containing the image he'd shot of the twisted section of aircraft skin Randi's crew had presented to her. The spare lenses and notch filters.

While his mind focused on the project ahead, he slammed the lid on the one he'd just terminated.

"I'll see you at OU on Monday, Anne."

"Pete! Wait!"

"We'll talk then."

It was well past six by the time Pete had sorted through the equipment, loaded what he needed into his pickup and made the drive back to Morgan's Falls.

A fat harvest moon rode high when he bumped across the cattle guard. Light spilled from the windows of the house like beacons in the frosty night. A crazy sense of homecoming struck him even before the front door opened and Absol bounded out to greet him.

But it was the woman silhouetted in the doorway who drew him like a bright steady flame on a winter night. Her hair was down and loose around her shoulders, a tumble of gleaming black that made Pete want to bury his fists in its silky mass.

He managed to restrain himself when he went inside, but the urge stayed with him through a dinner enlivened by Spencer's demand that Pete make good on his promise to teach him more tricks.

It was still with him long after Randi had put her protesting son to bed. It took on a sharp urgency when Lissa announced her intention of calling it a night and startled the heck out of Pete by wrapping him in a fierce hug.

"Thanks for charging to the rescue today. Thanks for *everything* you're doing to help my sister."

He smiled across her zebra stripes at the sister under discussion. "She's worth it."

"And then some!"

With a good-night for Randi, she went upstairs. Randi had made up a guest room for Pete but neither of them was ready to sleep. Pete settled on the worn leather sofa and stretched his legs toward the logs smoldering in the massive stone fireplace. Sinking down beside him, Randi tucked her feet under her. "It sounds really stupid and inadequate, but all I can say is thank you."

"I'm not looking for thanks from you."

Those blue eyes held his. "What *are* you looking for?"

It was becoming clearer to him by the moment that he wanted everything Miranda Morgan had to give. This wasn't the time to tell her that. She had enough to deal with right now.

"Sex would be good," he said. "Sex would be *very* good. But I'll settle for just holding you for a while."

She made a face but went into his arms with only a token protest.

She was still there when Absol poked his nose in Pete's face the next morning. That jerked him out of a sound sleep.

Thankfully, the violent start didn't disturb Randi. She'd dozed off just minutes after snuggling against his chest last night. Soon after that, she'd sunk into total unconsciousness. She hadn't stirred when Pete had nestled her against him and reached for a crocheted throw. Nor did she twitch now, despite the dog breathing in her face.

"Get away." Pete deflected the massive muzzle. "Let her sleep."

Easing Randi's weight onto the cushions, he tucked the throw around her. A couple of stretches unkinked his muscles. A walk with Absol in the cold, clear dawn recharged his brain. Luckily, he'd brought his shaving kit and overnight bag the night before.

He'd downed two cups of coffee and had dished up a short stack for Spencer when Lissa staggered into the kitchen.

"Caffeine. I need caffeine."

She gulped down a life-giving cup before helping herself from Spencer's plate.

"Hey! Get your own, Aunt Lis."

"Selfish little brat."

Ignoring Spencer's protests, she speared a second morsel dripping with syrup. Pete averted a squabble by sliding another stack her way. Between bites, she eyed him hopefully.

"You don't happen to have any unmarried brothers, do you?"

"Sorry."

"Male cousins?"

"One," he said with a grin, "in Vancouver."

"Hmm. When things settle down around here, I might just have to arrange a business trip to Canada."

"*If* things ever settle down around here," Randi said from the doorway.

With her eyes sleepy, her hair in wild tangles and

her shirttails hanging out of her jeans, she looked like a woman who'd spent the night somewhere other than her bed. A fact that didn't go unnoticed by Lissa. Or Spencer.

"I saw you on the couch when I came downstairs," the boy announced, "but Pete said I shouldn't wake you up. Why didn't you tell me you 'n him were having a sleepover?"

"Out of the mouths of babes," Lissa murmured with a gleeful grin. "Let's see how you handle this one."

"We didn't know we were having a sleepover." Refusing to meet her sister's eyes, Randi aimed for the coffeemaker. "Pete's driving in to the base with me this afternoon, so we decided it would be easier for him to spend last night here."

"Can he stay tonight, too?" Wiggling around, Spencer appealed directly to the source. "Can you, Pete?"

"Depends on what happens this afternoon. The tests I'm running will take a while. Your mom and I might have to remain in Oklahoma City tonight and finish up tomorrow morning."

That was news to Randi. She sent him a questioning look and got a shrug in reply.

"Better pack a toothbrush."

Randi packed more than a toothbrush. She packed a complete set of civilian clothes before zipping herself into her working uniform.

Her *stateside* working uniform, she explained to Pete when he looked over the gray-green flight suit, brown leather bomber jacket and flight cap with the dual silver tracks denoting her captain's rank.

"We wore tans at K-2. Tan flight suit, tan T-shirts, tan everything. Made for great camouflage while we were on the ground."

Pete was in his working uniform, too. Randi had grown used to seeing him in jeans and boots, but in keeping with his role as her "outside expert," he'd added a white button-down oxford shirt, navy tie and rust-colored tweed jacket. With his broad shoulders and thick brown hair shot with red, he certainly didn't resemble any professor she'd ever taken classes with.

Tossing her overnight bag in the backseat of his pickup, she used the long drive to Oklahoma City to fill him in on the organization and operation of the 137th Wing.

"You won't see much activity on base today, since it's not a drill weekend. Plus, we still have four birds at K-2, along with their aircrews and support personnel."

Sure enough, the base looked deserted to Randi once security had cleared them through the gate. A few vehicles were parked outside the Comm center, dining facility and headquarters building. The bay doors on the fire station were raised for instant egress by crash vehicles, but only three C-130s squatted on the parking apron. Another, Randi saw, was shooting touch-and-goes.

Following her directions, Pete parked in a visitor's slot in front of the Operations Building.

"Sledge said he'd get you access to the flightline. I'll go see if he's taken care of it."

Pete used the few moments while Randi was gone to get his bearings. The base looked a lot like others he'd passed through during his stint in the marines, only smaller and neater. He'd never worked closely with national guard personnel during his time in uniform. But he understood that, unlike members of the active-duty forces, they tended to remain in for the long haul. Men and women joined units near their homes, spent twenty or thirty years in that squadron or wing, and were generally experts at what they did.

The fact that he'd be dealing with extremely knowledgeable people was forefront in his mind when Randi reappeared with another officer in tow. Pete understood how the military operated. Allegations as serious as the ones Sam Keane had made against Randi demanded a full and thorough investigation. That didn't mean he had to like the officer appointed to conduct that investigation.

Shores surprised him, however. Tall, lean, with a jaw like a diesel locomotive, he didn't come across as a man with a hard-on for either his rank or his assigned task.

"Alex Shores." He returned Pete's shake with a no-nonsense grip. "I've had your vehicle cleared for access to the flight line, Dr. Engstrom. Put this in the windshield, please, and follow me."

With the pass prominently displayed on the dash, Pete started the ignition. He studied the other man as he folded himself into a red Camaro that had been polished to a bright, loving sheen.

"So that's your Sledgehammer."

"That's him."

"What does he do in civilian life?"

"He and his father own Shores Construction. They specialize in big-dollar asphalt and concrete projects. Roads, runways, bridges, stuff like that."

Pete relaxed by a few degrees. Shores understood the laws of physics and worked with them every day—both as a pilot and a construction engineer. He should be able to understand the comparative analysis process.

Trailing the Camaro, Pete passed through the entrance to the flight line and parked in a space outside the hangar. When he and Randi entered the cavernous building, Shores led them to the section of fuselage he'd had shipped in. It had been placed across a maintenance stand, exposing the jagged tear in its skin.

"This is a section from the right aft fuselage of a C-130 assigned to the Alaskan Air Guard," Shores said. "They fly the H models, same as we do. This particular bird got ripped all to hell when it skidded off the end of a runway at Bagram and triggered a fragmentation mine."

"Did they document the make of the mine?"

"A 1980s vintage Soviet POM-Z-2."

Pete had done considerable research on antipersonnel mines in the past few days. If he remembered correctly, the POM-Z-2 was the most common fragmentation mine sowed by the Soviets in their ten-year struggle with the Afghanis. It was also the most deadly, killing the majority of victims instantly.

Pete's pulse accelerated. He had a section of damaged skin from Randi's aircraft. He had a section from another C-130 pierced by fragments from a documented antipersonnel device. If he could demonstrate that the damage patterns showed similar blast effect characteristics, Randi would have hard physical evidence to support her assertion that Captain Ty Keane had triggered a lethal explosion.

"How about giving me a hand with my equipment?" he asked Shores. "I want to get to work."

Randi hated standing on the sidelines. Always before, Pete had integrated her into his team and put her to work. Now all she could do was stay out of the way while Sledge and several maintenance personnel helped carry in and set up the equipment.

She wasn't surprised when others drifted in to join the small group in the hangar. An aircrew checking out the status of their aircraft. A two-man security patrol. The chief of maintenance.

Word of the test would have spread. The 137th was a tight-knit family despite—or maybe because of—its demanding state and federal missions. Farmers and asphalt contractors and weather forecasters who might never bump into each other under ordinary circumstances reported for duty and melded into a highly trained, highly skilled military unit.

One of their own had died on a remote airfield in the Afghan mountains. Another now had to answer for his death. Whatever their personal opinions on the matter, these men and women wanted the truth as much as Randi did.

"Hey, Morgan. We just got down. How's the test going?"

Janice Overton threaded her way through the small crowd. Her copilot, flight engineer and loadmaster came with her. They'd flown a training flight this morning, as Randi knew from the call she'd made last night to her friend and fellow pilot.

"They're still getting set up." She pulled her attention away from the small group at the center of the drama. "You sure you don't mind if I swing by your house later and talk to you about the custody battle your ex put you through?"

"The battle he's *still* putting me through." Disgust contorted the former Miss Oklahoma's flawless features. "The prick found out that Kevin's been deployed and is making noises about taking me back to court. He says he doesn't think I can handle our three kids, Kevin's two, my military duties and six tanning salons, but I know he's just angling for me to agree to a decrease in child support. Like *that's* going to happen!"

Randi desperately wanted details, but Pete had his cameras mounted and was detailing the process to Sledge and the chief of maintenance.

"Come by the house around seven," Janice suggested. "I have to check the tanning beds at one of my salons after I leave the base, but I'll be home by then. Uh-oh. Look who's here."

Randi swung around just as the 137th Wing commander strode into the hangar. With him, she saw with a sudden thump of her heart, was Doc Russell.

As Sledge introduced Pete to the newcomers, she realized the key players who'd decide her future had assembled in this hangar. The inquiry officer who would recommend whether formal charges should be preferred against her. The colonel with the authority to bring those charges. The doc who might or might not return her to flight status when she told him about the incident up on the bluff. The fellow pilot whose vicious custody battle with her ex could give Randi fodder for her own pending battle with Sam.

And Pete, who'd put his job and his reputation

on the line for her. Whatever the outcome, whatever the results, she loved him for that.

No, she thought with a sudden jolt.

She loved him.

Period.

No caveats. No qualifications.

The man had walked into her life mere weeks ago, and now she couldn't imagine it without him. The realization flooded through Randi's veins with a hot rush. She let the warmth spread, let herself savor the unexpected and completely irrational sensation, as Pete explained his holographic imaging process.

The colonel absorbed the specifics of axial transmissive spectrographs. Brow furrowed, he listened intently while Pete described his approach to comparative analysis.

"I'll shoot the rupture from several angles to create three-dimensional images of every jagged inch. The computer will capture data on the angle, the depth and the thickness of the tears. Once the data's recorded, I can calculate the average, minimum, maximum and standard deviation for each variable. Then I'll compare the results to the data extracted from the images I've made of this."

Pete set the small, square trophy from Randi's crew on the maintenance stand, in full view of everyone in the hangar. The twisted metal shards constituted a vicious reminder that this wasn't some abstract scientific experiment. This was harsh, unforgiving reality.

21

"Pete got three perfect matches, Lis! Okay, not perfect but well within the standard deviation."

Excitement and relief pouring out of her, Randi jammed her cell phone to her ear. A crowd was still clustered around the colorful display on Pete's laptop, but she couldn't wait to report the results. Her first call had been to Sarah and Cal, who'd whooped at the news. The call to Lissa had her sister doing a happy dance. Randi could hear her banging pots and thumping walls as she waltzed around the kitchen.

"Does that mean this friggin' inquiry is over?" Lissa wanted to know when she finished her celebratory waltz.

"Not yet. Sledge still has to compare these test results with the additional data Warner Robbins supplied. But we're three giant steps closer."

"You tell Major Shores he'd better get his ass in gear or I'll take three giant bites out of it."

"Right," Randi drawled as the officer in question broke away from the crowd and headed in her direction. "I'll be sure to give him the message."

"You do that. Oh, and tell Pete a woman stopped by here looking for him. Anne Gillette, I think she said her name was."

"Tall? Gorgeous? Blond?"

"That's her. She said she's been trying to get in touch with him all afternoon and hasn't been able to reach him on his cell phone."

"I'll pass the word."

"You might also tell him she didn't sound happy."

"I will. And Lissa…"

"Yes?"

With Sledge just a few feet away she couldn't tell her sister how much she appreciated her support and unquestioning loyalty.

"Thanks again. For everything."

"You're welcome. Again. See you soon."

"We'll be late," Randi warned. "If we get back there at all tonight. I'm seeing Janice later to talk about custody issues."

"Well, I hope you do more than talk this evening! You should celebrate with a fat, juicy steak, a bottle of vintage merlot, and the professor. Not necessarily in that order."

"I'll think about it. Talk to you later, Lis."

"Your sister?" Sledge asked when Randi snapped the lid on her cell phone.

"Yes. She asked me to pass you a message. You want the sanitized version?"

"Give it to me straight."

"She suggested you get your butt in gear and wrap up this inquiry or she'd take a bite out of it. Your butt, not the report."

"I plan to write up my findings tonight. I have to run them by the JAG, but should be able to fax you and your attorneys a copy on Monday."

He had to play by the rules. Randi understood that. She wasn't expecting assurances at this point and he didn't give them. But she read the message in his eyes and felt a deadweight roll off her back.

While she was dragging in her first full breath in what felt like months, Sledge raised a brow. "Think that's slow enough to provoke your sister into following through with her threat?"

"Could be."

His cheeks creased in a flinty smile. "Now I have something to look forward to." He tipped her a two-fingered salute and walked away.

Randi kept her jaw from dropping. Was he thinking of going after Lissa? Now, *that* would be worth buying ringside seats for.

Torn between surprise and relief that one ordeal, at least, was almost over, she approached the flight surgeon, who was still studying the vivid imagery on Pete's laptop.

"I need to talk to you, Doc. Got a few minutes?"

"Sure. Chief, mind if Captain Morgan and I use your office?"

The NCO in charge of maintenance had no objections. Pete caught Randi's signal that she'd be right back and nodded.

With Russell perched on a corner of the chief's desk, Randi closed the door and rubbed her palms together. She hated to admit she'd lost touch with reality up there on the bluff. Hated even more that those terrifying seconds could keep her from ever climbing into a cockpit again.

"I blacked out, Doc."

His chin jerked up. "When?"

"A few days ago."

"How long were you out?"

"Two seconds. Maybe three."

She rubbed her hands together again. Her palms were already damp. The euphoria of a few minutes ago was gone.

"I didn't lose consciousness," she said slowly. "Just my grip on reality."

"Tell me exactly what happened."

Randi related every detail. The dull ache she'd woken up with that morning. The bone-jarring ATV ride up to the bluff. The hours of intense concentration. The extra-strength Tylenol Raynard had given her. The whirling images on the computer screen.

"They made me dizzy."

"Understandable," the doc said, relaxing. "I got a little dizzy watching the demo this afternoon, too."

"But a Viking didn't jump out of the computer at you, did he?"

"Uh, no."

"That's what happened to me."

She cringed at the admission. It sounded even more delusional here in this office, surrounded by charts listing the maintenance status of the wing's aircraft, than it had in the privacy of her own home.

"They were talking about this warrior," she said. "This Bjorn Strong Arm. Raynard—a Norwegian historian on Pete's team—got all excited and described the guy in such detail I could almost see him. Then," she said with an embarrassed shrug, "I *did* see him."

He was inside her head now. Sword raised. White-blond hair streaming. Eyes fierce blue flames.

Swallowing, Randi managed to continue. "He leaped off the computer screen and lunged right at me. He was so real, so damned terrifying that I stumbled back. Good thing," she added with a grimace, "since someone fired off a round about that time. It missed me, but the computer took a direct hit."

"What!"

"The sheriff thinks it was most likely a stray shot from a hunter."

No need to share her suspicion that Sam might have been behind it. She didn't have proof and didn't want to complicate the issue she'd just dumped in the doc's lap.

"Okay," he said after a brief pause. "Let's review the situation. You're recovering from a head trauma. You're under considerable stress. From what you've told me, you're also up to your ears in a project connected with dating these ancient runes. You stare into a computer screen for several hours, your head pounding, and see—or think you see—a prehistoric warrior."

"A Viking."

"A Viking."

"He was real to me, Doc."

"I believe you. I also believe that everything you've gone through these past months collided for a few seconds inside your head."

"That's what my sister said."

Randi wanted to believe that was it. That the powerful forces affecting her world had converged for those few, startling seconds. God, she wanted to believe grief and guilt and stress hadn't pushed her over the edge!

"We'll run another MRI," Russell said briskly. "We'll also schedule an appointment with a psychiatrist. But based on what you told me here, I don't see a serious problem. You didn't black out completely. You didn't keel over. You didn't lose your grasp on what was happening around you. On the contrary, your instincts and reflexes operated at such superb efficiency that you dodged a stray bullet."

Randi knew she wasn't home free, but the tight ball of worry she'd carried around since the incident up on the bluff diminished by measurable degrees.

"Thanks, Doc. I'll sleep a little easier tonight."

A *lot* easier, she reflected as she rejoined Pete. If she slept at all. Lissa's suggestion of a night on the town with the professor was sounding better and better.

Pete and a crew of volunteers had loaded his equipment, and he was waiting for Randi beside his pickup. "You still need to talk to your friend about the custody suit?"

"I do. She lives on the south side, just past 104th and South Penn. She said she'd be home around seven, so I figured we could grab something to eat before we swing by her house. We can head back to Morgan's Falls from there. Or not," she added, remembering the toothbrush she'd packed.

Evidently Pete was remembering it, too. With a wolfish grin, he slid the key into the ignition.

"I vote for not."

Randi's stomach tightened at the prospect of a whole night with this man.

"You said your friend lives on the south side," Pete commented as they left the base. "How about we stay at my place in Norman tonight? It's only a few miles further down I-35."

As exciting as the idea of spending the night with Pete was, the chance to look around his home tugged at something deep and visceral in Randi. She'd seen him immersed in his work. Watched him load a Winchester and pump three warning shots into the air with blinding speed. Witnessed his icy calm when he stepped between her and Sam.

Now she'd get a glimpse of his private, personal side. Intensely curious, she wanted to know his tastes in music, in art, in books, in furniture, in breakfast cereal.

"Your place sounds good."

"Be nice to me," he teased, "and I'll take you to the lab tomorrow. Show you where I spend all my days and most of my nights."

She intended to be nice to him. Very nice. But the reference to his lab sparked the memory of a belated message.

"Oh, I forgot! Lissa said Anne Gillette stopped by the house this morning, looking for you. She's been trying to reach you."

Frowning, Pete fished his cell phone from his pocket.

"Well, hell. The battery's dead. I've probably got several calls from the head of the physics department on there, too. I left him a message about shutting down the study."

When he dropped the phone into a cup holder, Randi slanted him a curious glance.

"Aren't you going to charge it and return the calls?"

"Nope. I'm not in the mood for a knockdown drag-out with either of them tonight."

Janice Overton and the Delta pilot she'd married some years after her messy divorce lived in a gated community that catered to young professionals. The houses were all brick, all beautifully landscaped and all pricey.

If the outside of her home was a serene blend of lawn and French-country architecture, the inside was semicontrolled chaos. Between them, Janice and Kevin had five kids, two dogs, a raucous mynah bird and video game paraphernalia attached to every TV in the house.

The video boxes were in use when Janice ushered Pete and Randi inside. So were the pool and air hockey tables in the game room.

"Sorry," Janice said over the electronic chorus and clack of balls. "The kids all have friends over for the weekend."

"This is Pete Engstrom, Jan. You saw him in action this afternoon."

"Yes, I did."

Ignoring the hand Pete held out, she went up on tiptoe and landed a smacking kiss on his cheek.

"That's for helping Randi fight Sam Keane's ridiculous allegations. All of us in the wing want this damned inquiry over and done with."

No more than Randi did. But with that battle almost behind her, she had to suit up for the next.

"Where can we talk, Jan?"

"In the kitchen. How about a beer while we're at it?"

"Sounds good to me," Pete said.

"Me, too!" a lanky teen called from the game room.

"In your dreams," his mother retorted.

Still in her uniform, Janice led them into the kitchen and shoved a pile of pizza cartons to one side of the cluttered counter. She supplied her visitors with longnecks and frosted mugs, then poured a foaming mug for herself.

"Okay," she said after a satisfying pull, "what's all this about a custody suit? Why's your ex trying to get Spencer after all these years?"

"He isn't. Sam Keane is."

Janice lowered her mug. "Well, hell!"

"That pretty well sums up how I feel about it, too."

The blonde's glance slid to Pete, then back to Randi. She didn't ask the obvious question, namely

Sam's grounds for asserting a claim to Randi's son. She knew her friend's history with Captain Ty Keane.

"In his petition for custody, Sam cited my frequent absences due to military duties. He's alleging that I neglected Spencer by palming him off on friends and relatives during drill weekends." Despite her best efforts, anger and bitterness seeped into Randi's voice. "He's also alleging I abandoned my son to pull that six-month rotation in Afghanistan."

She'd hoped Janice would flare up again, tell her the old geezer didn't have a leg to stand on. Dread curled in her stomach when her friend frowned and fingered the dew-streaked beer bottle.

"The prick I was married to tried that on me, too. He told the judge about the weekend my mom couldn't make it up here and I had to dump the girls at the salon where I worked at the time. Sandi, the attendant in charge, let them fool around with the tanning beds. Unfortunately, she got busy and my youngest daughter fried to a crisp."

Her neat, oval-shaped nail picked at the label on the soggy bottle.

"I almost gave up flying at that point, Randi. I needed the supplemental income desperately, but if it had come down to a choice between the girls and the guard... If it *ever* comes down to a choice between them and the guard, I'd hang up my uniform in a heartbeat."

So would Randi. Her son was the center of her universe. Her desire to serve her country, to employ the skills she'd acquired through years of training and experience, didn't count for squat compared to Spencer's future.

The problem was, he wouldn't *have* the kind of future she wanted for him if men and women in uniform didn't step forward to defend his freedoms. It was an age-old dilemma, one every military member confronted.

"The way I saw it," Janice said, echoing Randi's thoughts, "I didn't think I should have to choose between my family and my country. Men don't. People praise them for their noble sacrifice and offer all kinds of support when they march off to war. When a woman marches off, the arch conservatives trot out all the females-don't-belong-on-the-battlefield arguments. Particularly if the female's a single mom."

"So how did you fight them?"

"My lawyer and I managed to convince the judge that it was unfair to apply one set of standards to me, another to the male of the species. He cited every case he could dig up where the law afforded servicemen various protections while on active duty."

"That's what Sarah and Cal and I want to do, too. Could you put us in contact with your lawyer?"

"Sure. And I'll make you copies of the petitions he flooded family court with. I've got a whole drawer full of them upstairs. But…well…"

Wrinkling her forehead, she peeled off another strip of wet label.

"But what, Jan?"

"I don't see how any judge would even consider Sam's custody suit unless Keane can prove his son fathered yours."

"He's asked the court to require a DNA test."

"Are you going to let that happen?"

"When shit rolls uphill."

With Janice feeding her documents, Randi burned up the copier in the upstairs home office while Pete engaged Jan's noisy tribe in a no-holds-barred air hockey duel.

Her friend hadn't exaggerated. Her lawyer had indeed inundated family court with counterpetitions citing legislation and case law detailing the rights of custodial parents. The Soldiers and Sailors Civil Relief Act of 1940 popped up frequently. The bits and pieces Randi was able to skim as she ran them through the copy machine gave her hope she'd win this battle against Sam, too.

The thought buoyed her. Almost as much as the hope that she'd nearly put the nightmare of the inquiry behind her. She was still riding a crest of optimism when Pete turned into the driveway of a neat, fifties-era bungalow a few blocks from the University of Oklahoma.

So high a crest she forgot her curiosity about the house and what it would tell her about the man who occupied it. Poking around could come later, she decided as the door clicked shut behind them.

"It's not much," he said, tossing his keys onto a coffee table stacked with books and scientific journals, "but it's home. Want the five-dollar tour?"

"What do I get for a dollar?"

"Your choice. Kitchen or bedroom."

"Bedroom. First, though, I have to tell you something."

It was harder to put her feelings into words than she'd expected. Sliding her palms under the lapels of his tweed sport coat, she rested them on his chest.

"I want you to know that whatever happens between us tonight has nothing to do with gratitude."

"Didn't we have this conversation last night?" he asked, tugging the zipper on her leather jacket. "I told you then that I'm not asking for gratitude from you."

"As I recall, you said you wanted sex."

"I did. I do." He got the jacket off and started on the front zipper of her flight suit. "I also want everything else you're willing to give me."

"Everything?"

"Everything."

"Does that include, oh, I don't know. Love, maybe?"

"Love is good." He bent to nuzzle her neck. "Almost as good as sex."

"Pete, I'm serious."

"So am I."

His breath was hot against her skin. His hands were busy peeling her flight suit off her shoulders.

"Hey! Professor Engstrom! I'm trying to tell you I'm in love with you."

"That's nice to know, since I'm pretty sure I'm in love with you, too."

"You are?"

Surprise held her motionless. Pete, on the other hand, kept moving.

"Since when?" she asked as he nuzzled her neck.

He nipped at the cords in her throat and raised his head. "You want a date? A specific hour?"

"Just a rough approximation."

"I suspected I had a problem when you kicked me off your porch the first time we met. I spent the entire drive back to Norman plotting ways to get you into the sack instead of arguments that might convince you to let me take my team up to the bluff. I didn't realize I was a goner, though, until…"

He paused, his face furrowed in concentration.

"Hell, I don't know when I realized I couldn't see a future without you in it. But I suggest we adjourn to the bedroom and I'll show you just how bad I have it for you, woman."

Randi snuffed out any and all doubts as they

tumbled onto the unmade bed. She'd been married to David for three years. She'd been in and out of love with Ty Keane for most of her adult life. Yet she'd never felt this driving sense of urgency with either of them.

"Let me," she panted, shoving Pete's hands aside.

She got him out of his clothes and shed her own. His body fired her hunger. The hard muscles, the smooth planes, the hollows and ridges and heat of him stirred needs she'd never felt before.

The need to lose herself in him. The need to join with him. Not just her body. Not just her mind. All of her.

Raising her hips, she guided him inside her.

22

For the second morning in a row, Pete woke with Randi in his arms. She was curled tight, her butt to his belly. Her hair fanned out in a dark, silky tangle. A thick section was caught under his arm, pinning her to his pillow.

He raised his head to free her and squinted at the digital clock on the bedside table. Seven-ten. On a Sunday morning. With the gut-coiling tension of the damage assessment behind him and his team dispersed.

Pete had nothing on his agenda except this incredible woman.

His *immediate* agenda, he amended wryly. The crap would hit the fan when his boss received word that he'd shut down the runestone study. Bruhn might already have it. Pete probably had a dozen messages piled up on his cell phone and answering machine.

He'd get to them later. Maybe.

Right now there was only Miranda.

He could lie here beside her for hours, he thought with lazy pleasure, breathing in her warm, musky scent, cradling her body against his. Then she mumbled in her sleep, grunted and jerked her bottom against his groin.

Lazy went south. So did most of Pete's blood. Instantly hard, he was seriously considering a little early-morning tussle when someone leaned on the front doorbell.

Intent on a single goal, he ignored the interruption.

The bell buzzed again, a short angry sound followed by a longer, insistent one. With a muttered curse, Pete eased out of bed. He had a good idea who was on the other side of the door and knew he owed her more of an explanation than his terse phone call Friday evening.

The shifting of the mattress and the continued noise penetrated Randi's sleep. Lifting her head, she blinked owlishly.

"Whazzat?"

"Someone's at the door," he replied, stepping into his jeans. "Go back to sleep."

Still in a fog, she burrowed her face into the pillow. She had to be exhausted; the strain of the past few weeks would be enough to drain anyone's reserves. But Pete had done his best to relieve her of some of her tension last night. Smiling at the thought, he padded barefoot through his minuscule living room.

He put the erotic images out of his head before he opened the door to his lab assistant.

"I tried to reach you all day yesterday," Anne threw at him angrily. "Why didn't you answer your phone?"

"The battery was dead and I—"

"Dead, my ass! You just didn't want to talk to me."

"—and I was tied up with something important."

She was too incensed to heed the warning in the steely reply. "What could be more important than the process we've been working on for a whole frigging year?"

Reminding himself of the countless hours she'd spent in the lab, Pete stood aside. "Come on in, Anne. This isn't the kind of discussion to conduct on the front porch."

She swept past him, a bundle of rigidly controlled fury. He got a good feel for how close that control was to slipping, though, when she whirled on him.

"You can't shut us down when we're almost there, Pete!"

"I can and I have. Jack Beasley should be back in

Chicago by now. Raynard will fly home to Oslo shortly. Pauline and Brady—"

"We don't need them! Any of them! We can finish the project without them. I'll write up the findings, use them to validate the provisional patent and—"

"Jesus, Anne! You know damn well that poaching someone else's work is the surest way to commit academic suicide. This study was a team effort. If and when we finish it, we'll publish the findings jointly."

"If? When?" She banked her anger and voiced a desperate hope. "Are you saying you might still image the remaining runes?"

"Not all of them. But I told Raynard I'd think about reshooting the last rune up on the bluff."

"The old futhark *M*."

With a lightning shift in mood, she threw off her disappointment and refocused her formidable energy.

"That rune is our best hope of a match with the *M* on the amulet. The amulet is the key. If it originated in Newfoundland, like Keane said, it could be just the tie we've been searching for to link the Oklahoma runes to the Viking settlement at L'Anse aux Meadows. We need that certificate of authenticity Keane said he had."

Pete hated to crush her rising excitement, but he knew damned well they'd never see the certificate now.

"Forget it. Keane's not going to supply it."

Or anything else, including his ten-million-dollar grant.

"I'll talk to him. He'll listen to me." Her green eyes glittering, Anne swiped a tongue over her lips. "I'll make him listen. He's a man, after all. A little old and creaky in the joints, but still a man."

Disbelief rippled through Pete, followed by disgust. He'd intended to tell his young assistant about the images he'd shot yesterday at the 137th. He was already planning to submit his findings to the FAA, the Department of Transportation's Accident Investigation Board, and the International Advisory Group for Aerospace Research and Development based in France. A comparative analysis of aircraft structural damage caused by fragmentation mines would provide a far more technical validation of his imaging process than a study of symbols incised in weathered stone.

Anne's suggestion that she seduce Sam Keane into cooperating killed any impulse to share that information with her. It also confirmed his decision to ask for another lab assistant.

"Listen to me, Gillette. You're off the runestone study. I don't want you contacting Keane and I don't want you writing up the findings. You're not involved in any way from here on out."

The color drained from her face. Realizing she'd stepped over the line, she scrambled to recover.

"Okay, I won't contact Keane. But you need my

help with that last rune. You *have* to shoot it, Pete! You have to wrap up at least that much of the study."

"I'm driving to Morgan's Falls this afternoon," he said coldly. "If I do decide to shoot it, I'll get Randi to help me."

"But—"

"This conversation is finished. I'll see you tomorrow. We'll talk then about moving you over to assist one of the other professors in the department."

Her fingers curled into red-tipped claws. For a moment Pete was sure she'd go for his face. He was ready to bat her fists away when she blew out a shuddering breath.

"I'm sorry. It's just…" Tears blurred the hard brilliance of her eyes. "My dad…the doctor's bills…I'm really freaked right now."

"Yeah, I know." He softened his voice, if not his stance. "We'll talk tomorrow. I promise, you won't lose your fellowship or your assistantship. And I'll help with the bills."

Scrubbing at the tears with the heel of her hand, she nodded and turned to leave.

Pete closed the door behind her on a wave of guilty relief. When he headed back into the living room, he found Randi wearing a sheet toga and an expression of deep chagrin.

"Sorry. I couldn't help overhearing. Sounds like

I'm not the only desperate female to dump all her problems on you."

"I'm a big guy. I can handle anything you want to dump on me."

"But you shouldn't have to." She pursed her lips in disgust. "Difficult as it must be for you to believe, I don't usually lean on anyone. And I don't intend to do it again. I'm tired of being such a weak, helpless wuss!"

"You're about as far from weak or helpless as anyone I know. As for being a wuss…" He hunched his shoulders in a mock shudder. "You were pretty ferocious last night. Scared the crapola out of me."

That drew a reluctant smile.

"Yeah, right. Then why were you all set to repeat the ferocious performance this morning, just before the doorbell rang?"

"Noticed that, did you?"

"It was hard to miss. Literally."

"In that case…" With a predatory grin, he hooked a finger in the top of the sheet. "I vote we pick up right where we left off."

Their lovemaking lasted until hunger drove them out of bed. Randi used the shower first, then wandered through the house munching on wheat toast slathered with peanut butter while Pete was in the bathroom.

He needed more bookshelves, she decided as she

eyed the scientific journals and textbooks stacked haphazardly on every level surface. And more work space. And better lighting above his desk. He also needed to collect the dozen or so forgotten coffee cups, empty out the dregs and run them through the dishwasher.

She took care of that task and was fighting the almost overwhelming itch to stack the journals in a neat pile when Pete strolled out of the bedroom.

"Ready to go home?"

"You said you wanted to show me your lab."

"Later. Since I still have a whole crate of university equipment locked in my truck, I figure I might as well use it."

While he could. He'd probably be out on his ass this time tomorrow, with no access to a lab or equipment.

"What's the plan?" she asked. "Are you going up to the bluff to finish the last rune?"

"Yes. I was going to ask you to come with me, but I'm having second thoughts about putting you in someone's crosshairs again."

"Hey, didn't I say just a while ago that I was tired of wimping out?"

"Being cautious doesn't equal being a wimp."

"No, but it doesn't equal cowering behind locked doors for the rest of my life, either, waiting for another stray shot."

"And if it wasn't a stray?"

"I'll cover that contingency before we leave the house."

"How?"

"A simple phone call to Sam's place. If he's on the premises, I go up to the bluff with you. If not, neither one of us goes. Agreed?"

"No, I don't agree. We don't know Sam was the one who fired on you."

"It's my land. I'm going with you."

"Anyone ever tell you you're as stubborn as an Arkansas mule?"

"All the time, only they generally use less flattering metaphors. Grab your jacket," she ordered briskly, "and we'll get this show on the road."

Randi made the call to Sam Keane's residence short and sweet.

"Mr. Keane, please. No, you may not tell him who's calling."

Flanked by Lissa and Pete, she waited until Sam barked into the phone.

"I'm looking at caller ID, Randi. I know it's you. Whatever you have to say to me, you can damned well say through my lawyers."

Her eardrum just about shattered when he slammed down the receiver. Wincing, she dropped hers back in the cradle.

"He's home. Let's load up the ATVs and go."

Pete insisted on taking Absol with them as an

early-warning system. Spencer reminded his mother several times, very vocally, of her promise to take him, too. She reneged—again—and left behind an extremely unhappy child.

Absol, on the other hand, performed his assigned role with great enthusiasm. Loping ahead of the ATVs, he crashed into the brush after every squirrel and rabbit that crossed his path and several dozen only he could see or scent.

"Some early-warning system," Randi muttered as they topped the last rocky ledge and the lop-eared hound shot off after yet another prey.

"Better than none."

Dismounting, Pete scanned the ridge in all directions. Except for the hawks swooping across the sky, they might have been alone at the top of the world. Still, Randi took the Winchester out of its hard-sided carrying case and kept it handy as she and Pete carted his equipment over to the inscribed stone.

"We'll have to hustle," he said, eyeing the angle of the sun. "Another hour, and the rune will be in shadow."

Randi knew the drill well enough by now to be of real assistance as he mounted the cameras and angled them at the symbol. After watching him duck under the ledge, adjust the camera settings, and duck out again to check the data on the computer, she stepped forward.

"I'll feed you the data."

"That's okay. I'll manage."

"I can handle it, Pete."

"I don't want the swirling images to make you dizzy again."

She wasn't keen on the idea, either. But her head wasn't pounding the way it had the other time. Nor had she popped any painkillers.

If she *was* going to lose her grip on reality, she decided grimly, she'd rather do it here instead of in a cockpit, at the controls of a multimillion-dollar aircraft.

"I'll feed you the data. If I get dizzy, I'll let you know."

"You sure?"

"Yes, I'm sure."

Or she was, until Pete began to shoot the rune. The right-angled lens captured first one image, then another perpendicular to the first. Randi felt her throat tighten as the two brightly colored letters began to weave and spin.

"Read me the top data point on the vertical axis, Randi."

She ran her tongue over dry lips and squinted at the blue digits. "F-slash-one-point-six."

"Wait a minute. I need to recalibrate the vertical f-stop to one-point-eight."

The right image blurred and faded into the screen. A few seconds later, it burst back with startling clarity.

Randi's heart began to pound. Sweat stood out on her temples. She looked quickly at Pete and saw him contorted at the waist, his upper half folded under the ledge.

"We're set," he shouted. "I'm going to reshoot. Tell me when the two images merge."

Absol must have sensed her nervousness. Returned from his latest foray into the woods, he pressed against her calf.

"Okay," she muttered to the dog. "It's okay. No one's jumped out at me. Yet."

The twin images on the screen pulsed and moved toward each other with agonizing slowness.

"Almost there," Randi croaked.

"What?"

She cleared her throat. "Almost there. The images are three centimeters apart."

Her fists clenched. A low buzzing sounded in her ears.

"Two," she called out hoarsely. "One... Bingo!"

Her heart stopped. For a second, maybe two, a blue flame burned inside the holographic image. It flared star bright, agonizing in its intensity. The next instant, it was gone.

"Randi? You okay?"

She searched for the flame and saw nothing but a colorful, three-dimensional image of an ancient rune.

"I'm okay."

"We're almost done here. One more shot from another angle."

Giddy with relief, she wiped her hands down the sides of her jeans. That was when she saw that Absol had gone rigid beside her. A low, steady rumble emanated from the dog's massive chest.

"What is it? What do you see?"

As if in answer, he bared his fangs. His entire body quivered.

Randi swung around, searching the woods behind her. The pulse that had just slowed to near normal rocketed off the charts again.

What had Sheriff Jefferies said? A 7mm Remington Magnum boattail like the one fired at her a few days ago could bring down a mule deer at six hundred yards and make a clean kill at three.

"Pete!"

The call was soft, urgent. Too soft for him to hear tucked under the ledge the way he was. Randi focused on the Winchester she'd leaned against a rock less than a yard away and took a step toward it.

Before she could take another, Absol erupted into a furious mass of sound and speed and launched himself through the air.

When his prey stepped from behind a concealing pine, Randi's shoulders sagged in relief. The very next instant, she recognized the danger represented by a hundred-plus pounds of bared fangs and highly protective instincts hurtling across the rocky ledge.

"Absol! Stop! Sit!" Shouting the commands, she lunged after the dog. "Stop! She's a friend! She's just here to help!"

Or so Randi thought, until Pete's lab assistant brought up a high-powered rifle.

"No! Wait!"

Ignoring Randi's frantic shout, Anne pumped off a shot with unhurried precision.

Absol gave an agonized yelp. Somersaulting through the air, he crashed onto the rocks.

23

"Dear God!"

Randi fell to her knees beside the whimpering animal. She'd ripped off her jacket and wadded it against the gushing wound when her stunned brain registered several simultaneous impressions.

She heard Pete's shout and the thud of his boots on the rock. Saw Anne swing her rifle in his direction. Felt her blood turn to ice when the blonde issued a terse command.

"Stop right there!"

Still, the pieces refused to fall into place. Not until Pete spit out a vicious oath.

"It was you, Anne! *You* took that shot at Randi a few days ago."

"Yes, I did."

There wasn't a hint of remorse in her voice. Or in the glance she sent Randi.

"And if you hadn't jumped at just the wrong moment, I wouldn't be forced to take another."

Fists clenched, Pete took an involuntary step. "That business about your father," he snarled. "The stroke. The doctors. It was just a cover?"

"A very convenient cover, as it turned out. Dad did have a minor stroke. I did drive to Okemah. My mother will swear I was at the hospital with her the whole time. Except for the few hours she insisted I go home and grab some sleep. That gave me the perfect opportunity to slip back to the house, pick up one of Dad's hunting rifles and make a quick trek up into the mountains."

Her eyes hardened. Suppressed rage shimmered in their green depths.

"I did tell you Dad was a hunter, didn't I, Pete? That's how he kept food on the table most winters when I was growing up. We had nothing. Nothing!"

"You told me."

He didn't look at Randi. Eyes locked with Anne's, he kept her focused on him.

"Did your dad teach you to shoot?"

"What do you think?"

Randi understood what he was doing. He wanted Anne to talk, wanted to engage her while he edged closer.

Wanted to make himself the target.

Her breath coming hard and fast, Randi looked frantically at the Winchester still propped beside the computer.

Too far. Much too far.

They had only one hope. Divide and conquer. If they separated, rushed Anne from different directions, she'd have to choose. One of them might make it.

Blood dripping from her hands, Randi pushed to her feet. She closed her heart to Absol's pitiful whimper. Closed her ears to Pete's muffled curse. Closed her mind to everything but the blonde who whipped the rifle a few degrees to the right and aimed it at her chest.

"How do you intend to explain today?" Randi asked. "You can't use your father as an alibi this time."

"I don't need an alibi. Without Pete to tell the authorities about our little disagreement, there's no reason to suspect I had anything to do with his death *or* yours. The prime suspect—the only suspect—will be Sam Keane."

Randi had known in her gut that Gillette intended to kill them both. Her calm admission turned suspicion into icy certainty. It also told her the bitch was enjoying her absolute power over them.

"Ironic, isn't it? The old man hates you so much he provided the funding for our study, hoping to use the results against you. Now I'll help him by eliminating you—both of you—and use those same results to validate the process that's going to make me a very wealthy woman."

Absol whimpered again. His claws scraping rock, he struggled to roll over. Randi didn't look at him, didn't dare take her eyes off Gillette.

"That's what this is about?"

She had to keep the woman talking. Shaking with emotions she didn't have to pretend, Randi edged a few, imperceptible inches to the left.

Divide and conquer.

"You're going to murder two people for money?"

"What a stupid question!" Anne's cool facade slipped. Her face contorting into an ugly mask, she sneered at Randi. "You wouldn't ask that if you'd grown up eating rabbit. Or had to sleep with your high school history teacher to maintain your perfect four-point average so you could qualify for a college scholarship."

"Listen to me!" Pete terse command snapped her gaze back to him. "You don't have to do this."

"Unfortunately, I do. You've left me no choice."

Randi sidled another inch to the left. Pete must have sensed what she was doing. His body wire taut, he tried to buy her a few more seconds, a few additional inches.

"I did some work at the national guard wing yesterday. That aircraft damage assessment I told you about. We got three hits, Anne. Three near-perfect matches!"

"You think I care that you used our techniques to get this bitch out of a murder charge?"

"Of course not. But you might care about the fact that the process knocked the socks off the air force personnel. It also impressed a structural engineer who works at FAA. He wants us to demo the process to the accident investigators there. Take it to Washington and brief the National Safety and Transportation Board investigators."

Shoulders stiff, fists clenched, he took a step around a rocky outcropping.

Divide and conquer.

"It's what we wanted, Anne. What we'd intended all along. Commercial applications that could result in contracts worth millions. Hundreds of millions."

He had her full attention. Dollar signs were no doubt dancing in her head.

"It's all in the computer. The images. The data. The calculations."

Her green eyes locked on the laptop Randi had been standing in front of just moments ago.

Another imperceptible step to the left.

Another inch.

"All we have to do now," Pete said, his voice low and rasping, "is roll in hot."

Randi's heart stopped. Pete was sending her a

signal! Those words... That phrase... He was ready to launch an attack. For a frozen instant she was back on an abandoned runway in the Afghani mountains, twisting to peer over her shoulder while mortars and small-arms fire exploded all around her aircraft.

Then Pete dived forward.

Anne fired at the same second Randi lunged at her from the other side. The rifle cracked, Randi heard Pete grunt and saw the barrel whip to the left.

A second shot battered her eardrums. Heat singed her cheek. Then she plowed headfirst into Gillette's stomach.

The blonde went down hard. Her head slammed against rocky ledge. Mewling, she gave a half-hearted heave, trying to dislodge her attacker.

Randi buried her fists in the woman's hair, yanked her head up and smashed it down again.

The glossed mouth went slack. Gillette gave a little moaning wheeze and lay still.

Panting, Randi scrabbled for the rifle and rolled to her feet. A thin ribbon of blood trickled onto the rock beneath Gillette's head.

Randi didn't care if she'd crushed the woman's skull. Her only concern was Pete.

He was down on one knee, trying to push to his feet. He'd placed a palm on the ground and pressed the other against the red stain soaking his vest.

"Don't move!" Taking Anne's rifle with her, Randi sprinted across the rocks toward him.

"It's...just a...graze."

"Don't *move!*"

When she dropped to her knees beside him, weeks of intense Survival, Evasion, Resistance and Escape training kicked in. She didn't have a SERE kit with her, but she could perform the necessary basics.

The bullet had hit high, she saw. Too high to have nicked a lung, but she knew there were several critical arteries in the clavicle region. Hands already stained with Absol's blood unzipped Pete's down vest and peeled it to one side.

Red pumped from the vicious wound. Not in bright red arcs, thank God! In small, sputtering spurts.

She knew arteries severed at an angle would close in two or three minutes. She did a quick search for protruding bone or shell fragments, saw none and wadded the vest back into the wound. Applying pressure with the heel of her hand, she scrabbled for the cell phone clipped to her waist and stabbed a quick-dial button.

"Come on!" she breathed into the mouthpiece. "Come on!"

Lissa had to answer. it wasn't noon yet; she'd be waiting for Spencer. She could direct the EMT team up to the bluff.

"Morgan residence."

"Lissa! Pete's been shot."

"Oh, God!"

"Call 911. Tell them he has a gunshot wound to the right shoulder. He hasn't gone into shock and doesn't appear to be bleeding out, but he needs attention. You'll have to show them how to get up here."

"I will! Are you okay?"

"Yes. There's a blond bitch with a cracked skull the EMTs will have to attend to, though."

"What? Is she the shooter?"

"She is."

When Randi snapped the phone shut, Pete shoved at the hand she held pressed against his shoulder.

"I've…got it. Take care…of Anne."

"Screw Anne."

Despite the angry mutter, she slewed around. She found Gillette already on her feet and taking a few wobbly steps.

"If I were you," Randi growled, reaching for the rifle, "I'd plant your butt right back down."

Either the blonde didn't hear or was too desperate to heed the warning. She broke into a stumbling run, headed for the ATVs.

"Gillette! Don't even *think* you're going to—"

A vicious snarl cut her off in midsentence. Claws scrabbling for purchase, Absol lumbered up.

Randi realized his intent at the same second

Anne did. Gillette spun around, terror in her eyes, as the wounded animal got his powerful hindquarters under him.

"Absol! No!"

Randi threw herself at the dog, but he was already in full attack mode. The force of his body hurtling past knocked Randi onto her rear. By the time she scrambled to her feet, the dog was streaking after the fleeing Anne.

Randi grabbed for the Winchester, sick at the thought of having to bring the dog down, but by then Absol had crashed into Anne's back and slammed her into a pile of loose shale just yards from the runestone. Rocks and dirt flew as the screaming woman twisted and kicked and used all her strength to fight off her attacker. Locked in mortal combat, the two rolled over and over.

The tale her grandfather used to tell Randi flashed into her mind as she raced across the rock. Not far from this very spot, a puma had supposedly ripped out the throat of a French trapper.

"Absol!" Randi put every ounce of authority she possessed into the command. "No!"

Sides heaving, the dog lifted his head. His gums were pulled back and quivering, fangs exposed. His massive paws remained where they were on either side of Gillette. Saliva mixed with blood dripped into her terrified face. She, thank God, had the sense not to move.

Almost sobbing with relief, Randi slipped a hand under Absol's collar and dragged him back a few feet, allowing Anne just enough room to scramble into a sitting position.

"Don't try to run again," Randi warned in a hoarse growl. "Do *not* try to run!"

The blonde nodded, her eyes wild. The sharp-edged shale had cut into her arms and one cheek. Her blood mixed with Absol's saliva in watery rivulets.

Randi left the dog snarling into her face long enough to retrieve two bungee cords from the ATVs.

"Hands behind your back."

The bungee cords made for viciously tight bonds. Randi took pleasure in Anne's wince when she wrapped the second cord around the woman's ankles and hooked the ends together.

"Let's see you bust out of those," she muttered, pushing to her feet.

That was when she spotted the glint of metal. The dull gleam was almost obscured by a loose piece of shale. Intent on staunching the blood still spurting from Absol's chest, she didn't pay any attention to it until much later.

24

Sheriff Jefferies arrived with two husky deputies. An EMT crew from the local hospital followed hard on their heels.

The EMTs patched Pete's shoulder and put his arm in a sling. Anne Gillette got a once-over from the medics, a couple of Band-Aids for the cuts she'd sustained during her roll in the shale and a nice, shiny set of handcuffs.

The EMTs also did what they could for Absol. Promising to get him to a vet, they carted the heavily bandaged and sedated animal back down the bluff with them.

Sheriff Jefferies took separate statements from Randi and Pete. His droopy, hound-dog eyes grave, he advised Anne of her rights. She refused to give a statement until she'd consulted with an attorney.

"Fine with me, missy. Here, boys, you escort Ms. Gillette down to the squad car."

With a deputy on either side of her, Anne was hauled to her feet. Her hair fell across her face; looking both scared and defiant, she tossed it over her shoulder and twisted around.

"Pete, I—I—"

His stony expression had her biting back whatever she'd intended to say. Just as well, as Randi was in no mood to listen.

"Come on," she said to Pete. "Let's get you onto one of those ATVs and down the bluff."

The shuffle of their footsteps on the loose rocks reminded Randi of the metal she'd spotted earlier.

"Hang on a minute. I want to check something out."

Scraping at the shale and dirt with the toe of her boot, she uncovered two or three inches of metal. Her first thought was that it was a knife, lost by some hunter, maybe by her granddad during one of his many expeditions to the bluff.

"What is it?" Pete wanted to know.

"I'm not sure. Could be a knife blade."

Dropping to one knee, she brushed aside the dirt and loose rocks. More metal appeared. A long, narrow length of iron. Too long for a hunting knife. Frowning, Randi cleared away more dirt and uncovered what looked like an ornate crossbar. Below it was a hilt wrapped in decaying leather—with skeletal fingers clutching it.

"Holy shit!"

Startled, Randi rocked back on her heels. Her stunned exclamation brought Pete close to her shoulder, with Sheriff Jefferies ambling over to see what all the commotion was about.

"Well, well," the sheriff muttered. "What do we have here?"

"Unless I miss my guess," Pete announced in a voice rough with suppressed excitement, "what we have here is a grave. A Viking grave, judging by the carving on that sword handle."

25

Twenty-four hours later, Lissa locked her arms around her knees and shook her newly shorn head. She'd hacked off her fried hair and now sported a short, feathery cap of multi-colored curls.

"I still don't believe it. A Viking," she breathed, "up there on our bluff."

The house was quiet. With Spencer at school, the three adults could finally take a few moments to relax.

Randi had spent hours giving official statements, answering the flurry of questions from reporters and pestering the vet for updates on Absol's life-and-death struggle. She hadn't breathed easy until she'd learned the dog was going to make it.

Pete had also spent hours on the phone. Operating awkwardly with his right arm in a sling, he'd caught Pauline Lockwood at dinner, Jack Beasley at a concert and Raynard Jorgenson in bed. Additional calls went to Brady, the Oklahoma State Historical Society, the forensic anthropologist they referred him to, and, finally, his boss.

Pete hadn't shared the results of that conversation with Randi or her sister, but did feel compelled to offer a word of caution now.

"We don't *know* he was a Viking, Lissa. The sword and other artifacts in the grave appear authentic, but we'll have to date them using established scientific methods."

With a careless wave, Lissa dismissed the months of anthropological and historical research he'd warned her would follow.

"What do you think happened to him? How did he end up in that grave?"

"Hopefully, we'll find the answers to those questions when we examine the remains."

"Do you think he's *our* Viking, Randi?"

"The blue-eyed warrior?" she said slowly. "The one who supposedly fathered a child with a woman of the People?"

She had to admit the old family tale now held more than just fascination for her. The image of the warrior who'd jumped out at her remained all too vivid.

He was still inside her head when Sledge drove

up some hours later. When Randi answered the door, the fact that he wore full uniform caused her stomach to drop and land somewhere between her feet. She invited him in, all too aware of the rolled document in his fist.

"I drove out to give you a copy of my report," he said, his expression unreadable. "I ran it through JAG this morning. They concurred with my findings and recommendations."

Randi licked her suddenly dry lips. "Which are?"

"Give us the abbreviated version," Lissa snapped, coming to stand at her sister's shoulder.

Sledge's eyes widened a bit when he took in her new look. He didn't comment on it, however, or on Pete's sudden appearance.

Randi felt his solid presence at her back, sensed rather than saw the tension coiling through him. She knew he'd draw fire to protect her again, as he had up on the bluff.

Except this time he couldn't shield her. This time it was just her and this unsmiling representative of the Oklahoma Air National Guard.

"Tell me, Sledge. What are your findings and recommendations?"

"I found nothing to counter your account of the manner in which Captain Tyler Keane died. On the contrary, Dr. Engstrom's damage analysis offers evidence to support your claim Captain Keane was, in fact, killed by a land mine. I'm recommending to Colonel McLaughlin that no charges be brought against you."

Randi blew out a shaky breath. She didn't realize she'd slumped against Pete until his lips brushed her temple.

Lissa, on the other hand, huffed disdainfully. "Took you long enough, Shores."

"You think so, Morgan? Maybe you'd like to have dinner with me sometime and tell me how I could've done it faster and better?"

"I'll consider it."

"You do that. Your sister has my number. Call me when you make up your mind."

Handing Randi a copy of the report, he gave her a salute, nodded to Pete and left.

Lissa started whooping before the screen door banged shut behind him. "You did it, Randi! You did it! You pounded Sam and his absurd allegations right into the dirt!"

"Not me. Pete."

"You," she said, landing a loud, smacking kiss on her sister's cheek, "*and* the professor!"

She grabbed Pete's arm so she could lay one on him, too. Unfortunately she grabbed the wrong arm. Letting out a grunt, he went a little white around the gills.

"Oh, hell! Sorry 'bout that."

Stretching his lips in a strained smile, Pete forgave her.

"This calls for a celebration," Lissa announced. "I say we break out the champagne."

"Or your granddad's favorite scotch," he suggested. "I'm in the mood for something with a real kick."

Lissa waltzed into the den. He began to follow, then saw Randi staring at Sledge's report and halted.

"You okay?"

She bit her lip. They'd won a major battle, but not the war. She still had to fight Sam's custody suit in court. And God knew how those remains up on the bluff would affect his apparent plan to challenge her ownership of Morgan's Falls. Then there was the question of whether she'd ever get back into a cockpit again. She faced another round of tests, and at least one session with a shrink.

It wasn't either of those considerations that kept her from celebrating, though. It was the document in her hand. The report refuting Sam's allegations that she'd left his son to die.

"I need to go somewhere, Pete."

"Now?"

"Right now."

"Okay." Digging his good hand into his pocket, he fished out his keys. "You'll have to drive."

"I didn't mean you had to go with me. Your arm... You should rest."

"You drive, I'll rest."

Pete figured Randi had one of two goals in mind. Either she was heading to Sam's place to whack him in the face with the report or she wanted to lay her ghosts to rest.

He wasn't sure which during the short trip north, but when he spotted a sign for the turnoff to Fort Gibson National Cemetery he breathed a little easier.

His relief lasted only until Randi pulled into the gravel parking lot and shifted into Park.

"I'll be right back. I just need to—"

She broke off, swearing softly under her breath as she spotted a lone figure amid a field of white crosses.

"Oh, hell," Pete muttered. "Isn't that Keane?"

Randi nodded, her eyes on the man standing beside a grave covered with patches of sod that hadn't yet grown together.

"You think he's read the report?" Pete asked.

"I'm sure he has. The governor probably faxed him a copy personally."

"You can't rub it in, Randi. Not here."

She studied Sam's slumped shoulders and bent head. "No," she agreed after a long pause. "But I can talk to him."

"You think he'll listen?"

"Probably not. I have to try, though. Wait here, okay?"

Pete caught her arm before she could reach for the door handle. "You're not armed, are you?"

"No, you idiot. Just wait here."

Dead, dried leaves crunched under her feet as she wove her way through the crosses. So many warriors were buried here. Soldiers who'd served at nearby Fort Gibson from its founding in the early days of Indian Territory. Men in blue, men in gray—victims of the war that had almost ripped the nation apart. The fallen from Verdun, from the Argonne, from Midway and Inchon and Khe Sahn, brought home to lie with their comrades in arms.

Like Captain Tyler Keane.

Her heart aching, Randi halted beside Sam. He didn't speak, didn't acknowledge her presence at all. For long moments, they stood side by side and relived their separate memories of the man they'd both loved.

Finally, Sam faced her. His sunken, red-rimmed eyes stirred Randi to both shock and pity.

"It's not over between us," he rasped.

"I know. I've been thinking…"

She had to force out the words. Each one cost her more than he would ever know.

"I've been thinking, Sam, it doesn't ever have to end between us."

"What the hell does that mean?"

"My son doesn't have a grandfather. You could play that role if you wanted to."

Abruptly he lifted his head. Triumph flared in his face. "Are you saying you'll agree to a DNA test?"

"No. Spencer's paternity is not now, nor has it ever been, the issue. I'm saying it doesn't matter."

"It does to me."

"Why? You know I loved Ty. You know my son *could* have been his. If you want to believe that, if it gives you joy or comfort to think you'll live on through Spencer, then go ahead."

She reached out, dismayed at the brittle boniness of his arm.

"Be part of his life, Sam, just as you were part of mine. Teach him to hunt and ride and be proud of the land that bred him. Help me raise him."

He stood silent, his eyes burning into her. Randi knew he couldn't simply turn off his hate. She had to give him time.

"Think about it," she said softly. "You lost your son, but you don't have to lose the child who could have been your grandson."

Still he said nothing. Randi made another attempt to breach the barriers.

"Did you hear we found a grave up there on the bluff?"

The only answer to her question was a brief flicker of acknowledgment.

"The grave holds artifacts that may date to Viking times," she said quietly. "The find would have thrilled Ty."

Sam's intense stare dropped to the marble headstone marking this newer, fresher grave. Weeping inside for the son he'd lost, the friend she'd shared so many dreams with, Randi made a final appeal.

"You could still make the find a tribute to Ty's memory. Fund the rest of the study, Sam. Honor your pledge to OU."

The rigidity went out of his shoulders. Looking old and tired and frail, he unbent as much as Randi suspected he could at the moment.

"Maybe."

She left him standing beside the grave. She would come another time to say her goodbyes to Ty.

She was shaking when she climbed back into Pete's pickup. He didn't ask any questions, just waited until she got the tremors under control and started the ignition. Five miles from the cemetery, he had her pull into a turnoff.

"Tell me," he said simply.

"I said I wouldn't agree to a DNA test. That's something Spencer can decide for himself when and if it ever becomes an issue for him. But I also said Sam could be part of my son's life if he wanted to."

"How?"

"Spencer needs an adult male he can turn to. One who'll teach him to hunt and fish and put on a condom when the time comes."

Pete cocked his head. "I could probably teach him about that. The kid's bright. He picked up that egg trick fast enough."

Randi's breath caught. "Are you planning to hang around until Spencer gets to the rubbers stage?"

"I might." He waggled his brows. "If you ask me nicely."

The regret and sorrow Randi had carried inside her since Ty's death eased a little more. She hadn't said her goodbyes back there at the cemetery, but she knew that she could now remember their good times without a constant, aching sense of loss.

Pete had filled that void.

She'd tell him about the possibility that Sam might continue funding the study later, she decided. They could talk about her situation, too, and the question of whether she'd fly again.

Right now, all that mattered was the fact that he was painting a picture of a future that included her and Spencer. A smile forming around her heart, she asked him as nicely as she knew how.

"Please stick around, Pete." Leaning across the console, she brushed his mouth with hers. "Pretty, pretty please."

Merline Lovelace

32181 THE LAST BULLET	___$6.99 U.S.	___$8.50 CAN.
32172 THE MIDDLE SIN	___$6.99 U.S.	___$8.50 CAN.
32164 THE FIRST MISTAKE	___$6.99 U.S.	___$8.50 CAN.
32075 UNTAMED	___$6.50 U.S.	___$7.99 CAN.
66707 A SAVAGE BEAUTY	___$6.50 U.S.	___$7.99 CAN.
66649 THE CAPTAIN'S WOMAN	___$6.50 U.S.	___$7.99 CAN.

(limited quantities available)

TOTAL AMOUNT	$ _____
POSTAGE & HANDLING	$ _____
($1.00 FOR 1 BOOK, 50¢ for each additional)	
APPLICABLE TAXES*	$ _____
TOTAL PAYABLE	$ _____

(check or money order—please do not send cash)

To order, complete this form and send it, along with a check or money order for the total above, payable to MIRA Books, to: **In the U.S.:** 3010 Walden Avenue, P.O. Box 9077, Buffalo, NY 14269-9077; **In Canada:** P.O. Box 636, Fort Erie, Ontario, L2A 5X3.

Name: _____
Address: _____ City: _____
State/Prov.: _____ Zip/Postal Code: _____
Account Number (if applicable): _____

075 CSAS

*New York residents remit applicable sales taxes.
*Canadian residents remit applicable GST and provincial taxes.

MIRA®

www.MIRABooks.com

MML1105BL